ROUGH WORLD

The Misadventures of Some Random Guy
and His Friend Tannic

V. KIM KUTSCH, DMD

ROUGH WORLD MEDIA, LLC

Hardcover: ISBN-13: 978-0-9974972-0-5
Paperback: 978-0-9974972-1-2

ROUGH WORLD MEDIA, LLC

www.roughworldmedia.com

PRINTED IN THE UNITED STATES OF AMERICA
Signature Book Printing, www.sbpbooks.com

This book is for my grandson,

James Carson Bowers,

and his vivid imagination.

PREFACE

The places and characters in this novel are the product of James's video game creation *Rough World* and his cartoon strip characters Some Random Guy and his friend Tannic. The story doesn't follow James's depiction of Rough World exactly. I took some artistic liberties and wove a story out of his ideas and a few of my own. This is a work of fiction. The places and the characters are not real. But as I wrote the story, these characters became very real to me. They came to life. I hope you have as much fun reading it as I had writing it. Obviously this story never really happened. It's fiction. Of course, there's always the random chance that it could have happened. I'm just sayin'.

INTRODUCTION

It all started as just another random day. Of course, when your name is Some Random Guy, every day's pretty random, but this one was randomly different. Only he didn't know it yet. This day would turn out to be anything but random. It would be a day he and Tannic would never forget.

Some Random Guy wasn't his real name. His parents were huge Stevie Ray Vaughn fans, and they loved the blues. So it was only natural that they'd name their first-born son after a blues singer. After a long debate over everyone from BB King to Jimi Hendrix, they finally agreed, and he was named after Stevie Ray Vaughn. After all, even BB King had declared Stevie the best blues guitarist of all time. So his *official* name was Stevie Ray Guy, and his dad even pretended his last name was a tribute to another blues great, Buddy Guy, but in reality that was just a random coincidence, like so many other random coincidences in his life.

His parents called him Stevie, which he hated. He was 10 years old and it wasn't cool to have a name that sounded like a little kid's name. The other kids at school teased him relentlessly about it, the way kids do. But he just ignored them. In his own world, his initials, SRG, stood for Some Random Guy. And that was cool all by itself. In his mind, it defined him, and he was the definition of cool. Definitely cool.

He didn't actually come up with the name himself. It was given to him by his best friend Tannic. Tannic took his initials and came up with Some Random Guy, he liked it, and it stuck. Mind you, Tannic wasn't exactly a real best friend, at least not in the normal sense. He was more of a cross between Drop Dead Fred and Hobbes. He had been with SRG for about as long as he could remember, ever since he showed up out of nowhere one day and said, "Hi, my name's Tannic." SRG had never even wondered where he came from. He just accepted his new-found friend the way children will. Tannic wore medieval clothing, but SRG never gave that a second thought. He didn't have a middle name or a last name, either, just Tannic. But that didn't bother SRG. In fact, he thought that was pretty cool too.

SRG was also the only one who could see and hear Tannic. This created a lot of problems, as you can imagine. He'd told his parents lots of times that Tannic was real, but they always laughed and said, "Sure he is, Honey," and went along with it even though they clearly believed Tannic was one of those imaginary friends that kids eventually grow out of. "It's just a stage," they said, and they didn't worry much about it.

Only it wasn't a stage. Tannic was very real. He was just invisible, except to SRG. But only SRG seemed to understand that.

So Tannic and SRG became best friends, and wherever SRG went, Tannic was there with him. He even went to school with him. It raised a few eyebrows when SRG always seemed to be talking to himself or lost in some fantasy world, but SRG did his best to ignore those worries too. He never tried to explain Tannic. After all, who would believe in an invisible friend? His parents certainly didn't. They only got annoyed when Stevie tried to blame some unfortunate event on Tannic, like a broken lamp or a stain on the carpet, to avoid facing up to his own actions. That was the biggest problem.

Except for the time Tannic convinced Some Random Guy that he could fly. The contraption they built broke a big hole in the neighbor's fence, and that all ended up being a big hairy mess. Luckily the contraption broke his fall, too, and SRG only got a few bruises and no broken bones. But everybody was upset, and SRG was grounded from video games for a whole month. That was unbearable, and he accused his parents of cruel and unusual punishment, to no avail.

Tannic, meanwhile, had conveniently disappeared just as the fence broke, leaving Stevie to take all the blame. In truth, even SRG was upset at Tannic for throwing him under the bus on that one, but it was two years ago now. Aside from a little paint on the sidewalk, a little hole in his bedroom wall, and a big tear in his brand new jeans, he and Tannic hadn't really gotten into too much trouble since. And that was pretty normal boy stuff anyway. Well, there was also the little incident with Mrs. Kibbitch's lawn, but that was a year ago too. Anyway, that was all about to change in a random way that wasn't all that random.

Chapter 1

Rough World

S RG woke suddenly to a loud and obnoxious alarm buzzer. Tannic was already awake and ready for another exciting summer day. He poked SRG on the shoulder. "Come on, sleepy head, get out of bed!" He prodded him again. "Your dad left for work at 6:30, your mom left over an hour ago, and it's high time you got up."

SRG slammed his fist on the alarm clock and groaned as he rolled over. "Just let me sleep more . . . Come on . . ."

But it was no use. He needed to get up and get going. His mom had left a list of chores for him. Today it was mostly just mowing the back lawn, but that was more than plenty. He tried to go back to sleep, but the snooze alarm started beeping just as he was drifting back into that morning daze between sleep and reality. Then Tannic clobbered him on the head with a pillow and gave him an unimpressed look. He was watching him impatiently and holding the pillow at the ready to clobber him again.

"Okay, okay, I'm coming! Geez, can't a guy catch a little break around here? I didn't expect you to be my mother's agent and make sure I did my chores. You're supposed to be on my side! I just wanted a few more minutes of sleep!"

"I just don't want you to get in trouble and blame it on me the way you always do," Tannic replied. "I want to play Rough World today, and you know you have to get your chores done first or you'll get grounded and we won't be able find out if Dr. Denton defeats the Evil Boss."

So SRG got out of bed, took his morning shower, brushed his teeth and flossed, combed his hair, got dressed, and went downstairs to make some breakfast. Being invisible and somewhat imaginary, Tannic didn't need to eat at all, so SRG always ate a little extra for him. Luckily he was always just hungry enough for that.

Most mornings his dad fixed waffles for SRG and his two younger brothers, but during summer vacation he went to work long before SRG made it to the kitchen, so he was on his own for breakfast. This morning it was cereal and milk. After he finished the second bowl he noticed the note on the kitchen table reminding him to mow the lawn—and to please not offend Mrs. Kibbitch, the weird neighbor next door, in the process. The note didn't say she was weird, he just read that part into it. SRG had a talent for offending the poor old lady, and he didn't really know how. Tannic said she just had a bad case of the grumpy pants, and there wasn't any cure for that. He wasn't sure what her problem was, she just seemed to be unhappy about everything in life, especially him. He didn't know why he randomly had to live next door to someone like that, but it wasn't something he could change, so he just tried to make the best of it, ignoring her and avoiding her as much as he could.

After reading his mom's note, he knew what the day would bring, or at least he thought he did. He called Tannic into the kitchen. "So here's the deal. I need to pick up the house, put my dishes in the dishwasher, clean my room, make my bed, and mow the lawn. After I have all of that done, if I can possibly get all of that done in one single day, then you and me can go back to playing Rough World and see what happens to Dr. Denton." He stood up.

"Hey, wait a minute, I have an idea," Tannic said. "It's really too wet to mow *now*, I mean, the grass will take a couple of hours to dry from the sprinklers, so, well, you really shouldn't mow the lawn until at *least* this afternoon. But also, you know, Mrs. Kibbitch takes her nap from about one to two in the afternoon, which we know from experience, you remember, so you probably really shouldn't mow until after two o'clock. And anyway it only takes about an hour to mow the yard, and your mom won't be home until three thirty. So if you mowed the lawn between two and three, I was just thinking, then we could play Rough World *first*, then you could do the inside chores while Mrs. Kibbitch is taking her nap, and then at two o'clock you can mow the yard. Then your mom gets home at three thirty, all the chores are done, the lawn is mowed, Mrs. Kibbitch got her nap, everybody is happy. Your mom will never know we played first and did the work after!" He paused. "How's that for a brilliant idea?"

"Yeah, that's an idea all right. But Mom gave me specific instructions that I'm not supposed to play until after I have all of my chores done. And if I do a really good job, we get to go out for pizza tonight when Dad gets home. I know you could care less about pizza anyway, but I love it. Especially three cheese pizza from Pizza King. But I have another idea. How about I do all of the inside chores first, then we play Rough World until the lawn looks dry enough to mow, and then we just pause the game when we have to, and go back after the lawn's mowed, and also we can play during Mrs. Kibbitch's nap."

"Okay, that's a deal! You start on the inside chores and I'll turn on the TV and the Wii and set up for the game".

"Uh . . . I don't think that's a good idea. You're not very good at turning things on and off. Remember what happened last time?" SRG reminded him.

"Oh, that's right. Well . . . I'll pick my spot on the couch and wait for you. I get the center cushion!" Tannic yelled.

"Do not!" SRG yelled back.

"Whoever gets there first gets it! That's the rule, Compadre," Tannic insisted.

"Okay, whatever. You're as big a nuisance as my brothers. Would it hurt you that much to help me do the chores?" SRG asked.

"Hey, they're your chores, not mine. Don't drag me into this."

So Some Random Guy carefully picked up his breakfast dishes and rinsed them in the sink and put them in the dishwasher. Then he went to his room and made his bed and put all his dirty clothes into the hamper his mother had bought especially for them. Then not seeing anything else that needed immediate attention, he went back downstairs to join Tannic in the family room. His brothers were spending a few days with their grandparents, so the rest of the house was unusually clean. They were a couple of real knuckleheads. What one didn't think of, the other one did. They were always wrestling and making messes and were basically a cyclone waiting to touch down, and he usually got stuck helping clean up. There was no way he wanted to pick up the messes they usually generated. But today was different. They were gone, the house was quiet, and it was just him and Tannic and Rough World. Well, and a back yard that still need to be mowed, before his mom got home and hopefully not during Mrs. Kibbitch's nap. But he was already thinking about Rough World.

The family room was a cozy place with dark plush carpeting and over-stuffed leather couches. The far wall was mostly bookcases. A large flat-screen TV hung above the fireplace in the center, and there were a couple of paintings on the walls between the picture windows. SRG's mom had done all the decorating herself, and she was fussy about making sure the colors blended and set the right mood for the room. Tannic was sitting proudly on the center cushion when SRG got there, patiently waiting for his best friend and another adventure in Rough World.

Now, you have to understand, Rough World was their favorite video game, and it was like no other game. It had ten levels in each world, and every level was full of exciting and unexpected and dangerous adventures. Once you started playing, you could just get lost in it, it seemed so real. And it was appropriately named. It really was a rough place.

The hero of the game was Dr. Denton, who invented good things to help the poor people of Rough World survive, which was ruled by the Evil Boss. His name was Mr. Eville which may or may not have been a random coincidence. As it turns out Mr. Eville was really well named, as he was basically evil to the core.

The point of the game was for Dr. Denton to figure out a solution and create something helpful, like a special weapon, to get the players out of each jam. He would also coach them on things to expect and strategies they could use as they entered each new level. The end of World One was Level 10, and if they made it that far, the players got to use the number one weapon of the game, the Fortran sword, which was forged from Excalibur itself and Sideral steel. They would then confront the Evil Boss, Mr. Eville, in his inner office and save the people of Rough World. If they were successful in defeating him, then they could enter the Transport Chamber and travel to the next world, which would have ten new levels, each harder and more dangerous than in the previous world. Then they would repeat the process. All told there were ten worlds that each had ten levels. If the players made it through all of the levels of all of the worlds, they would confront Mr. Eville one last time, and if successful, he would be defeated for all time and presumably Dr. Denton would become the new leader of Rough World.

Then they'd probably change the name to Peaceful World or something like that. Some Random Guy and Tannic didn't really care what happened after they helped Dr. Denton defeat Mr. Eville. They just wanted to get that done. Of course they each wanted to be the player who won the Fortran sword. Only the player whose turn it was got to wield the weapons. However, aside from just being there to help him, the other player also acquired a special skill, like being able to jump higher. And that skill was different for each world. The problem was that skill only became apparent as the players progressed through the levels, and sometimes it was not obvious at all. So there was some competition between them, even though they were playing as a team and had to help each other just to survive. But they'd never made it past Level 5 of the first world, so they still had a lot of work to do. And a lot to learn about Rough World.

Some Random Guy turned on the TV and the Wii. The TV hummed, the picture appeared, and the Rough World screen came to life. He hit Resume Play and the screen returned them to Level 5 of Rough World One. He assumed his position on the right cushion, which gave him a bit of a disadvantage, but he figured he'd reclaim his favorite spot after making an amazing move somewhere. This was the furthest they'd ever been, and they were about to embark on a new adventure. They just didn't realize how big an adventure at that moment.

It was still SRG's turn as player, and he was carefully guiding his figure through a maze of vegetation. Level 5 looked like a prehistoric jungle, even though it was named the Rough Forest and was just on the outskirts of the Jagged City. They had to negotiate their way through the Rough Forest to make it safely to the edge of the Majestic Meadow, next to the Jagged City, which they both hoped was Level 6.

"What's that thing?" Tannic asked nervously.

"I don't know, some kind of snake? Do you think it's poisonous, should we use the Taser?" SRG asked in reply.

Suddenly it moved, and they saw that it was a slimy moving appendage attached to another, much larger appendage, which was attached to a still-larger body, which was attached to a gigantic head with razor-sharp teeth. Some Random Guy and Tannic screamed at the same time. It was a Weevil Beast, one of the Evil Boss's creations to keep people from leaving the Jagged City and enjoying the forest.

"Quick! Use the heat-seeking Taser!" Tannic screamed. Since it was SRG's turn, Tannic's character wasn't carrying any weapons, but he had lots of stamina and other helpful skills. He was there to offer encouragement and support. They were both focused intently on the screen and the Weevil Beast.

All at once a flash of light filled the room, and there was a moment of eerie silence followed by a loud explosion. They both screamed again. This time it wasn't on the TV—it was in the house.

"What was that?" Tannic asked nervously.

"I have no idea," SRG responded. "Could it have been lightning and thunder?"

They ran to the kitchen window and saw rain pouring down. The sky was covered with ominous black clouds dumping rain, and as they watched there were more flashes of light and loud booms, some closer and some further away. They both stared out the window, transfixed by the light show in the back yard. Summer thunderstorms might be normal in some parts of the U.S., but they were very rare in the Willamette Valley of Oregon, where Some Random Guy had been born and raised. They were witnessing a rare event.

"Well, that pretty much takes care of mowing the lawn today," Tannic pointed out cheerfully.

"Yeah, it'll never dry out in time now. Well, Good Buddy, it looks like we'll just have to spend the rest of the day playing Rough World. It can't be helped."

"Yeah, it really is too bad about the rain. Oh well. You'd better get ready, then, because today I'm going to school you on how to get to Level 6!" Tannic bragged.

"Are not!"

"Am too!"

"Are not!"

"Am too!"

"Are—oh no, the game . . ." SRG suddenly realized.

"What about the game?"

"The lightning! We have to turn the TV and the Wii off. If lightning hits the house it could burn up the circuits in the TV and ruin it. And the Wii too." He ran for the family room. "I'd be grounded for forever, like until I go away to college anyway. Mom will be mad, Dad will be pissed! Hurry! Run!"

They scrambled to the sofa, and of course they both dove for the center cushion, and a wrestling match started. Bursts of lightning continued to light up the room, and the thunder was rattling the windows. The flashes and the thunderclaps were coming at almost the same time now.

"Give me the controller, it's still my turn!" SRG yelled.

"Not a chance, Compadre! I want a turn!"

"Didn't you hear anything I just said? I need the controller so I can turn it off! We've got to turn it off now! Give me the controller!"

They kept fighting for control of the controller as they began slipping from the sofa to the floor. SRG wanted to turn it off and Tannic wanted a turn. They both had their hands on it, but neither one had control and neither one was willing to give it up.

Suddenly the room was filled with the brightest flash of light yet and a noise that sounded like a bomb going off. Some Random Guy thought he smelled smoke for a second, and then everything went quiet and dark. Really dark, as in you-can't-see-your-hand-in-front-of-your-face dark. Scary dark, if you were afraid of the dark even a little. And eerily dead quiet. Tannic and SRG froze.

Chapter 2

Dr. Denton's Lab

"Some Random Guy. Psst. SRG. Are you there?"

"What just happened?" SRG whispered back. "I'm here, but I'm not sure where *here* is."

"Me neither! Wow!" Tannic giggled. "That was awesome! I mean, wow!"

"If you say so," SRG responded. "I just hope the TV is okay or we're going to be in big trouble. And I mean big trouble."

"Correction, Compadre, you're going to be in big trouble. I'm invisible and imaginary, remember?"

"Yeah, some friend you turned out to be!" SRG said under his breath. "What just happened?"

The room began to lighten up a little and Some Random Guy could see Tannic, but everything was a bit foggy or smoky. They were both intact and none the worse for the lightning strike. They studied each other silently for a few seconds.

"The lightning must have struck the house," SRG said. "Do you smell anything odd?"

"Just stinky 10-year-old boy," Tannic taunted.

"Now isn't the time to start with that. We need to figure

out what just happened. It smells strange in here. I mean, the air smells weird," SRG said. "And I'll have to come up with a story too, no thanks to you, Good Buddy."

"No problemo, Compadre, happy to help!"

The family room grew lighter and lighter as the fog started to dissipate. Only they weren't in the family room anymore. They were standing in the middle of what looked like a large scientific laboratory. Some Random Guy didn't see anything he recognized. He looked blankly at Tannic, who shrugged his shoulders. They were surrounded by lab benches covered with scientific equipment and there was sophisticated machinery everywhere. Two large television screens hung on the far wall, opposite the door. There were several computers humming, but otherwise the place was quiet. There was nobody else there. They were alone, and it definitely wasn't the family room.

"Where are we?" SRG whispered to Tannic.

"Beats me," Tannic replied. "I have no—uh, wait a minute. This place looks kind of . . . Isn't this Dr. Denton's lab in Rough World?"

"Yeah, right. I mean, it does kind of look like Dr. Denton's lab," SRG responded. "But that's not possible! What happened to the family room?"

"I don't know, but it sure looks like Dr. Denton's lab." Tannic turned around curiously. "Isn't that the door we go through when we start each level?"

SRG was trembling. "It sure looks like it, but how can it be? Are we in the game for real? That's not possible! I want to go home! I have to be dreaming! Quick, slap me and wake me up! Slap me back into reality! Please!"

So Tannic quickly slapped Some Random Guy a few times, like maybe six times.

"Ow, ow, ow! Stop it!" He covered his face. "What was that all about?"

"You told me to slap you!"

"Okay, fine, but I didn't mean it! And you didn't have to slap me more than once!" He took a deep breath. "I just want to go home and wake up in my own bed. I want to start this day over. This can't be real!"

"Somehow I don't think that's an option, Compadre. Look at that TV on the wall. That's the reverse of your TV screen, and that's your family room it's showing. And it's empty. There's nobody there. We're in here." He frowned. "At least it seems like we are. Can that be possible?"

"You're imaginary to everybody but me, and you're asking me if this is real? Of course there's nobody there, and somehow we're here. Perfect, just perfect!" SRG spit out sarcastically. "Somehow we got transported from the family room into the game? This can't be happening, but if it is then this must be Dr. Denton's lab. But where is he? Yoo-hoo, Dr. Denton! Are you here? Dr. Denton? Hello . . ."

There was no answer. The computers were running but nobody was in the lab. Not even a lab rat. The place was as deserted as a grade school on a Saturday morning. The quiet suddenly felt ominous.

Tannic spoke first. "Okay, let's not jump to conclusions. Let's just go over to the door and open it and see what's outside. Maybe we walk through the door and we're back in the family room. What do you think?" He didn't sound confident.

So they both slowly—*very* slowly—slowly enough that they took turns pushing each other—walked through the lab to the door that looked like the starting point of Level 1. Later on they would each claim to have dragged the other one kicking and screaming to that door. But the truth is that they were both a little nervous, a little unsettled, and, well, certainly a little scared. Really scared, in fact. Some Random Guy was silently wishing he had mowed the lawn during Mrs. Kibbitch's nap. That would have been a much better adventure. That would have been something he could live with. This was unsettling. This just couldn't be happening. This was not possible.

Tannic slowly opened the door. The handle creaked a little bit as he pushed on it. The door led outside to a meadow covered in lush, tall, and very green grass, strewn with flowers of every color. The sun was shining brightly. There was a slight breeze. And it was quiet. Too quiet, even. Not just randomly quiet. Almost a creepy kind of quiet. It felt somehow deserted.

It certainly wasn't the family room. In fact, it looked just like the Majestic Meadow from Level 1 of Rough World. They both stared out the door as the realization hit them.

"Okay, Good Buddy, go ahead and step outside," SRG suggested.

"I'm not stepping outside. You step outside, Compadre."

"Oh, come on. If this is really the Majestic Meadow, there's nothing to be afraid of. We've beaten this level lots of times. So, uh, you go," SRG half-commanded.

"All right, all right. You don't have to push me. If this is really the Majestic Meadow, it's a piece of cake." Tannic boasted.

"Yeah, except for last time when you died on Level 1, remember?"

"That was an accident and you know it! Anyway—if this really is the Majestic Meadow—it's still your turn," Tannic argued.

"Okay wise guy, let me show you how it's done."

"Let's see you just do that."

"Uh-oh . . ." SRG gasped.

"Uh-oh what?"

"There's three Life Wedges above your head. I can see them, just like in the game."

"Oh no. Compadre . . . I can see three Life Wedges above your head too. They're illuminated just like in the game. We're in the game. Can that be possible? We're in the game for real."

In the game each player was given three Life Wedges for each level. If either player lost all three wedges, that player died and the other player tried to finish the level alone. If they lost all three wedges, the level was over. Then you simply just hit the reset button and played the level over and over again, without limits until you succeeded. That was the video game. This was real life. Or at least it seemed to be real life. And there was no reset button.

Chapter 3
The Majestic Meadow

They stood silently before the door until Some Random Guy, remembering something, glanced toward the corner. There waiting for him stood the Dragonwrigley Sword. He picked it up in his right hand. It was heavier than he'd expected. He looked it over closely. The blade was shiny and sharp. It looked well-polished. The grip was wrapped in leather and contoured perfectly to fit in the palm of his hand. The Dragonwrigley emblem, a dragon in the middle of a circular labyrinth, was engraved on both sides of the blade just below the cross guard and it glowed in a faint green color. The sword was more beautiful in real life than it had looked in the game. It was a work of art.

The Dragonwrigley was more than just a sword. It could shoot fireballs, like a dragon, when it was pointed at an enemy, and it could also throw crescent blades through the air when you swung it. Of course, it could also be used as a regular sword, and its edge was exceptionally strong. But that was nowhere near as cool as fireballs and crescents. Some Random Guy turned it around in his hands to admire it. As the main player, he would carry the Dragonwrigley Sword through the entire game. He swung it through the air a couple of times to get the feel for it. He accidentally fired a couple of fireballs which flew out the door and into the meadow and sizzled out in the lush green grass. They looked at each other in amazement.

Tannic wouldn't have a weapon. He would have a special skill to help SRG with. In some levels there would be other, special weapons available, but it was SRG who would carry and use those weapons too.

"It's real, it's official . . . we're in the game." Some Random Guy stepped through the door, sword in hand. "I don't know how else to explain it, and it doesn't make any sense at all, but here we are. So . . . now we just need to get past the Minotaurs and the Ender Dude, and avoid getting killed by the Chomp Cheap Carps in the ponds, and find the Rainbow Star."

"We're going to have to work as a team, Compadre. I don't have a weapon."

"Okay. Well, here we go. Keep your eyes peeled for Minotaurs, or who knows what."

In legend, the Minotaur is a fearsome beast from the island of Crete, a heavily muscled creature with a man's body, a bull's head, and hooves on its feet, and as strong as an ox—literally. The people of Crete sacrificed young men and maidens to it to satisfy its cannibalistic hunger. In Rough World there were numerous Minotaurs on each level. Minotaurs walk upright, and though their bodies are mostly covered with hair, they are fond of wearing pants. They don't swim and they rarely bathe, so you can smell them before you see them. On the other hand, they have great hearing but can't smell very well, which might explain their not bathing. Their vision is about average. And they have really bad tempers. A lot like a Cape Horn Buffalo, which, in case you've never heard of it, is a really bad-tempered buffalo. And the Minotaur's eyes will stare straight through you. They look at you like they own you, and your lunch money too. They would scare the life out of the worst bully on the playground. They were nothing to be trifled with, but unfortunately they can be found in abundance on most levels of Rough World.

The door closed behind them with a loud clank. SRG and Tannic looked at each other.

"What if we don't play the game, what if we just go back inside of Dr. Denton's lab and wait for somebody to show up?" Tannic asked.

SRG shrugged and then turned around and grabbed the door handle. He pulled hard on it. It was locked. The door wouldn't open. He pounded loudly on the door and waited, but there was no answer.

"That appears not to be an option!" SRG stated the obvious. They both looked ahead at the meadow.

"Well, what if we don't play the game? Maybe there is an outer boundary to the meadow and we can just go to the edge, go through it and escape. Maybe if we can do that we'll end up straight back in the family room!" he offered hopefully.

"That would be totally random, but what if we end up someplace else? At least here we know where we are! I mean, I think we know where we are, if you can believe it."

"Yeah, maybe you're right. I'm straining my eyes in every direction and I don't see an end. This meadow seems to go on forever. At least as far as I can see, so I guess that's maybe not an option either."

"I think we just play this level out and see what happens and go from there. What do you think?"

"I'm right behind you Compadre!"

Showing a healthy fear of Minotaurs, Some Random Guy and Tannic tip-toed slowly into the meadow, step by step, looking both ways. The grass was lush, dark green, and waist-high. They needed to get to the other side of the meadow and somehow find the Rainbow Star, a radiant rainbow color gem about the size of a baseball, which would open the way to Level 2. And they needed to not get killed in the process. They would have to face the most dangerous enemy of each level, the Ender Dude, to capture the Rainbow Star. They'd have to collect Rainbow Stars from all ten levels to battle the Evil Boss and proceed to World Two. Of course, they'd never gotten past Level 5, let alone made it to the showdown with the Evil Boss—Mr. Eville, as he called himself. With Dr. Denton's help, they were supposed to defeat him using the Fortran Sword. And now it looked like they had to do that for real, and they seemed to be on their own. None of it made any sense. They should be sitting in the family room. SRG still had the lawn to mow, and there was a promise of cheese pizza tonight. But instead they were about to face a life-and-death battle in Rough World!

And it was about to get really rough.

Fifty yards or so into the meadow, they started to relax. The sun was in the middle of the sky and the air was warm. They could see the far side of the meadow, only a half-mile away. And even the meadow looked more beautiful than it had on the TV screen. If it were anywhere else, it would be a great place for a picnic, but this was Rough World. *No worries*, Some Random Guy told himself. This was Level 1. They'd defeated it lots of times, even if there had never been this kind of pressure. They would make it through and they could worry about Level 2 after that. And they could do that too, for sure. They'd done it dozens of times. It was just that none of this made any sense at all. He must be dreaming.

His thoughts were interrupted and he instinctively froze.

"Tannic! Don't move!"

At the sound of his voice, Tannic jumped to the left and straight into the arms of a Minotaur towering out of the grass. The Minotaur looked just like they did in the game, only bigger. Its bull's head was covered with hair and sported sharp, curved horns. It was covered with muscles and wore a pair of ragged pants. It glared down on them with menacing red eyes and grunted angrily, clutching Tannic as if about to break him in two.

SRG slowly raised the Dragonwrigley. It was heavier than he'd imagined. Of course, when you were playing a video game you couldn't tell how heavy anything was, or how hot the sun was, or how cold the water was, or how bad the Minotaurs smelled. But right now he needed all his strength just to lift it and point it at the Minotaur. Tannic hung limply in the monstrously muscled arms. He wasn't breathing. One of the Life Wedges above his head flashed brightly and then faded away. There were only two wedges now. SRG mustered all his strength, aimed the Dragonwrigley at the Minotaur, and sent a fireball at it. The ball of flame lit up the air and hissed as it shot toward the Minotaur. Tannic opened his eyes and raised his head to see the fireball coming towards the Minotaur, who still had a death grip on him. But the Minotaur moved just in time, and the fireball caught Tannic in the middle of his chest. SRG froze in horror, and another Life Wedge briefly glowed and faded away. Now SRG could only see one wedge remaining above Tannic's head. One left. Panicking, he swung the sword at the Minotaur. A sharp crescent arced toward it, its blade shining in the sun. It caught the Minotaur in the throat and sent it stumbling backwards, blood gushing out of its neck. Tannic dropped to the ground, fell down into the grass, and lay still. Dead still. SRG rushed over to Tannic. He was lifeless and quiet. He wasn't breathing. SRG's heart was pounding in his chest. "Tannic! Tannic!" he screamed. Tears welled in his eyes as he stared at his friend.

For a long minute Tannic lay dead still and didn't respond. SRG didn't know what to do. Tannic had raised his head after the first Life Wedge disappeared. He seemed to momentarily come back to life, just like in the game, before the fireball caught him in the chest and his second Life Wedge was lost. Was he dead? Would he come back to life again just like in the game? SRG was trembling as he looked over his best friend's lifeless body. Finally Tannic gasped lightly and took a shallow breath. He stirred and opened one eye. SRG let out a deep sigh of relief.

"That was a close one, huh, Compadre? . . . When I saw the fireball coming . . . my life flashed before my eyes," Tannic said wearily.

"I thought you were dead," SRG responded quietly. "I was scared Tannic!"

"Well, I'm not dead yet! It looks like we get restored after we lose a Life Wedge just like in the game. I didn't feel anything. Everything just went black for a moment. How long was I out?"

"Probably less than a minute but it seemed like eternity Tannic!"

"Cheer up Compadre, you made a great shot. You killed him. We can laugh about it now. I mean, I still have two Life Wedges left. I thought I was a goner for sure. But you saved me, Compadre! That was amazing." He closed his eye, but his breathing was steadier now.

"Uh . . . that's not exactly what happened," SRG stammered.

"What do you mean?" Tannic opened an eye again. "What did happen . . . exactly?"

"Well, the Minotaur took one of your Life Wedges when he was wringing you out like a wet sponge, before I could even get a shot off, and then, uh—"

"Then . . .uh. . . what exactly Compadre?" Tannic demanded.

"I, uh . . . well, the fireball actually hit you. Not the Minotaur."

"It—You . . . what? You shot me with it? Oh, way to go, Compadre. I should call you 'Old Dead Eye' instead. So what now? You're telling me I only have one Life Wedge left?"

"Yeah, something like that. I'm sorry. We're going to have to be more careful. Much more."

"Yeah, and you're going to have to be a better shot. Much better. No margin for error now, Compadre. I only have one Life Wedge left! What does that mean anyway? What happens if I lose my last Life Wedge? Would I be permanently dead? Is there any way to reset this level? What happens?"

"I don't know and I don't want to find out. But I can't imagine that it will be anything good. I don't know how we could possibly reset this level and play it again. I don't know what to do!" SRG lamented.

"Well, we definitely need to be more careful, just in case. How'd that happen anyhow? You're always so good with the Dragonwrigley when we play the game."

"Well, the Dragonwrigley doesn't weigh fifteen pounds when we play the game. It's not the same as using a controller. It's all I can do just to lift it. And I've never used a real sword before. That was my first time. And, well, that Minotaur was huge. It scared me."

"And it was deadly . . ."

"Okay so listen, we just need to be really careful now until we find the Rainbow Star," SRG said.

They were now wide awake and on edge and giving their full attention to their surroundings. They walked slowly toward the first pond. They studied every blade of grass, ready at every moment for another surprise. They didn't have to wait long. Some Random Guy and Tannic were focused on the grass in front of them and not paying attention to their back trail. Suddenly Tannic noticed a shadow passing over them. He turned around, and as if on cue the Minotaur following them rose to its full height out of the grass and towered over them. It took him a second to realize what he was seeing.

"Compadre!" he shouted. "Look out behind you!"

The Minotaur moved quickly now. It lunged at SRG. This time he spun on his feet and raised the Dragonwrigley just in time to shoot a fireball at the Minotaur before it reached him. It caught the creature full on, and it grasped at its face before falling forward right on top of SRG. He was pinned to the ground and couldn't move. He could barely breathe.

"Help me, Tannic! Get this thing off of me!" he screamed.

"What did you say? You're mumbling! I can't hear you!"

"I said 'get this stinky creature off of me' . . . I can't move! Help me!"

Tannic still couldn't hear him clearly, but he ran over and tried to lift one of the Minotaur's arms. It was no use. The thing was too big and too heavy. He tugged and tugged, but the corpse didn't budge.

"It's no use," he panted. "I can't move him."

"I can't hear you either! What are you doing out there?"

"I said 'I'm trying to get him off of you but he's too heavy'... and you'll have to talk louder!"

"So will you!"

"I am talking louder! You talk louder!"

"I am talking louder! Can you hear me now?"

"I don't know. Can you hear *me* now?" Tannic shouted through a broken giggle.

"I can hear you fine and I don't find this funny! I can't stay under here for the rest of the game. Another one will find us. I can't move my weapon either, and you don't even have one, Good Buddy. You'd better think of something. And fast!"

"What if I look for a pole or branch? Something I can use to lever him up enough for you to crawl out?"

"Okay, just make it fast. It's not just the danger—he stinks! I can hardly breathe!"

"Don't worry, I'll be right back," Tannic reassured him.

With that, Tannic began searching through the grass, crouching low so he wouldn't be seen, and hunting for anything he could wedge under the Minotaur. The meadow was nothing but grass and flowers. He couldn't find anything useful. He began feeling around the grass with his hands.

After a while something caught his eye that might work. It was dark and hard, and at first he thought it was a big stick, but when he grabbed at it, it refused to move. It was stuck or attached to something. He hauled on it with all his might, and finally it moved toward him. As he got a better look at it, he recognized the hoof of a Minotaur. Tannic jumped up and ran toward SRG. The Minotaur was running too, close behind him and gaining. He dove toward the dead Minotaur head-first like he was sliding into home plate. He actually slid under the edge of the Minotaur before coming to an abrupt halt.

"What are you doing under here?" SRG asked. "You were supposed to be getting a stick!" Tannic just looked wide-eyed at Some Random Guy and didn't say a word.

A second later the Minotaur was upon them. Seeing SRG and Tannic hiding under the corpse of his cousin, he started lifting the dead mass out of the way. As the dead Minotaur shifted, SRG managed to wriggle his arm a bit and slowly move the Dragonwrigley. He inched the tip of the blade in the direction of the live Minotaur. He could almost see it, and if he could reach just a little further he would have a clear shot at the beast. As the live Minotaur lifted the dead one off him, SRG waited patiently. Just a little bit more and he and Tannic could squirm free. Just a little bit more and he'd have a clear shot. He carefully aimed the sword at the lifting Minotaur's chest and fired. The fireball missed. He'd done nothing but provoke the beast. It was grunting loudly as it lifted the corpse higher. It looked enraged.

SRG fired again, and this time the fireball found its target. It struck the Minotaur in the side of his chest just under its armpit. The Minotaur fell back, stunned. It stood motionless for a moment, and then ever so slowly began to teeter back and forth. When it finally tipped over, it fell straight onto the other Minotaur. And now instead of being pinned under a dead Minotaur, they were pinned under two dead Minotaurs. They looked at each other in the dark beneath the bodies.

"Oh, this is perfect!" SRG exclaimed. "Just . . . perfect. Good job, Good Buddy! You were supposed to get this thing off me, and now we're trapped under two of them! Any idea what we should do now?"

"Hey, I wouldn't be so critical. You're the one who shot me, remember? I couldn't find anything to use, and then I ran into that Minotaur. I was lucky to get away from him at all, with you stuck under here the whole time."

"Okay, yeah, you're right. Let's not fight about it. We're in a real jam and we need to figure out how to get out of it. Wait a minute. Why are you under here?"

"I don't know. I just ran and dove to get away from the second Minotaur and I ended up under here. I didn't know what else to do. I just slid under here to escape him."

"Wait, that's good news. That means the ground's soft enough for you to slide under here. It should be soft enough for us to dig our way out. I think we should give that a try. I don't know what else to do."

"Dig our way out? Are you serious? With what, Compadre? Did you bring a shovel? I can barely move."

"Do you have a better idea? We'll have to use our hands," SRG said. "Come on. We have to. It's our only way out."

"Really, Compadre?" Tannic argued. "How can we dig our way out if we can't move?"

"We'll just start slowly and eventually we'll be able to move more. We can do it! We have to."

So they scratched at the dirt with their bare hands, trying to create enough space to dig more and eventually move their arms. Unfortunately for the duo, the commotion had attracted the attention of yet a third Minotaur, which came quizzically over to have a look. It was shocked to find two of his companions piled together and both apparently graveyard dead. He grunted loudly and started to shift the top Minotaur. Some Random Guy and Tannic had heard the approaching enemy and felt the pile above them move just a little bit. They both instinctively froze, but it didn't really matter because they couldn't really move anyway. They could feel the dead weight shift more and they could start to see daylight as the new Minotaur lifted up the top one with his left hand and then tugged at the bottom one with his right hand. He was just managing to lift both corpses enough for SRG and Tannic to wiggle.

SRG carefully slid the Dragonwrigley alongside his body and began aiming the tip towards the live Minotaur. The Minotaur stared at the boys momentarily and cocked his head as he tried to figure out what he was looking at. The sun was behind the Minotaur's head and SRG had to squint to make out its form. He just managed to point the tip at the Minotaur and shoot a fireball at it. He could tell immediately from the high pitched squeal and the smell of burning hair that he had hit his target. He was just about to sigh in relief when the unthinkable happened. Before he and Tannic could wink, blink or think, the Minotaur dropped both of the corpses back and then wedged his own dead weight on top of them. Now they were buried under three dead Minotaurs and could move even less than before.

"Perfect, just perfect! What do we do now? I can barely breathe!" SRG grunted in disgust.

"You know what they say! Two's a party, three's a crowd!" Tannic replied.

"What's that supposed to mean?"

"I don't know. It just randomly popped into my head. You know, like if they tell you not to think of something, you immediately think about it. Like don't think about a dead Minotaur. You can't help but think of a dead Minotaur. It just popped into my head. I thought maybe it fit the situation…" he giggled.

"Yeah, well, it's not funny. But I think they're right.

Three Minotaurs is a crowd, as in it feels crowded under here. I think we have to go back to plan 'A', unless you have any better ideas. We need to get out of here before we end up stuck under a mountain of these stinky things!"

"Yeah. Like what's worse than being stuck under a pile of three dead Minotaurs? Being stuck under a pile of four dead Minotaurs! Tannic giggled again.

"I'm glad you think this is funny!"

"Who but us would even get that joke?"

So they struggled, bit by bit, handful by handful of dirt, the plan worked. After what seemed like hours, they managed to crawl out from under the dead Minotaurs. Tannic emerged first, followed by Some Random Guy. They were covered with dirt and immediately started dusting themselves off.

"These things really do stink," Tannic observed.

"I told you they do!" SRG replied. "Three of them stink even more than one!"

They looked over the three dead Minotaurs lying heaped behind them. They were like huge triplet ogres, all muscular and hairy. But each of them had a bull's head, with sharp curved horns. The Minotaurs were incredibly strong and could kill you easily. And after you lost your three Life wedges it was game over. If you were playing from the comfort of your own home, of course, you would just reset the game and start the level over again. But they were in the game for real. There were no resets. No do-overs. Just three Life Wedges apparently standing between life and death, real death. The only saving grace would be if they could find a Heart Gem. But those were randomly hidden on random levels and not easily found. They were an invention of Dr. Denton. They would replenish all three of your Life Wedges.

But they had limits. They still only returned you to three Life Wedges; you couldn't bank them. The most you could have at a time was three Life Wedges, so if you found a Heart Gem when you had three Life Wedges, it didn't help you at all. And you had to find it while you still had one wedge left, or you were dead anyway and it was game over. There was, technically, one exception: if you fell onto a Heart Gem right after you lost your last Life Wedge, it would restore all three wedges and you would be whole again. But what were the odds of that, falling on to a Heart Gem just as you lost your last wedge? That would be a very random event and would require a tremendous amount of luck. Some Random Guy and Tannic had actually discovered that loophole once while playing the game. But it had only happened once. Tannic had fallen onto a Heart Gem as he was dying on Level 3. But the odds of that happening again were too slim to contemplate. And neither SRG nor Tannic was feeling particularly lucky at the moment. In truth, they'd only discovered a couple of Heart Gems in all the games they'd ever played. When you replayed a level, the Heart Gem wouldn't be in the same place, if there even was one. And at present, SRG was still worrying about mowing the grass when he wasn't worrying about what would happen to them next. Tannic was putting on a brave face, but deep down he was scared. He only had one Life Wedge left, and there was a long way to go yet on Level 1. They'd encountered only four of the level's Minotaurs, and they hadn't even seen the Ender Dude yet. And there were still the Chomp Cheap Carps in two random ponds. This was all a living nightmare. It couldn't possibly be real.

"Now what do we do?" Tannic looked with concern at SRG.

SRG thought over the game's layout for a minute.

"Well, I think our best bet is to get to the center of the meadow. We have to cross the first pond, get farther across the meadow, and capture the Rainbow Star in the second pond. We just have to do that without any more Minotaurs noticing us. And who knows where the Ender Dude is, or what he looks like in real life. So we'll just have to deal with him when we find him. We just need to keep our senses alert and be prepared for anything. Are you up for it? I say let's go and get this over with!"

"Yeah, I'll be ready," Tannic said. "We usually run into the Ender Dude about the second pond. Do you think it's possible to find the Rainbow Star without meeting him? I don't know what we're going to do if we do find him."

"I don't know either. I'll be happy if it works out that way. Anyway, we should head off. We still have a long way to go, and we need to keep moving."

"You should go first, Compadre. I only have one Life Wedge left, remember?"

"Oh, be happy you've got one. We've still got a chance. Quit acting like a little girl about it."

"I am not!"

"Are too!"

"Am n—" he raised his voice.

"Okay!" SRG whispered. "Listen, we need to be quiet. There are probably more Minotaurs here, and I don't want to see another one. No, make that, I don't want another one to see us."

"Too late!" Tannic screamed.

A Minotaur was running through the grass toward them. SRG and Tannic ran toward the pond. This time there was no arguing about who would go first. They were racing each other to outrun the Minotaur, and they'd completely forgotten about the Chomp Cheap Carps in the water. SRG started out ahead, but he was carrying the Dragonwrigley and Tannic was running for his life. He passed SRG, and as he approached the shore he kept speeding up. When he hit it he just kept right on running, over the top of the water and across the pond. Chomp Cheap Carps were leaping into the air and chomping at the wake he left in the surface.

SRG watched in amazement for a moment and slowed down. Then he remembered the Minotaur.

"Wait up, Good Buddy!" he shouted. But Tannic was most of the way across the pond already.

The Minotaur was closing in as they approached the pond. SRG stopped for a second at its edge and looked at the Chomp Cheap Carps still chasing Tannic in the distance. He hesitated, and looked back. The Minotaur was rushing toward him with its arms outstretched. It held a scythe like weapon in its right hand. SRG swung the Dragonwrigley at it and sent a flurry of crescents, but they fell short of the target. It was too far away to shoot at. He didn't really want to get into a close range battle with this armed Minotaur. He looked at the pond.

Without thinking, SRG dove in. He would just have to take his chances with the carp. The armed Minotaur wasn't really a good option. The water was ice cold when he hit it. The sword was still clutched in his right hand, and he struggled a bit trying to swim while holding it, but he kept going as if his life depended on it. After all, it really did, and that helped. Luckily, the carp were still focused on Tannic, as he ran off the water and up the bank at the other side. SRG started to swim away from the Minotaur and into the dangers of the pond.

With difficulty, he yelled to Tannic. "When were you . . . going to tell me . . . could walk on water . . . Good Buddy?"

"I'm sorry, Compadre! I would have told you before, but I didn't know!" Tannic yelled back.

Some Random Guy glanced back. The Minotaur had stopped at the edge of the pond. He was glaring at Tannic and SRG but wasn't going anywhere near the water. *Why isn't he coming after me?* he wondered. Was it that he couldn't swim? Was he afraid of water? Were they outside his territory now? Or were the Chomp Cheap Carps so bad that even Minotaurs were afraid of them?

In fact, it was just because in real life Minotaurs can't swim, but SRG and Tannic didn't know that.

Perfect. Just perfect, SRG thought as he swam. *I escaped the Minotaur by swimming with man-eating carps that even Minotaurs are afraid of.* He'd heard that you could swim with piranhas as long as you swam very slowly. You just had to avoid panicking and be sure you weren't bleeding at all. One drop of blood in the water and it was game on. You could probably do the same with sharks. After all, some people swim with them. But Chomp Cheap Carps? Who knows? In the game you could swing the Dragonwrigley while you were swimming well enough to fend them off. It was different in real life, though. There wasn't much chance SRG could swim and attack the carp at the same time. Luckily Tannic could run on the water and keep their attention while SRG struggled slowly across the pond, but how long until they noticed him? Maybe he could swim with them and survive if he didn't excite them, but being in the water to find out didn't appeal to him.

The Minotaur was still pacing on the bank like it was anticipating something. It was watching Some Random Guy intently. He tried to swim calmly without attracting attention, but it was no use. It was too hard to carry the Dragonwrigley and swim at the same time. He was splashing and making noise, and a few carp had already spotted him and were coming back, razor sharp teeth clapping in the bright sunlight and reflecting off the dark blue water. The sight sent a chill down his spine and he started to panic. He momentarily had a random thought. Carp in real life were bottom feeders. They didn't have teeth but had large sucker type mouths. These carp were an idiosyncrasy. Either that or they were poorly named. But they did look like giant carp, just with rows of teeth. His random thoughts were interrupted as he took in a mouthful of water. The Dragonwrigley was weighing him down like a scuba diver's lead belt, and his arms and legs were getting tired. He had to struggle just to keep his head above the water, and he was regretting not paying better attention in his swimming lessons. He could get by and felt comfortable enough in the water, but his dad always told him he needed to be able to swim better. He'd always thought so himself, he just hadn't expected that this was why he would need it!

He was still criticizing himself as the carp approached. His thoughts immediately returned to the fish. He braced himself for the attack.

"Tannic!" he screamed instinctively. "Tannic!"

"Hang on, Compadre! I'm coming!"

'No! You only have one Life Wedge left!"

But it was too late. Tannic was already running back across the pond. Unfortunately, his diversion arrived a little too late. A Chomp Cheap Carp attached itself to Some Random Guy's right leg, intent on eating it for lunch, and began gnawing relentlessly at it. SRG felt a sharp burst of pain but was helpless to stop it as he tried to keep himself afloat. Blood slowly tinged the water red, and he began feeling faint. He tried to raise the Dragonwrigley but couldn't manage.

Tannic's heart sank as he saw a Life Wedge flicker and expire above his friend's head. SRG was lying lifelessly on the surface of the water. Tannic shouted encouragement to him.

"Hang on, Compadre! Don't give up! Use the sword! I'm coming! I'll get their attention and draw them away from you! Swim across the pond slowly! I'll keep them occupied!"

Some Random Guy stirred and looked up when he heard Tannic's instructions. Tannic ducked down and started slapping the surface of the water as he ran along on top of it. The waves drew the attention of the carp. He ran in circles until they were all chasing him, then he skidded to a halt on the water, jumped over the ones behind him, and started running in circles the other way. All the carp were focused on him, chomping at his heels and chasing him across the pond while he just managed to stay ahead of them. He was the perfect bait for the school of man-eating fish pursuing him. But now that he had their full attention, he couldn't slow down or stop. So he just kept running and slapping the water, taunting them.

In the meantime, SRG took a deep breath and lifted the Dragonwrigley. In one stroke he smoothly disconnected the fish from his leg with a swipe of the blade. His energy was returning slowly, and he started swimming carefully toward the far shore. Every now and then Tannic churned by with a wave of carp swimming close behind him. SRG marveled at Tannic's stamina, it must have been part of his special talent.

The Minotaur looked tempted to enter the pond and chase him, but his instincts prevailed and he quietly slipped back into the green grass of the meadow and disappeared.

Ten long minutes later, a SRG pulled himself onto the far bank and dropped face-down into the sand, motionless. He was too spent to move. He'd swum that distance a couple of times before, in lessons, but it had been nothing like what he'd just done. Swimming classes hadn't prepared him for dragging the Dragonwrigley across a pond full of man-eating fish. He was breathing deeply, trying to catch his breath and compose himself. Finally he lifted his head and looked back at the pond. It seemed bigger and more ominous in real life.

Tannic came hurtling proudly toward him and ran straight onto the bank like a speed boat flying up a ramp. He wore a huge grin. Several carp were so focused on him that they swam right up onto the bank behind him and started flopping around. Their teeth were still chattering non-stop and making a racket. Tannic smiled as he kicked them back into the pond one at a time. He seemed to enjoy that.

"Did you see that? That was awesome!" Tannic laughed. "I mean, I ran circles around those fish and never even got tired. That was fun, that was . . . even better than being able to fly. That was so awesome! Could you believe it? Have you ever seen anything like that before?" Then he looked at Some Random Guy lying face down in the sand. "Hey . . . are you okay, Compadre?"

"Oh, I'm perfect, just perfect. Never better, really. Perfect. Really," SRG answered drily. "You can't even swim, much less run on water. You wouldn't even take swimming lessons because you said little kids peed in the pool. Where did your new-found love of the water come from?"

"Well, your grandpa helped me out last time we were at his pool. He told me not to worry about the little kids, they didn't really pee in the pool. So I got into the water and he helped me learn to swim."

"Wait, my grandpa told you that?" SRG asked in amazement.

"Yeah. After your grandma took you guys into the house for chocolate chip cookies. I don't eat, so I stayed in the pool with your grandpa and he gave me some pointers. They really helped. I'm not scared of the water anymore."

"Oh, well, that makes sense—hey, wait a minute! Grandpa could see you? Nobody's been able to see you except for me! How do you explain that?"

"I don't know," Tannic replied. "He just looked at me and said, 'So, you must be Tannic.' I asked how he could see me. He said he didn't know, but he thought maybe he still had the imagination of a 10-year-old boy. He said he was a 10-year-old boy in a 60-year-old man's body. I didn't really understand what he meant. But it made sense to him, so I just left it at that. You know how your grandpa is."

"Yeah. I could see that, actually. Sometimes he does act like a giant kid. Sometimes Grandma gets mad at both of us for getting into some kind of trouble. She says he should know better. He just smiles and ignores her. I think he never grew up all the way," SRG said thoughtfully.

"So I figured I could swim," Tannic continued, "at least enough to not drown. Although it didn't really matter, I just wanted to get as far away from the Minotaur as I could. But I didn't know I could run on water. That caught me by surprise. But it might come in really handy here, especially since I don't have a weapon."

"Wait a minute, that's it! That's your weapon! Unless

you have any other skills we don't know about yet. Your special skill for World One must be running on water, and you had incredible stamina. And I really appreciate you saving my life out there. I wouldn't have survived without you distracting those fish. It was all I could do just to swim and carry the Dragonwrigley."

"Hey, no problem Compadre. But you're down to two Life Wedges now. We're going to need to be more careful!"

"Really, Tannic? Is that your best advice, to be more careful? We're in Rough World, Tannic! There's a reason it's called Rough World!" SRG spit out the words tersely.

"All I'm saying is we need to be afraid, Compadre! Brave men can get careless, and if we're careless here we'll get killed in short order! I think we should stay scared."

"Yeah, you're right. I'm sorry, Tannic. I'm just a little on edge here, after the Minotaurs and the Carps. I thought I was a goner out there. But we need to figure out what to do now. Any ideas?" SRG asked.

"I say we creep through the grass with the stealth of a leopard, go to the second pond, and look for the Rainbow Star. What say you to that?"

"I think you're right! That's a good plan. You go first."

"I'm not going first. I went first last time. You go first."

"You did not."

"Did too!"

"Okay, okay. I can't really remember. So just to show you I'm not chicken, I'll go first. But right after you." SRG gestured Tannic onward.

"Nice try, Compadre, but I didn't fall for it!" Tannic laughed as he pushed SRG forward. "Your knucklehead brothers might fall for that one, but not me."

So they set off into the meadow again, on their hands and

knees this time. SRG was soaked to the bone, and Tannic was as dry as a bone. The sun was bright, though, and it warmed SRG up a little. The grass was knee-high and thick enough to make their passage slow. They struggled through it one behind the other, SRG in the lead gripping the Dragonwrigley in his right hand. It was heavy, but he managed to keep the tip from dragging on the ground. The second pond, up ahead held more Chomp Cheap Carps, and maybe the Rainbow Star . . . and maybe, too, the Ender Dude.

Ender Dudes are the strongest enemies on every level. Their job is to protect the Rainbow Star and not let players capture it. They're huge and heavily muscled, like a cross between Minotaurs and ogres, and they have hands like the Hulk's. They fear no one and nothing. And they have a really bad attitude. They're so mean that Minotaurs cut them a wide berth, and even the Carps are afraid of them. SRG could picture an Ender Dude picking up a Chomp Cheap Carp and biting its head off for a snack. Ender Dudes are also tough. They're immune to most conventional weapons, including the Dragonwrigley. It takes cunning and creativity to get past them.

Of course, all it really took was getting hold of the Rainbow Star. That would immediately end the level and transport you back to Dr. Denton's lab, where you could watch highlights from the level you just finished—or look through the reverse-screen monitor to see who was playing the game. In the game, Dr. Denton was there to answer your questions. You could ask for clues, and he would have advice about the next level, its special weapons and enemies and anything else you should look out for. Sometimes he knew where the Rainbow Star would be located and have suggestions on how to get it.

Right now SRG just wanted to find out how to escape this bizarre predicament and go home. *How do I get back? I already miss my parents. I even miss my brothers. Well, not really, but almost. I just want to go home.* He looked over at Tannic, but Tannic was walking along quietly, lost in a world of his own thoughts.

It must have been close to noon. The sun was high in the sky, and it was getting warm. In full sunlight it was even hot. There were no trees in the meadow, and the thick grass offered little in the way of shade. The air was dead still and stuffy. SRG's shirt was almost dry on his back. Every now and then one of them stuck his head above the grass to take their bearings and then dropped down again to crawl slowly onward. *Just like leopards sneaking up on their prey,* he thought. Except that they were more like the prey than the leopards. In fact, they were the prey. But it was better to be optimistic.

"Hey, it's like we're doing the leopard crawl!" SRG whispered.

"How do leopards crawl? And how would a 10-year-old boy know how leopards crawl?" Tannic asked.

"I don't know. I think they kind of creep along crouching close to the ground. I saw it on a nature channel. They sneak up on their prey undetected that way. Kind of how we're sneaking along now. Then they suddenly pounce on it. I think. I'm making this up as we—Listen! . . . Did you hear something?"

"Phew, more like smell something. Something I've smelled before and I didn't like it one bit! It smells like you ate burritos for breakfast, it stinks, like you—wait. You know what that means," he whispered. "Uh-oh, it smells just like a . . ."

Some Random Guy and Tannic clung to each other motionless in the grass and didn't make a sound. The stench of the Minotaur got stronger, and soon they heard its footsteps. Minotaurs were known to never bathe or shower. Was that because they couldn't swim and were afraid of the water? It would explain the reluctance of the Minotaur at pond. Or did they just enjoy their own rank stink? It didn't really matter now. As SRG and Tannic watched, a shadow began moving closer through the grass, until it covered over them. They were hiding in the shadow of the Minotaur. They froze, afraid to move. The creature paused for a moment and snorted. Then it started sniffing the air, turning slowly left and right for any sign of movement. They could smell its pungent breath and feel the hot air on their necks, but they stayed statue still against the ground. Some Random Guy was holding his breath. Tannic was doing his best to be invisible, but unfortunately invisibility wasn't a skill he had in Rough World. He was about as invisible as waving a red flag to a bull—or to a man with a bull's head. The Minotaur lowered its head into the grass and parted it with its horns for a better look. Slowly the head panned left and right, coming within inches of SRG and Tannic through the grass. SRG looked at Tannic with panic in his eyes. They were about to be discovered. He gripped the Dragonwrigley tighter, looked at Tannic again, and nodded almost imperceptibly toward the Minotaur. He readied himself to draw the blade, and was planning his shot when it abruptly raised its head. It gave a low grunt, stood upright, and started running back toward the first pond. Tannic looked at SRG, who sighed deeply. They both had a relieved look in their eyes.

"Whew! That was a close one," SRG whispered. It was obvious, but he needed to say something.

"Yeah. Too close for comfort," Tannic answered.

"I was about to draw the sword when it stood up. I was trying to wriggle it free without making a noise."

"That was lucky!"

"Yeah, but was it good lucky or bad lucky?" SRG asked.

"How could it be bad?"

"What can you think of that would make a Minotaur run away?"

Tannic's eyes widened. "The Ender Dude!" They both said it at the same time.

"So what do we do now?" Tannic asked nervously.

"I think we keep going to the second pond. If it is the Ender Dude, maybe we can sneak past him like we did with the Minotaur. If not I'll have to hold him off with the Dragonwrigley. I don't know what else to do. I'm not looking forward to meeting *him* in real life."

"And I can run on water, that might help," Tannic added.

"Do you think the Ender Dude can swim?" SRG asked.

"They never do on Level 1. In the game, I mean. But being here for real doesn't seem to be exactly like the game. This is a lot harder, and scarier. We can't just hit reset and start over again. I don't know if the Ender Dude can swim or not. I think we should assume he can. Anyway, I think we need to keep moving. We need to find that Rainbow Star."

They continued leopard crawling through the grass. They were a couple hundred yards from the second pond, and it was still early afternoon. SRG's clothes were finally drying out from his swim, but now they were both sweating. If he'd had more time he would have wrung his clothes out and laid them on a rock in the sun to dry. His grandpa had taught him to do that one year when they were fly fishing together in the Steen's Mountains. It was the year after the Great Luigi

Incident—that's what his family called their 2010 trip. But that's a story for another time. In 2011, his grandpa told him to get off the wet rocks before he slipped and fell into the creek. But in true SRG style, he hadn't paid attention, and the next thing he knew he was neck-deep in ice-cold mountain water and bobbing downstream. It turned out that wet rocks really were pretty slippery. Luckily his grandpa caught hold of his collar and dragged him onto the bank before he drowned. He was cold and shaking, and it was shaping up to be a long day until his grandpa got him to dry his clothes on the rocks. He didn't know how his grandpa had learned about things like that, but he reckoned it was from personal experience. His grandpa had always been the "voice of experience." At least that's what his grandma called him. She called herself the "voice of reason."

Today there was no chance of drying out his clothes. They couldn't risk taking the time. There was still the risk of Minotaurs to worry about and an Ender Dude hanging around somewhere protecting the Rainbow Star. The sooner they reached the second pond, the sooner they would complete Level 1. That would take them one step closer to getting home. Well, maybe. SRG hoped they would be going home. But he didn't really know.

Tannic was a little scared, but he was also somewhat imaginary, so where was home for him, really? His thoughts drifted back to the present as he continued forward through the grass.

Even apart from the risk of losing your Life Wedges, Rough World was scary, but it was fun at the same time. And it was quite a while since he and Some Random Guy had had an adventure like this. This was one they would tell their grandchildren about. That is, if they lived. And that was a pretty big *if.* They'd never been on an adventure to match this one. Their last real adventure happened the year before, when they were caught digging for buried treasure in Mrs. Kibbitch's back yard. They'd tried to explain the treasure map to her, and assured her the grass would grow back. But she was just unreasonable and didn't want to hear any of it. She was even grumpier than normal, if that was possible. So they offered to divide the treasure with her when they found it. But she still wanted no part in it. She was just unhappy about the huge hole in her perfectly manicured lawn. In the end, SRG's dad called a landscaper to repair it, and SRG was grounded for a month. In addition to getting a stern talking-to, his dad had been pretty upset over the deal. (What SRG didn't know was that his dad and mom had laughed about it in bed later that night.) And Mrs. Kibbitch still wasn't over it, even though it had happened almost a year ago. You couldn't even see the scar in the lawn now, well, not unless you looked really close. Anyway, Mrs. Kibbitch was scary enough, but she didn't hold a candle to a Minotaur. Minotaurs were *really* scary. Dangerous scary. They were big and mean and strong and smelly. She was just a grumpy little old lady. Tannic said she had been grumpy ever since the house fell on her sister. Some Random Guy pictured her driving a broom, although he had never actually seen her do it.

But now they had other problems. SRG and Tannic weren't sure what an Ender Dude would look like in the flesh. They were scary enough in the game. In real life they might be worse. So Tannic was scared and nervous, but he was excited too. And he could walk, or run at least, on water, which was really cool. All in all, it was shaping up to be the adventure of their lifetimes, if they lived.

Some Random Guy and Tannic continued their slow crawl toward the second pond. They kept their eyes out for Minotaurs and the Ender Dude and just kept moving at a slow, easy pace. They were closing in on the second pond. They hadn't stumbled onto a Heart Gem, but they hadn't run into another Minotaur or the Ender Dude either. They could smell the cool water ahead and could see a clearing at the water's edge, with a small sandy beach where they'd be able to assess the situation, and they were inching toward it. Any other day, a swim in the cool water would have been a welcome treat, but today was different. They were close to the clearing, though, which was the good news. And a moment later they got more good news, when they saw the Rainbow Star sitting atop a tiny island right in the middle of the pond. Beams of colored light radiated in every direction from it. It looked like a brilliant rainbow bursting out of a single spot. They stopped and stared at it in silence. They were transfixed.

"Wow, the Rainbow Star is beautiful in real life," SRG exclaimed. It was mesmerizing.

"Unbelievable," Tannic nodded.

"Now we know why they call it the Rainbow Star. It doesn't look anything like that in the game. It's just sort of a rainbow-colored star-shaped rock."

They needed the Rainbow Star to finish the level, and they'd need all ten Rainbow Stars to get into the Evil Boss's private headquarters at the end of Level 10 to finish World One. The lock was a wall-sized ring of indentations that the Rainbow Stars would fit into. When all ten were in place, the large, carved wooden door would open from the center like a giant steel jaw, and you would walk into the most dangerous part of the game—up to that point, anyway—the Evil Boss's private office.

Neither of them knew what happened next. But that's getting ahead of the story anyway. There were still lots of enemies to defeat, booby traps to dodge, and clever plans to make up and carry out. And that's good news, because there was no guarantee they'd survive the Evil Boss. Nobody had ever made it far enough to confront Mr. Eville before, they didn't know what to expect.

Bad news, however, was just about to arrive in waves—literally.

"Oh no! Do you see what else I see?" Some Random Guy asked.

Tannic nodded, in a trance. His eyes were fixed on the Rainbow Star.

"Hey! Stay focused for me, Good Buddy! Look in the pond. Directly between us and the Star."

Tannic finally looked, and then gasped. The Ender Dude was swimming halfway between them and the Rainbow Star. It couldn't have been a coincidence. There were no co-incidences in Rough World. Nothing was random. The game had been carefully planned by a team of experienced gaming engineers. It was possible to win, but it was rough enough to challenge even the most experienced gamers.

Nobody had actually defeated the Evil Boss yet. That was part of the game's draw—nobody even knew what happened afterward. Or if someone did know, they were keeping it to themselves. Winning had become a kind of Holy Grail, and the game was becoming a legend. Whoever defeated it for the first time would be famous. It was human nature. People want to know what others don't know, they want to have what others don't have, and they want to go where no one has been before. It was like a club that everybody wanted to belong to, but that was so exclusive there weren't any members at all yet. At least, as far as anybody knew. But in the meantime everybody was talking about it in the gaming chat rooms, and everybody was making predictions about what would happen after you defeated the Evil Boss. Even at Super Smash Brothers contests, the topic inevitably came up. And the conversation always ended with speculations about Mr. Eville.

That was part of the reason Some Random Guy and Tannic loved the game too—at least, when it was a *game*. Rough World in real life was a different story altogether. It was no Mario Kart 2. It was more like Donkey Kong meets Jurassic Park. This place might even put Navy Seals on edge and make their pulses race. Rough World kept the best gamers challenged and interested, and right now it had all of SRG and Tannic's attention. In fact, the Ender Dude himself had all their attention, as he swam menacingly about the pond, glancing about with an air of casual indifference. Even the Chomp Cheap Carps left him alone. That couldn't possibly be good news.

"So now what?" Tannic asked.

"One of us will have to create a diversion while the other one swims to the Rainbow Star," SRG answered.

"You mean, one of us will be the bait while the other one gets the glory? Isn't that what you're saying, Compadre?"

"Well, I wouldn't put it exactly like that, Mister I-Can-Run-On-Water."

"Whoa, wait a minute! That was fun, being chased by the carp, but this is a whole different story. I don't think I want to be the bait for the Ender Dude!"

"You have a better suggestion?" SRG asked.

"Yeah! You be the bait! I'll run over the water to the

island, grab the Rainbow Star and we'll be done with this stupid level!"

"What if the Ender Dude defeats me before you get the Star? Then I'm dead, Good Buddy! And then you're dead!"

"Hey, you still have two Life Wedges, I only have one. At least you get to make one mistake. I don't get to make any."

"I don't know," SRG replied. "The Dragonwrigley's really heavy, and in the water it's really awkward. I barely managed to cut that carp off of my leg. And you did a great job of distracting them. Better than I could have."

"Yeah. But what if he can walk on water too? Or what if he can swim faster than I can run?"

SRG smiled. "I guess that's a chance I'm willing to take."

"Nice try. I vote no."

"Overruled."

"I appeal!"

"Overruled again!"

"How come you get to overrule everything? I want to overrule you!" Tannic complained.

"Listen, I honestly think it's our best chance. Until we find out how fast he can swim or run or whatever. We know that you can run on water, and we know that I'm a slow swimmer, especially with the sword. I think it's the best plan."

"I don't like it."

"Do you have a better idea?" SRG asked.

"Yeah, you distract him from the beach. Get him to swim this way. Stay out of the water and keep shooting fireballs at him the whole time. That should keep him occupied, and I'll skedaddle across the pond, pick up the Rainbow Star, and we're off to Level 2!"

"That could work. What if he decides to chase you instead of me?" SRG asked.

"Then I'll have to keep him entertained while you try to swim to the island. But if he catches me or comes back for you then we're both dead. Well, I mean, I guess we could always politely ask him, could he swim to the island for us? And please would he mind terribly getting the Rainbow Star and bringing it to us? I guess that's another option."

"No time to be a smarty pants, Tannic," SRG scolded.

"All right, whatever! What do you want to do? I think both of our plans could work. It all depends on the Ender Dude and what he's capable of." Tannic stared at SRG.

"What? Hang on, give me a minute, I'm thinking!" SRG replied.

"Well, don't think too long or we'll be too nervous to try anything. If we die, at least we die trying, not sitting here thinking about it. And if we die, I just want you to know you were my best friend. You and Katie from down the street."

"What? Katie? Are you freaking kidding me? Don't be getting all soft on me now, Good Buddy. Remind me to slap some sense into you when this is all done! Who likes girls, anyway? Yuck! What's happened to you?"

"Hey, just a minute there, Mister I'm-Too-Tough-To-Like-Girls. You love your mom. I've seen you cuddle up next to her on the couch. So don't start with me! I like Katie, okay? So get over it!"

"Okay, whatever. Never mind. I hate to admit it, but I like your plan best," SRG admitted. "I'll distract him while you run out to the island and grab the Rainbow Star."

Some Random Guy rose slowly out of the grass until he was in full view of the Ender Dude. The Ender Dude seemed to ignore him, though, and kept swimming back and forth as if he didn't care. Tannic began slowly edging to the left, keeping carefully hidden in the grass and preparing to make a daring run as soon as SRG had the Ender Dude's full attention.

"Hey, you! Yeah, I'm talking to you, dog face! You're ugly . . . and stupid, and . . . you're ugly and your mother's ugly too! That's if you even have a mother! You're so ugly, when you look up "ugly" on Wikipedia, there's a picture of your face! You look like something a dog would puke up on the lawn. You look like week-old roadkill that dried up in the sun after the buzzards got done eating it! You make the Minotaurs look like beauty pageant winners! Yeah, you, uh . . . lizard brain! I'm talking to you!" Some Random Guy shouted at the top of his lungs. "You want a piece of this? You got nothin'! You got nothin'!"

The "lizard brain" comment must have gotten the Ender Dude's attention. He turned and started swimming toward SRG, fast.

He was much faster than they'd expected. Tannic was still looking for an opening to run to the island. It was going to be close. He needed to go now to have any chance of getting the Rainbow Star before Ender Dude destroyed SRG. He was still feeling confident about the plan, though. He ran.

He sped right onto the surface of the water at full speed. It felt just like running on soft grass, he thought. It was amazing. He felt like he was racing down a soccer field—or across Mrs. Kibbitch's yard to retrieve a ball. As he pondered that, however, he forgot to ponder the Chomp Cheap Carps at all. But they hadn't forgotten about him. Suddenly they were chasing him, jumping out of the water and nipping at his heels. He could feel their razor-sharp teeth brushing the heels of his sneakers. These ones were bigger and faster than the Carps from the first pond. He hadn't considered that.

And the Ender Dude was almost on top of SRG, who was still dissing him loudly from the beach. SRG was making it pretty personal.

There are moments when you're executing the best-laid plans in the world, and everything morphs into a time-warp-zone and life moves in slow motion. That was happening to Tannic right now. To SRG, though, it seemed like his life was about to flash before his eyes.

And that's when it happened. The thing they hadn't planned for at all. The thing they hadn't even thought of. The thing they certainly had no contingency plan for. A Minotaur stepped out of the grass a few feet behind SRG. It raised its arms high, grunted loudly, and then it was moving toward SRG. Tannic couldn't believe it. The plan had suddenly gone horribly wrong. SRG had the Ender Dude closing the gap in front of him and a Minotaur closing in on his back. Tannic was struggling to stay ahead of the man-eating fish as SRG turned and sent two rapid volleys of fireballs at the Minotaur. The Minotaur ducked and dodged both. SRG swung the sword wildly at the Minotaur, releasing wave after wave of razor-bladed crescents, and the Minotaur started . . . dancing. He danced like a silver salmon putting on an aerial display at the end of a taut fly line. He dodged around the shiny moon-shaped blades from side to side like he was bending time. Tannic kept running toward the island while watching the action on the bank over his shoulder in horror. His heart was pounding in his ears. It was going to be close.

SRG turned back to the pond just in time to see the Ender Dude stand up out of the water. He gasped. The Ender Dude must have been eight feet tall and easily weighed 500 pounds. He looked like an ogre—even more so in real life.

And he wore a smile that seemed out of place. It was a confident, contented smile, as if he were about to squash a bug and enjoy it. He seemed to be completely in control of the situation. There was no hesitation in his movement.

The Minotaur, which had just dodged the last crescent, looked up to see the Ender Dude rising out of the water. It squealed, turned, and dashed whimpering away into the grass. Now SRG needed to face the Ender Dude one on one, *mano a mano*, man to man. Or rather, boy to huge monster. He was reminded of David and Goliath as he raised the Dragonwrigley and sent two fireballs directly at the chest of the Ender Dude.

Both shots were perfect hits into the middle of his body. The Ender Dude just stood there unfazed, and then starting laughing. He roared as he laughed out loud. SRG's mouth went dry and he couldn't swallow. Fear was welling up inside of him. He felt like he was going to puke. The Ender Dude slowly began approaching, and now SRG had nowhere to go. He swung the sword and fired a flurry of crescents. They all hit the Ender Dude spot-on, and once again they made no impact whatsoever. They just bounced off with a metallic tinkling sound and fell to the ground at the Ender Dude's feet. The Ender Dude kept walking. He towered over SRG and looked down with his satisfied smile. He was in no hurry. He was in total control. He was savoring the moment.

SRG wanted to run, but his legs wouldn't respond. They weren't even listening to his screaming brain. It was like they had turned to ice. He was frozen in place. He drew what would probably be his last breath and thought about his family. He was really going to miss his parents. Heck, he was even going to miss his brothers, the knuckleheads. He was sorry he hadn't mowed the lawn, though. He was sorry he didn't get to say goodbye. He was sorry that they'd probably never know what happened to him. The headline would read *10-Year-Old Boy Mysteriously Disappears from North Albany*. He thought all the random thoughts you think when you know you're about to die.

He was jerked out of his thoughts and back into the present when the Ender Dude picked him up with one hand. SRG couldn't believe his strength. The Ender Dude looked at him the way SRG would look at an ice cream cone or a maple bar. He smiled again and licked his lips. SRG squeezed his eyes closed and opened his mouth to scream. He could feel his heart pounding in his chest. He tried to scream, but no sound came out.

Tannic had not been idle. He'd barely escaped the Chomp Cheap Carps, but he'd finally made it to the island. He ran straight to the Rainbow Star, and his hand landed on it just as the Ender Dude's teeth were closing down on SRG's head.

Some Random Guy's body went completely limp, and a Life Wedge above his head glowed briefly and began to fade.

Chapter 4

The Underground Mining Car

And just like that it was over. The Ender Dude was gone. The Majestic Meadow was gone. Some Random Guy was standing next to Tannic in Dr. Denton's lab. Dr. Denton was looking them up and down, obviously trying to figure out what had just happened and where these two lads had come from.

SRG hugged Tannic. "Whew! You saved my life, Good Buddy." He took a deep breath and blew it out slowly between his lips. He was still trembling. "At least I'm pretty sure you did. I thought I was a goner for sure. What happened out there?"

"I got the Rainbow Star just as the Ender Dude was about to make a meal out of you. That was way too close. I can't believe we made it. But we actually made it, Compadre! We finished the first level!"

Then they both looked in amazement at Dr. Denton, who was quietly staring at them with a confused look on his face.

"Hi, Dr. Denton, my name is Some Random Guy, well, that's not my real name, I mean not really, but you can call me SRG for short too if you want to. And this is my best friend Tannic. That's his real name and he doesn't have a last name, at least I don't think he does," SRG introduced himself rambling on. "We recognize you from the game. You know, from Rough World."

"It's nice to meet you boys, but what are you doing here?" Dr. Denton asked.

"We don't know. We were playing the game in our family room, and I think lightning hit the house! Do you know what could have happened? How did we actually end up here for real? I mean, we are here for real. At least it sure seems real to us."

"I really don't know what happened. This is Rough World, the *real* Rough World," Dr. Denton replied. "That's really most unusual. I'm not sure I can explain it, but it sounds like it had something to do with a temporal electron neural transport initiated by the lightning strike. Let me think. Ah, yes! Consider the phenomenon Marty and Doc experienced in Back to the Future. They used a temporal flux capacitor to transport electrons through time. In this case, you were both transported from the real world into the video game world, which is just like a real world once you get here. That's the best explanation I can hypothesize at the moment. But I've never really heard of this happening before. It's most unusual, most unusual indeed. I'm not sure what to say."

"H-H-How do we get home?" SRG stuttered.

"Hmm. I'm not sure. I don't want to scare you, but to be honest, I don't know," Dr. Denton responded. "I'll have to do some investigating. I'm not even sure if it's possible to reverse the process and send you back. I have no experience with anything like this. But I'll do my best to look into it and help you boys however I can."

SRG began to tremble. "I just want to go home!" he cried. He bit his lip.

"Listen, I'll work on it and see what I can come up with. Don't worry. I'll work on it. I'm here for you. Do you want to review highlights from Level 1?" Dr. Denton asked.

"No!" SRG blurted. "I'm done with the Majestic Meadow. I don't care if I never see it again!"

"Well . . . I would kind of like to see the part where SRG shot me," Tannic added. "I can't believe my best friend shot me! Who would do that, anyway?"

"Nothing doing, Good Buddy. We don't need to examine the past. We're going back out there to Level 2, the Underground Mining Car. We don't need to replay our past mistakes. We need to keep moving forward until we get out of here!"

"In that case, I wish you both the best on Level 2," Dr. Denton said. "It's a challenging level as well, and they'll continue to grow more difficult as the game progresses. Please be safe out there! I'll be here trying to figure out what happened, how you got here, and how to reverse the process."

"Any advice for Level 2?" Tannic asked.

"Well, nothing terribly specific comes to mind. It's pretty straightforward. Don't get yourselves killed . . . watch out for the Mining Minotaurs . . . capture the Rainbow Star . . . avoid the Ender Dude. Oh yes, you'll have headlamps as your special accessories for this level, but use them sparingly. You'll only have a couple of hours of battery power, so make it count. And you'll notice that the Dragonwrigley is now a *psword* instead of a sword—it's a combination sword and pick axe. It will still shoot fireballs and crescents, but you can use it as a pick axe too. That might come in handy in the mine. The Rainbow Star will be at the very end of the mine shaft, on a ledge next to the bottomless chasm. Just like in the game, I would think." He smiled. "That should about cover this level. Do you have any questions?"

"Uh, yeah, Doc. If we lose all three Life Wedges on any level are we dead? I mean like dead for real? Is there any way to reset the level?"

"I'm afraid not boys. This is the real Rough World and you're the players here. You get three Life Wedges at the start of each level. If you lose a Life Wedge you will die temporarily and then be reset complete and intact, just like your characters did in the video game. However, here if you lose all three Life Wedges, well, you'd be very certifiably dead for real. I'm sorry. There is no reset here." He gave them a serious look. "There's one more thing you should know. If you happen to lose the Dragonwrigley to an enemy and they kill you with it, it doesn't matter how many Life Wedges you have left, you will be permanently dead and it will be game over. So no matter what, do not lose the Dragonwrigley!"

"Wow! That's not like in the game. I was kind of afraid of all that, Doc. But thanks, it helps a lot. It really does and we've actually played Level 2 before, so we're pretty familiar with it. Except in the game, the Dragonwrigley doesn't become a psword. So that's new. And it's a lot heavier in real life than I imagined. But we've defeated this level a bunch of times before. We've never had to deal with a Bottomless Chasm in real life, though. If one of us died we just hit reset and played the level again. That was pretty tame compared to being here for real. Okay, I think we're about as ready as we'll get. We appreciate your help," SRG answered. He and Tannic walked over to the lab's outer door.

"That's what I'm here for. Now, you boys be careful out there. I'll be waiting for you back here in the lab, cheering you on! And I'll see what I can figure out about how you got here in the meantime. Good luck!"

The Dragonwrigley stood waiting for him in the corner. He picked it up and looked at it. There was now a pick axe blade jutting out of the sword about halfway down its length. The new psword was a bit heavier with the addition. He nodded to Tannic and they picked up the headlamps and put them on. Some Random Guy flipped the switch to test his. It was pretty bright. He nodded in approval, then switched it back off, shrugged his shoulders, and opened the door for Tannic.

As Tannic stepped through the door, SRG glanced longingly back at the reverse screen on the wall. The family room was still empty, and the game controller was sitting off-kilter on the ottoman. He couldn't tell if it was still raining. He took one last look at home, and then waved goodbye to Dr. Denton and followed Tannic out of the lab.

They stepped over the threshold and directly into a mine shaft. After the door closed behind them, it was absolutely dark. They couldn't see anything. It would take a few minutes for their eyes to adjust. They could hear faint voices and activity further ahead in the shaft. The air had the cold feel of a damp basement that seemed to penetrate all the way to your bones. It smelled musty and damp, and it was so dark that it even smelled dark. And a faint odor of Minotaur stink mixed with fresh dirt hung heavily in the air that wafted by them.

Eventually his pupils dilated and SRG could just make out Tannic's form in the darkness. He looked down and found what looked like railroad tracks. They were narrower than normal train tracks, so he supposed they were for a smaller train that carried ore through the mine. SRG could feel a weak vibration in the tracks under his feet. A low humming murmur accompanied it. They paused to listen for a couple of minutes, but nothing changed in the vibration or the sound.

Finally, SRG spoke. "Psst. Tannic. Can you see me now?"

"Yes. May I say you look just like Justin Bieber in the dark, Compadre?" Tannic teased.

"Enough nonsense. We have work to do. We need to focus and be sharp. Seeing as we barely made it through Level 1, I'm frankly a little worried about this level. It's quite a bit harder, and we don't really know what to expect. We had enough trouble defeating this level when we were playing the game."

"Sorry, Compadre, just trying to lighten the mood. You know, lighten, since it's so dark in here." He paused for effect. "Get it? It was a pun . . . oh forget it, you never have any fun."

"Fun? You think this is fun? We're at Defcon 5 here, Good Buddy. Any one of these levels could to be our last. I don't feel like making jokes about it. I want to go home. We need to be serious!"

"Sorry again, Compadre. I mean it this time. So what's the plan? How should we approach this level?"

"Well, I was thinking," SRG said softly, "Since I went first last time, maybe you should go first here, and I'll be right behind you with the psword."

"Nice try!" Tannic retorted. "But you have the only weapon. And I don't remember any water for me to run over in this mine shaft, so that won't be of any help. I'd say that leaves you in charge. So lead on!"

"Oh, all right. Hey—do you think you could run across the bottomless chasm? I mean, like, just pretend it's water and run straight across it? What do you think? Think that's possible?"

"Only one way to find out, and I'm not about to try." Tannic answered dryly.

"Okay. It was just a thought. Well, how about I lead and we try to find a mining car and ride it past the Mining Minotaurs? Then we can figure out how to get past the Ender Dude and grab the Rainbow Star once we see what we're up against?"

"That sounds like a plan. Anything that has you in the lead sounds like a plan to me. I've never told anybody this, but I'm kind of afraid of the dark. I'd feel better if I could use my headlamp."

"You can't turn on your headlamp now or the Minotaurs will see us. And you're afraid of the dark? Really?" SRG asked. "Now's a fine time to tell me that. Besides, if we could see everything in here it might be even scarier!"

"It never really came up," Tannic responded. "There was no reason to mention it. Anyway, I'd just feel better if I could have a light on, that's all."

"Well, you'll get over it fast. We need to travel in the dark so we aren't discovered. Come on. Keep quiet and follow my lead."

So the two best friends, with only a Dragonwrigley psword and their wits to protect them, proceeded silently down into the guts of the mining shaft, leaving Dr. Denton and whatever safety his laboratory provided behind. There was no turning back. You couldn't open the lab door from the outside. They had already tried that. Once you left the only way back was to capture the Rainbow Star, and risk death in the process.

The mine shaft descended deeper and deeper into the earth. Eventually they saw a curve in the tracks up ahead. As their eyes adjusted to the dark they also noticed a faint glow on the walls, and the humming sound in the distance was growing louder. When they reached the corner, they hugged the outside wall and crept carefully around it. Just past the turn they saw their first Mining Minotaur. It was much smaller than the ones in the Majestic Meadow. It was shorter, and its horns were also shorter and more rounded at the tips. However, it was still well muscled and dressed in ragged, dirty bib overalls with red suspenders. It also was wearing a yellow hard hat with a miner's headlamp that lit up the area immediately in front of it. The horns protruded through the hard hat and made a funny sight. Some Random Guy and Tannic both wanted to laugh but caught themselves. They couldn't be discovered now.

The Mining Minotaur wore leather gloves over its huge hands and was swinging a pick axe repeatedly into the shaft wall. Its headlamp illuminated the area it was working on, and another on the floor flooded the region in warm yellow light. The Minotaur started shoveling a pile of dirt and debris into an open mining car. It was grunting while it worked, and it seemed to be humming too. It was so busy that it hadn't noticed them at all. SRG and Tannic crept quietly along the wall, moving invisibly, or so they hoped, in the shadows. They timed their movement to the Minotaur's. If they could sneak past unnoticed, they could avoid creating a ruckus until they knew where they were, how many more Minotaurs there were, and what they should expect. The Dragonwrigley was also now heavier and a bit more awkward to swing. Still, it was the only protection they had.

Some Random Guy was still leading the way. Tannic stayed within arm's length behind him, grinning sheepishly. For all his complaints, and even though he really was afraid of the dark, for all outward appearances he was still having fun.

SRG hadn't noticed the grin. His eyes were focused on the Minotaur. It had gone back to swinging its pick axe at the wall. A pile of dirt was growing on the floor of the shaft. SRG was breathing in time with the pick axe, trying not to be noticed. This move would take all of their concentration.

Tannic tugged his arm. "We need to time it just right as we pass this guy. We don't want to attract any attention," he whispered.

"Yeah. We should sneak past the car one at a time when he's facing the wall," SRG agreed. "I'll go first. If anything goes wrong just drop to the ground and freeze. I'll confront him with the Dragonwrigley. If that happens, be ready for anything. Stay close and follow my lead."

SRG waited until the Minotaur had turned back toward the wall and raised his pick axe. He dropped to his knees and slipped into the shadows behind the mining car. He paused and waited for the Minotaur to put down the pick axe and pick up the shovel. When it began scooping up the loose dirt again, he moved carefully again beyond the mining car and safely out of the Minotaur's view.

Tannic followed SRG's example and waited until the Minotaur turned away from the mining car and swung his pick axe at the wall. The pick axe drove into the wall and the Minotaur tugged at it, pulling a pile of dirt to the floor. Tannic moved with purpose to hide behind the car. The Minotaur then turned and grabbed its shovel as before and sent up a cloud of dust as it threw a load of dirt into the car.

Tannic sneezed.

He couldn't help it. It was the dust. He tried not to, but it was no use. He couldn't hold it in. Sneezing is just a reflex. Some people can hold their sneezes in, but Tannic wasn't one of them.

So he sneezed. He muffled it as much as he could, then he held his breath and froze. The noise startled the Minotaur and he abruptly looked up.

Some Random Guy had a panicked look on his face. Tannic squatted as low as he could and held his breath as he waited. The Minotaur was looking around for the source of the noise. SRG was looking on in horror. He tightened his grip on the psword, but he really didn't want to attract the rest of the Minotaurs before they'd even gotten started on the level.

Fortunately he didn't have to. The Minotaur scanned left and right, but not seeing anything, shrugged its shoulders and turned back to its shoveling. When it picked up its pick axe, Tannic carefully maneuvered through the shadows between the track and the wall and caught up with SRG. They were now safely out of the Minotaur's view. They looked at each other. SRG rolled his eyes and nodded at the Minotaur.

"Whew, that was close!" Tannic said. "I thought he was going to find me."

"Why did you sneeze?" SRG asked. "Couldn't you hold it? You just about blew it."

"I tried, but it just came out. I'm sorry."

"Well, try harder next time. We may not be so lucky again. Come on, let's sneak farther along and see what's happening down in the mineshaft."

"What was the object of this level again?" Tannic asked.

"Come on, Tannic, wake up! This is the Mining Car Level. We need to collect bits of ore from the mining cars, and they turn into Boss Coins. Once we have ten, we can jump far enough to get across the bottomless chasm at the end of the mine. We've played this level like thirty times before. Don't you remember anything? The Ender Dude is on this side of the chasm, and we have to either trick him into falling in or get around him. The Rainbow Star's on the other side of the chasm," SRG whispered.

"That's right, now I remember," Tannic whispered back. "Shhhh, look out. Here comes a Minotaur."

The Minotaur was a dark shape walking slowly toward them from deeper in the mine. His headlamp lit his way as he wandered along. Tannic and SRG backed up against the wall as tightly as they could, but there was nowhere to go. Randomly, there was a small depression in the wall right behind them, and they pressed into it as best they could. It was a good thing they were best friends, as it was a tight fit. Tannic had his back to the wall and SRG was in front protecting them, the Dragonwrigley pulled tightly in between them to keep it from reflecting the Minotaur's lamplight. It was so snug in the depression that they would have had to take turns breathing, if they weren't already holding their breath.

The Minotaur stopped a few feet away and studied the railcar tracks carefully. A bead of sweat trickled down SRG's forehead and into his eyes. He blinked as it burned, but he didn't dare move any more. He could feel the handle of the psword, but it was wedged between him and Tannic and it wouldn't be easy to draw.

The Minotaur picked up a chunk of ore. It shone brightly under his headlamp. He shook his head, grunted, and dropped it into the pocket of his bib overalls. Then he picked up his pick axe and walked by so close that he almost touched them. But he was focused on the tracks and not paying attention to the walls. SRG and Tannic both sucked in deep breaths after he was out of earshot. They exhaled slowly.

"I'm getting tired of these close calls, Compadre. Did

you have to squish me against the wall so tight? I could barely breathe."

"Hey, we're lucky that depression was deep enough for the both of us. I was scared the whole time that you were going to sneeze!"

"And I was scared the whole time that you were going to fart!" Tannic snickered. "So what do we do now Compadre?"

"Let's follow the tracks to the end of the mine. I'm sure we're going to see more Minotaurs and mining cars. And did you see that ore? It was awesome! Come on, we need to find some. We've got ten coins to collect."

Some Random Guy and Tannic slowly and carefully worked their way down the shaft and around the next corner. A hundred feet ahead of them was a string of mining cars, with an engine at the nearest end. In what appeared to be "shovel ready" jobs, each mining car was being loaded by a Mining Minotaur with pick axe and shovel. There were flood lights illuminating the entire area, but the noise from the work created a palpable din in the air. If they were patient and careful, SRG and Tannic would be able to proceed unnoticed to the engine car or, maybe, the first mining car. But after that, they'd be partially exposed in the light and would need a plan.

They were squatting behind a rock, watching and trying to work out a plan, when a Minotaur stepped onto the platform of the engine and fired it up. He was dressed like the others, in bib overalls and a yellow hard hat with his horns protruding through it. The motor groaned and coughed as it turned over and gradually sprang to life. It made a loud humming sound. The Minotaur put it into gear, and the whole train slowly clattered forward. SRG and Tannic exchanged worried glances. Then it came to an abrupt halt with a screech of steel wheels on steel tracks, and the Minotaur stepped off of the train engine. He picked up his tools, set up another flood lamp, and started working on a fresh area of the mine shaft wall.

The rest of the Minotaurs shifted forward after him and went back to their rhythmic dance of picking and shoveling. They'd simply been shifting position to work on a new part of the wall. The first Minotaur gathered the other flood lamps and set back up to illuminate the new section. The mining activity created the same loud noise and provided good cover for the boys. After a few minutes, all the miners were back at their jobs, picking with their axes and shoveling ore into the string of mining cars. There was a shallow shadow behind the train cars now. It would provide enough cover for them to sneak along undetected if they were careful and timed their movements. They watched the miners work, getting a feel for their rhythm.

After a couple of minutes SRG spoke up. "I'm thinking," he said. "What if we get as close as we can and then wait till the Minotaur starts the engine again. Then we move in close and lie down next to the track, in the shadows. When he drives past us we can hide behind the cars, and time our moves like we did with the first car. What do you think?"

"I don't know, it sounds risky. What if he sees us?"

"Really, risky? Did you think we were going to just walk past all the Minotaurs to the end of the mine shaft and just pick up the Rainbow Star while the Ender Dude watches us? Everything about Rough World is risky. That's why we like playing it so much. It just not as much fun when it's for real!"

"Okay, you're right. I can't think of a better plan. Let's try yours," Tannic agreed. "We can make it work. It just makes me nervous. And I feel a little bit confined in here, like the walls are closing in on me. That and the dark. I just feel kind of . . . what's the word? Anxious about being penned in?"

"Claustrophobic? I think that's the word. My dad felt that way when he had an MRI and they stuck him in this big machine. He said he focused on his breathing and it helped. Just take slow steady breaths and focus on the task at hand. Think about the Rainbow Star, think about whatever you need to. Just be alert and focused. Take your mind off of everything else. We have enough to worry about right in front of us. There are more Mining Minotaurs than I imagined. We'd be totally outnumbered in a fight, so we have to avoid them. Are you with me?"

"Yeah, thanks, that helps a lot. I'm going to focus my thoughts on my breathing."

Tannic started counting his breaths and focused on keeping his breathing slow and steady, never taking his eyes off the Minotaurs. SRG crept along the wall toward the engine car with Tannic just behind him. He held the psword behind his back so that it wouldn't reflect any light. They stayed between the tracks and the wall, as deep in the shadows by the wall as they could get. SRG kept his eyes on the ground, making sure he didn't trip or kick any rocks. They moved in time with the rhythm of the workers. It took a few minutes of stopping and starting, but they finally made it safely to the engine car.

A shiny piece of ore next to the track caught Tannic's eye. He bent down and picked it up carefully. It immediately turned into a Boss Coin right in his hand. He tapped SRG on the shoulder and showed it to him, keeping it low and in the shadows.

"Look!" he exclaimed quietly. "Our first coin! Now we only need nine more."

The coin was brilliant and beautiful. It was a shiny gold color, with the Dragonwrigley emblem on one face and a bust of a strange man on the other. He looked mean and evil. Tannic made a face.

"Who do you think that is? The Evil Boss? Is that Mr. Eville himself?"

"Good work. I don't recognize him, but it makes sense that it would be Mr. Eville. That's probably why they're called Boss Coins. Now we just need to wait until the Minotaur moves the train again. Get as low as you possibly can and don't move. Don't make any noise," SRG instructed him.

"How long will that take? In the game, we just confront the Minotaurs and you shoot them with the Dragonwrigley as we collect the coins while we're running past the cars until we get to the end of the mine shaft. Then we just jump across the bottomless chasm."

"Yeah, but how many times did we both get killed doing that?" SRG asked.

"Uh . . . too many times?" Tannic answered with a question.

"Exactly. Too many times. We can't risk that this time. I think we should sneak through as much as we can. We just need to be patient. The fewer fights we get into with Minotaurs, the better, and the less attention we collect, the better. It would be great to get to the chasm with all our Life Wedges. That way we'd have the best odds of getting the star. I mean, I'm just saying."

Tannic sighed. "I just wonder how long this will take. It makes me nervous, lying here waiting."

"Why? Do you have something else to do? We're here, and we need to do this to get out of here," SRG whispered.

"Geez, I just said I wondered how long it would take. That's all. You're being pretty grumpy."

"Sorry, Good Buddy, I'm just a little on edge. We haven't seen this many Minotaurs all at one time before. I'm a bit nervous too. But we can do this. We got this."

"Okay, I'm with you." Tannic took a deep breath and started counting again.

Time dragged by and it felt like hours passed as they lay face down next to the engine car. In reality, after about twenty minutes, the lead Minotaur stepped back onto the platform and started the engine. It sputtered and coughed again as it turned over, and the exhaust pipe was next to Tannic's head. It blew a cloud of smoke and dust right into his face. His face turned black, and SRG wanted to laugh. But his eyes grew big when he realized Tannic was about to sneeze. He froze in fear.

"Ah . . . *choo!*" Tannic sneezed loudly. "*Achoo! Achoo!*"

But the Minotaur didn't hear him over the chugging of the engine. The train was slowly tugged forward, and they lay completely still until the second car passed them. Then they stood up just enough to move and snuck along the moving rail cars in a crouch. When he got a chance, SRG would reach over the rim of the nearest car, grab a piece of ore, and pocket the coin it turned into. Tannic was grabbing ore too. Their plan was working and they hadn't been detected yet.

The train screeched to a halt again, and SRG and Tannic hit the deck facedown again and waited. SRG watched the feet of the Minotaurs under the train as they walked one by one to catch up with the train. He realized too late that he should have counted them. All he knew was that there were a lot of them, and he had been right that they were seriously outnumbered. Sneaking past undetected was still the best plan.

The Minotaurs reset their flood lamps and returned to

work in unison. SRG and Tannic continued their coordinated dash along the hidden side of the train, waiting for each Minotaur to turn away before moving to the next car. As they were approaching the end of the train undetected, SRG looked at Tannic and smiled. Tannic nodded. They were feeling pretty pleased with themselves as they moved on through the shadows. Their plan was working perfectly.

"What do we do when we get to the last car, Compadre?" Tannic whispered. "How far is it to the end of the mine shaft?"

"No idea. Could there be more workers too? Or do you think this is it? Maybe another train?"

"In the game there was only the one train. So this should be it. I think it's all downhill to the end of the mine. But it's still pretty dark in here. I don't know how far it is."

"Yeah, let me think." SRG thought. "Remember that time we hopped into the last car and pulled the pin and rode it to the end of the tracks? And we knocked the Ender Dude right into the bottomless chasm? Maybe we should try that again."

Some Random Guy's dad had read a book about crossing the chasm and talked to him about it. He couldn't remember what the book said, and now he wished he'd paid better attention. He silently promised himself that if he ever made it home, he'd listen better to his dad.

He continued. "Although . . . now that I think about it, that was after we'd killed all but one or two of the Minotaurs. If we ride the car now I bet we'll have a whole car of Minotaurs chasing after us. And hitting the Ender Dude slowed us down before the bumper at the end of the track. If we missed him we might have flown into the chasm instead. I don't know. Maybe it's too risky. We don't even know how long this mineshaft is."

"Yeah, and we weren't even going that fast. Do you think there's a bumper at the end of the track here?" Tannic asked.

"I don't think we can count on anything here. It's too risky. I think we should just keep sneaking along the track to the end of the mine. It can't be that far. We'll just have to be patient. Once we get past the last car we'll be back in the dark and we can hide better," he concluded.

They were squatted next to the last mining car planning when a spotlight began playing over the walls nearby. A Minotaur was walking down their side of the track and was halfway down the train. He hadn't noticed them yet, but it was only a matter of time before his light hit them. There was nowhere else to go, so without thinking they jumped into the last car.

It was mostly empty, and they had both hoped they could hide in the shadows inside it. But they'd been too late. The Minotaur grunted in surprise as they clambered over the top, and it began howling loudly. Somewhere an alarm bell started sounding. The entire hoard of Minotaurs turned and started running toward them brandishing pick axes. When SRG was halfway over the rim of the car, he heard the Minotaur shout, and did the only thing he could think of. He leaned down between the cars and pulled out the connecting pin.

Once it was loose, the tracks were just steep enough for the car to start rolling backward into the depths of the mine. The Minotaur that had spotted them was running, though, and closing the gap to the two boys.

"I thought you didn't want to do that!" Tannic cried out.

"No choice! There were too many of them and you don't have a weapon! Unless you think running on water can help us!"

"Well excuse me! You didn't think it was so lame on Level 1!"

"Never mind—I just didn't know what else to do! Hang on tight, Good Buddy! We may have to jump!"

As the car gained speed, it slowly pulled away from the running Minotaur, but it kept up its pursuit. In anger, it hurled the pick axe at them, but it fell short and clanked down on the tracks behind them. The Minotaur grabbed it again as he ran by, and now all of the other Minotaurs were behind him, running down the tracks and shouting in a large angry mob, their headlamps bobbing in the dark.

So much for sneaking through the level, SRG thought. They'd almost made it, but almost wasn't good enough. Still, they were building a small lead, and they'd have a little time—but only a little—to get the Rainbow Star before the Minotaurs arrived. And they had to deal with the Ender Dude first. This was all happening too fast, and the rail car was moving too fast for comfort. It started swaying from side to side as they wound their way deeper into the mine, they held on tight to the rail car as it ran over small bumps and around curves. The steel wheels were clattering loudly on the tracks. Tannic was whimpering quietly, but SRG couldn't hear him over the noise. They knew there was a small rise in the grade ahead, but the shaft was dark now that they'd left the Minotaurs behind, the kind of dark where your other senses are heightened because you can't see anything at all. They rocketed down through the dark in their out-of-control car toward the bottomless chasm that loomed somewhere ahead.

The wind was blowing hard in their faces. They began to make out a faint light in the distance ahead, like the light at the end of a tunnel. The mine began to lighten as they hurtled at the speed of light—well, it seemed that way—toward the light. The Minotaurs were minutes behind them now, and SRG and Tannic started feeling more comfortable about them. And less confident about the Ender Dude and the bottomless chasm that waited in front of them—that is, if they didn't crash and die first. Their eyes were big as they looked at each other in fear.

"Hold on tight!" SRG shouted.

"What? I can barely hear you! I am holding on! I can't see anything!" Tannic shouted back.

"Turn on your headlamp!" SRG shouted louder.

"Good idea! I forgot about that!" Tannic turned on his lamp and promptly shined it directly into SRG's eyes.

"Thanks a lot! Now I can't see either!" SRG shouted.

"Oops, sorry!"

The car slowed down a little as it went over the rise, but it gained speed again as the mineshaft got steeper. They could now see the end of the tunnel approaching. It opened onto a large chamber with a bright light overhead. There was a sturdy-looking bumper at the end of the track and a fire hose coiled on the left-hand wall. The bottomless chasm yawned straight ahead, beyond the bumper. It was nothing but an ominous black hole at the end of the tracks. Across the chasm was a ledge holding the Rainbow Star. On the ledge next to the star lay the Ender Dude. He seemed oblivious to the rail car racing toward him at breakneck speed. Then he heard the noise of the wheels on the track and he looked up in amazement. It took him a couple of seconds to realize that there were two foreigners in the car.

"I think we're going to have to jump!" SRG yelled.

"Uh-uh! At this speed? Are you crazy? I'd rather take my chances in the car."

"I don't think the bumper will stop us at this speed. We

have to jump, Tannic!" SRG shouted again.

"I still don't want to! We're going to die either way, and I'm afraid of falling into the chasm!" He paused thoughtfully. "If it's really bottomless, would we just keep falling forever?"

"I have no idea! I don't want to find out! Get ready, Tannic! We both jump at the same time. Hang on to me and I'll try to use the pick axe on the Dragonwrigley to slow us down!"

SRG and Tannic climbed on top of the car's side wall. On the count of three they jumped. Tannic was anchored tightly onto SRG's left leg, and SRG drove the pick axe into the wall to drag them to a stop, like a mountain climber breaking a fall with his ice axe. Dust flew everywhere and the rail car smashed through the bumper, shattered the retaining wall and sent debris everywhere, and launched like a shot into the air. It followed a long arc before plummeting down into the middle of the chasm. SRG hung onto the Dragonwrigley for dear life, and the blade slowly brought them to a halt just shy of the chasm. One of Tannic's feet dangled over the edge.

The commotion had roused the Ender Dude, and he was up on his feet now giving them his full attention. He paced back and forth on his ledge, staring at them and then down into the chasm. The rail car had disappeared into the murky depths.

"Whew! Did you see that? It's a good thing we jumped! I thought we were going to die!" SRG exclaimed. "That was way too close!"

"Me too!" trembled Tannic. "I thought it was game over."

"We don't have much time. I thought the Ender Dude was supposed to be on this side. I was hoping we'd knock him into the chasm or something. What are we going to do now?"

"I don't know. I was hoping the same thing!"

They stood up and SRG picked up the psword. He took aim at the Ender Dude and shot a couple of fireballs at him. The fireballs lit up the chasm briefly as they crossed it. The Ender Dude didn't bother to move, and he didn't flinch as the fireballs hit him in the middle of the chest and sizzled out. He let out a loud, boastful laugh. They could now hear the commotion of the Mining Minotaurs from the mine shaft behind them. It wouldn't be long now. They were running out of time.

"Quick, Tannic, get out your Boss Coins. I'll hold them in one hand and the psword in the other hand and we'll jump across. I'll try to knock the Ender Dude off balance so he'll fall into the chasm."

They pooled the Boss Coins from their pockets.

"Seven, eight, nine . . . uh, bad news, Compadre. We only have nine coins. We can't jump. Now what?"

The noise of the Minotaurs was getting louder, and their headlamps had appeared in the distance. The first one was only fifty yards away, its headlamp bouncing as it ran toward them.

"I don't know! Even if we defeat the Minotaurs, there's no way for us to get across—hey, wait a minute . . ." SRG eyed the fire hose hanging on the wall. "You can run on water."

"Uh, Compadre, there's no water in the chasm. And, uh, it's bottomless," Tannic responded.

"No problem, Good Buddy. I'll make some." He picked up the hose and turned it on full-blast. The stream of water just reached across the chasm. Now the Ender Dude was looking on with curiosity. "You just run across the stream to the ledge. I'll distract the Ender Dude with fireballs and crescents while you grab the Rainbow Star! And then we're back in Doc's lab and on to Level 3!"

"No way, Compadre. How do we even know if I can run on a stream of water coming out of a hose?"

The first Minotaur was closing in on them, with the hoard of others not far behind him. The situation was growing more tense by the second and the clock was ticking. They looked back at the Minotaurs and then at each other.

"You got any better ideas? We're running out of time!"

The Ender Dude just stood there looking in anticipation at the boys and the approaching Minotaurs. He smiled. This was going to be good!

Tannic put his head down and ran toward the water stream as fast as he could, preparing himself mentally for falling into the Chasm and meeting certain death. But as he stepped onto it, the stream supported him. He kept going, but slowed to a walk in amazement. The water kept holding him up. He was standing directly over the middle of the bottomless chasm.

"Look at me!" Tannic cried. "It's working!"

Now the Ender Dude had seen enough. He smiled and walked toward the water stream. His eyes on Tannic, he confidently stepped onto the stream himself. And he passed through it, and kept going, down, down, down into the bottomless chasm. He screamed as he fell until they could no longer hear him.

Tannic ran the rest of the way jumped onto the ledge. He quickly peered over the edge into the dark chasm. "Down goes Frazier! Down goes Frazier!" he shouted.

SRG was holding the fire hose tightly in both hands, the psword lay in the dirt at his feet, when he looked back. The first Minotaur was almost on top of him and had raised its pick axe to swing it straight into SRG's head. SRG closed his eyes and prepared for the worst. He thought about his family. He waited for the blow. He wondered if it would hurt. He waited. Nothing happened. When he opened his eyes again he was standing next to Tannic in Dr. Denton's lab. Dr. Denton was looking at them both with relief. Tannic had a big grin on his face. Some Random Guy let out a deep sigh. He looked at the Rainbow Star in Tannic's right hand. It was glowing and radiating colored light all over the lab. Then they both started laughing at their good fortune.

Chapter 5

The Sunken Jolly Roger Lake

"That was awesome!" Tannic shouted. "Did you see the Ender Dude go into the chasm? He went down like a heavyweight boxer whose face had met one too many boxing gloves!"

"I'm sorry I missed that Tannic, but I was a little bit pre-occupied with a Minotaur that was about to . . ."

Doc interrupted him. "My friends, that was a close one. I was watching from here in the lab, and you had me worried to death. I didn't know if you'd make it. But now that you're back, I have some news. I've been doing some research, and I think I've determined how you arrived here. It's a bit complicated, but it's a process called temporal electron neural transport—TENT for short. I'd only heard of it before. I'd never actually observed its occurrence. It's extremely rare, but it has been reported when people are connected to or touching something electronic at the same moment that a huge power surge passes through it. They can then be transported temporally—that is to say, like time travel, kind of like Doc and Marty in Back to the Future, as I mentioned before—or they can be transported geographically, to another place in the same time frame. Or, as in your case, they can transported digitally into a computer or video game. I'm fairly certain that's what happened to you when the lightning struck your house."

"Okay, I think I understand," SRG stated less than confidently. "So how do we get home?"

"Yeah, how do we get back to SRG's house, Dr. Denton?"

"Well, that part I haven't determined yet, boys. But I'll work on it. In the meantime, Level 3 is waiting for you. That's where—"

"Yeah, we know," SRG sighed. "The Sunken Jolly Roger Lake."

"We've played the game a lot, so we know the first five levels pretty well," Tannic added.

"Well then, you know that your accessory for this level will be a scuba-diving apparatus. However, you only get one between the two of you, so you'll have to decide how you'll divide up the use of it. And I'm afraid your Dragonwrigley won't do you much good here. The fireballs will fizzle out underwater. The crescents will work, but they'll move much slower. You might not want to risk taking it into the lake with you. Of course, then you'd risk an enemy getting his hands on the Dragonwrigley." He paused to think.

"Oh, yes—watch out for the Boss Bass. They don't have piranha-sharp teeth like the Carps, but the real danger is that they'll try to drown you and swallow you whole. And they're as big as you are, so they can do it. They lurk beneath the surface of the lake, especially in the abandoned pirate ship at the bottom, which is also where you'll find the Rainbow Star. That's about all I can tell you. Good luck, boys!"

So SRG and Tannic mustered their courage and walked to the lab door once again. As he grasped the doorknob, SRG looked back at Dr. Denton, standing there confidently in his white lab jacket. "Just in case I don't see you again, I really appreciate all your help, Dr. Denton."

"Me too," Tannic added.

"Now, now, boys, what kind of talk is that? I'm happy to help you. That's what I do. You boys just be careful out there, and I'll see you back here when you're done!"

They walked out the door and into the Sunken Jolly Roger Lake level. SRG picked up the air tanks, regulator, face mask, and fins, and tried to carry the Dragonwrigley under his other arm. Tannic could only look on apologetically and watch him struggle.

"Maybe I should carry the scuba gear," he offered.

"You're not that great a swimmer, remember?"

"Yeah, but I can walk on water and you can't!"

"Well, maybe you'll need to use that while I'm diving for the Rainbow Star. Besides, you got the first two. It's my turn now."

"Okay. What's your plan, Compadre?" Tannic asked.

"I don't have one. I'm thinking."

The lake really was a lake. It must have been several miles across. But it wasn't all that deep. Some Random Guy and Tannic walked through the waist-high grass to the water. The lake was a beautiful blue color, and there were snow-capped mountains in the distance. Trees lined the lake's perimeter. They were dark green and reflected in the water. It was a sunny day without a cloud in the sky. Between the blue water, the green trees and the mountains in the distance, if it hadn't been a game they were stuck in, it would have been a breathtaking view. Unfortunately, neither of them was in the mindset to notice or appreciate it. They paused at the water's edge.

"Do you think there are Minotaurs on this level?" Tannic asked.

"Well, there never have been any in the game when we play it, but we both know that doesn't mean anything now Good Buddy! There could be Minotaurs lurking here anywhere for all I know. I think we need to be ready for anything."

"What about the Ender Dude? Where do you think he is?"

"I don't know that either, but he has to be somewhere close to the Rainbow Star."

"Do you think he's underwater?"

"In the game he's on a small island next to the sunken ship and jumps into the water to defend the star if you get close. But I don't see an island on this lake. I don't know what that means."

"So what's your plan Compadre?"

"I still don't have one. The lake will have Chomp Cheap Carps in it, I think. Then there are the Boss Bass. Doc made a point of warning us about them. And then there's the Ender Dude. . . Whew! I don't know how we're going to get through this. This is a lot harder than playing the game."

"Don't fret, Compadre. There are two of us working together! We're a team! We've got this!"

"You're right. Hey, I have an idea! I'm thinking just like on Level 1, you run out onto the water and make a big scene and distract the carp, while I swim down to the sunken ship and grab the Rainbow Star."

"Uh, what about the Boss Bass?"

"I'll take the Dragonwrigley. Maybe I can hurt them enough to make them leave me alone. Anyway they won't be able to drown me, because I'll have the scuba gear. And they can't catch you, so we should be okay. The only unknown is the Ender Dude."

"But we don't know that the bass can't catch me."

"Trust me, when you see how big they are in real life, you'll run faster than you every thought you could," SRG laughed.

"Well, I'm glad *you* think it's funny!"

"Hey, why are you getting all serious, Mister I-Can-Run-On-Water?"

They both heard the noise at the same time and looked up. Two Minotaurs were running through the grass toward them.

"I'm starting to hate these stupid Minotaurs!" SRG exclaimed. "Don't they know they're not supposed to be on this level? Gee whiz, give me a break!" He turned and started firing the Dragonwrigley at them. He hit one and missed the other. Now there were two more.

"Run, Tannic!" he yelled.

Tannic did run, right into the arms of yet another Minotaur. Now there were five of them. SRG had managed to kill the first two before he looked over at Tannic just in time to see the Minotaur hoist Tannic above his head. One of Tannic's Life Wedges illuminated briefly and then faded away. Tannic lay limp in the Minotaur's hands.

The closest Minotaur came at SRG. He raised the Dragonwrigley and let loose a barrage of crescents. They caught the Minotaur mid-step and he went down hard. His body bucked twice and then he was still.

The last one was still coming. SRG was firing wildly and missing his target. He glanced at Tannic to see a second Life Wedge fading away. He had to work fast. He ran toward Tannic, firing at the Minotaur as he ran. He couldn't wait. He had to risk hitting Tannic again to save him from the beast. Finally a blast of crescents hit the Minotaur full in the chest, just missing Tannic. It was close, but he'd killed the Minotaur just in time to save Tannic's last Life Wedge.

The final Minotaur was closing in angrily. It ran towards them growling, its arms extended. As Some Random Guy spun away, the Minotaur caught his right leg and hauled him into the air. Tannic was lying helpless in the grass. As the Minotaur lifted SRG, in desperation he swung the Dragonwrigley at its head and killed it instantly. They both collapsed to the ground.

It had been a trap. All five Minotaurs had been lying in wait for them. Now they all lay sprawled dead on the grass. Some Random Guy and Tannic looked at each other in relief. SRG shook his head as he looked at the dead Minotaurs. They lay scattered on the ground like bowling pins after a strike, only blood was flowing everywhere and flies were suddenly buzzing around them. It looked like somebody had spilled buckets of red paint. SRG just shook his head in disbelief and then he started looking through the grass for his scuba gear. The attack had been so fast and unexpected that they'd barely survived, and now Tannic had only one Life Wedge left, and they hadn't even gotten into the water yet.

"Well, this changes things a bit," SRG said. "But we should be safe from Minotaurs now. Most levels in the game only have about five or six. So I hope that's how it is here."

"Safe from the Minotaurs, maybe, but not from anything else," Tannic observed.

"Yeah. Wait, I have another idea. What if we drag a couple of Minotaurs over to the water to distract the fish. Give them something to feed on while we slip past. Maybe they like fresh Minotaur meat."

"As long as it doesn't turn into a feeding frenzy. But I don't know, those Minotaurs are pretty heavy. I'm not sure we can even move them."

"If we work together maybe we can roll one through the grass and into the lake. They're not as big as the ones on the first level. All we have to do is get it into the water."

"Ha ha, that's it! We'll roll them! I bet we can do that."

So they put their backs into it. They picked the Minotaur closest to the water and started heaving and pushing until the beast finally started to roll. It took a few minutes, and it was covered in mud and blood by the time they got it to the water, but it quickly started turning the water red. It would attract the fish without a problem. In fact, they had barely climbed out before the first carp showed up and started ripping big chunks out of it. Soon a whole school was feeding on it. SRG and Tannic returned shortly with another Minotaur. Now there was plenty of bait to distract the fish. The Boss Bass would be another problem altogether, but SRG thought he could handle them. Of course, he hadn't seen them in real life just yet, so he wasn't certain of his prospects.

He hauled the scuba tanks onto his back and secured the waist straps. He turned on the regulator, put on the facemask, and took a breath to test everything. He sat down to put the fins on his feet, then stood up and walked awkwardly backwards toward the lake.

"You look like a real scuba diver," Tannic commented. "I wish I had a set of gear too."

"You'll be helping me by distracting the rest of the fish." SRG picked up the sword. "I think I'll take the Dragonwrigley with me just in case. It'll be harder to swim, but I like the idea of having a weapon. I just hope all this stuff works. I've never scuba dived before. It can't be too hard, you just breathe through the mouth piece, and the shipwreck is only thirty feet down."

"So what's the plan now?" Tannic asked.

"Just like we talked about. You run out to the center of the lake and attract the Boss Bass while I dive down to the shipwreck and find the Rainbow Star. Here we go."

"What about the Ender Dude?"

"What about him? Maybe he's not here."

"Yeah, right. He's always there. What are you going to do about him?"

"I don't know, I'll make something up if I run into him. I don't think the Dragonwrigley will be much help, but I'll think of something. I mean, I have to."

"Okay, well, once you're underwater I won't be able to help you. You'll be on your own, Compadre."

"Just distract as many Boss Bass as you can. You'll know we've succeeded when we're standing in Dr. Denton's lab. I only have thirty minutes worth of air, so if we're not in the lab in thirty minutes, well . . ." SRG went silent and gave Tannic a worried look. Then he shrugged and shook his head. He wanted to say something, but he couldn't make the words come out.

"Hey, Compadre, don't talk like that. We're a team. We've got this! Go get that star!"

With that, Tannic sped off. The water was bright blue and it was a great day for a run. Then he laughed out loud. A great day for a run indeed, if you could run on water. He was still getting used to his new skill and his unbelievable stamina. It was fun but a little weird too. He wished he could take it with him if they ever got home. He was thinking about home as he ran along, creating as much commotion on the water's surface as he could. Then he realized he hadn't seen a Boss Bass in real life yet and started worrying. What if they were faster than he was? What if they were so big they could swallow him whole? The thoughts put him on edge, and he ran faster.

SRG moved slowly to the water's edge and waded in. The carp were well occupied by feeding on the dead Minotaur carcasses. SRG noted that they probably had enough food there to keep them occupied for at least half an hour, but then again, he only had about 30 minutes of air anyway, so it wouldn't matter. He thought for a second about the carp and again it struck him as ironic. Carp back home were bottom feeders and didn't have any teeth. They just sucked up bits and pieces off of the bottom of a river or lake, looking for food. They were pretty much harmless. Here in Rough World they had teeth and they were ripping chunks of flesh off of the dead Minotaurs. Of course they would do the same thing to you if they caught you. SRG was thinking they should have been named something else, although this was Rough World, and the rules of the real world back home no longer applied. He refocused on his current task as he waded into the water. When he got to about his waist deep he leaned forward and started to swim to the approximate center of the lake, where hopefully the shipwreck would be. It was awkward swimming with the Dragonwrigley in his right hand so he transferred it to his left hand as he was much stronger swimming with his right arm. Occasionally he would look up and he could see Tannic running around in the middle of the lake. He was hoping that the Boss Bass were chasing Tannic and would give him a clean shot at getting the Rainbow Star. He had the facemask on and could see down into the water. It was pretty clear and he could make out the bottom as the lake continued to get deeper. Tannic was running around slapping the water and for all outward appearances looked to be enjoying himself. Except that SRG knew he was likely scared to death and just staying ahead of the huge Boss Bass that would easily pull Tannic under and make a meal out of him. He could see the one illuminated Life Wedge over Tannic's head, a grim reminder that there was no margin for error with his plan. They were only going to get one chance at this.

Some Random Guy struggled to swim, although the fins were a blessing. He was still moving slowly and awkwardly, but he would never have been able to carry the Dragonwrigley without them. He was getting tired and beginning to wish that he'd listened to his swimming instructor better and swum more laps during swim class. Instead his mind had always drifted to thinking about playing Rough World. The irony struck him. Here he was swimming in Rough World for real and wishing he was at his swimming lesson instead. At least the swimming pool didn't have man-eating fish in it. He'd never take that for granted again.

The water kept getting deeper, and SRG continued to make slow progress. He was still on the surface and hadn't used any of the air, so he'd have a full thirty minutes when he finally went below. He could barely see the bottom. He looked around to see that Tannic was okay, and just then Tannic ran by and a wave washed over him. Under the surface he could see a few Boss Bass chasing Tannic. He was shocked at how big and how scary they were. *Keep running, Tannic*, he thought, *and I'll keep swimming.*

Twenty yards on he saw a sinister-looking shape at the bottom of the lake. Gradually he began to make out a pirate's ship sitting upright on the lakebed. All three masts, the main mast, foremast, and mizzen mast, were toppled over each other across on the deck. The shipwreck was lightly covered with silt, but he could still make out the Jolly Roger flag, the skull and crossbones, hanging from the crow's nest. He swam until he was right above it. He didn't see any bass or other dangers, so he put the regulator in his mouth and tested it again. He took a deep breath and then exhaled. It seemed pretty easy. He looked at his watch and made a note of when his thirty minutes would be up. Then he wondered whether his watch was actually water proof. It said it was. *But what can I trust at this point?* He'd never really cared if it was waterproof or not. He certainly hadn't tested it in the pool. And now his life might depend on it.

SRG pulled the facemask off, spit into it, and wiped his spit around the inside of the glass. Then he rinsed it out lightly. He had learned that trick playing with a facemask in his grandparents' pool. It would keep the glass from fogging up, which might be critical. Then he ducked his face into the water and started to kick-dive his way into the depths. He held the Dragonwrigley out in front of him like a beacon leading his way down. When he was about ten feet down, his ears popped loudly. That was a new experience, and it hurt a little bit, but not enough to slow him down. The mask fit pretty well, and only a little water had gotten into it. The glass was still crystal clear. He glanced at his watch, and it was still working. He was breathing normally through the mouthpiece. It was strange to breathe underwater.

Something moved in his peripheral vision. He turned as a Boss Bass swam out of the ship's hold, eyed him curiously, and swam slowly up toward him. This one was bigger than he was. It had large eyes and a huge mouth with several rows of teeth. It wouldn't even need the teeth, though. It could easily swallow him whole. It swam closer, and its mouth was open for business.

Some Random Guy pulled the Dragonwrigley up and

aimed at the oncoming beast. He fired a couple of times, but Doc was right, they were more like fizzle balls. The bass swallowed them like they were appetizers. SRG struggled to swing the sword underwater and released a flurry of crescents, but they moved too slowly to do any damage, and the bass swam easily around them. Then it darted close and grabbed his right leg. SRG struggled to free his foot as the bass started to dive, taking him along. He realized that it hadn't actually bitten into him. It didn't hurt. The fish was trying to drown him, not knowing he could breathe underwater. SRG gave up fighting against the bass and pulled the Dragonwrigley alongside his leg. But it was no use. He couldn't get a swipe at the bass without cutting his own leg. The bass was returning to the ship's hold with its new meal.

At twenty feet, his ears popped again. This time it hurt more, but he couldn't do anything about it. He was breathing fast and his heart was pounding in his ears. Air bubbles rose in a steady line to the surface above them.

They reached the deck, and the bass tried to swim through the hatch, but it couldn't fit with SRG in tow. They got wedged into the opening. SRG looked at his wristwatch. He had twenty minutes left. The bass was wiggling, struggling hard to push him through. He went limp. Moving slowly, he could just bring the Dragonwrigley up to the bass's head. It was still pushing them into the hatch, wedging them in more tightly. They were firmly stuck now. SRG was patient and finally managed to set the Dragonwrigley's tip against the bass. Abruptly, he shoved the blade between the fish's head and neck. He felt it force its way through the scales and enter the fish's flesh. He twisted it. The Boss Bass squirmed and pushed SRG hard against the ship. Blood started streaming out of the wound in a ribbon of red that wafted up through the water and mingled with SRG's bubbles. SRG kept twisting and plunging the blade into the bass. Each time the fish tensed up and flexed hard. After a few moments, it jerked twice, tensed up once more, and then relaxed and stopped moving completely. SRG pulled the Dragonwrigley out. The fish was dead. Unfortunately they were both wedged in the hatchway, and he couldn't move at all. He looked at his watch. He was down to fifteen minutes. He looked up and could see Tannic's silhouette as he ran across the surface with a school of Boss Bass in hot pursuit.

All SRG had to do was get free and find the Rainbow Star. There was still time, he just needed to move the dead fish that was pinning him in place. He wriggled, but was barely able to move his legs. Then fear came over him as he saw movement to his right. He turned to see an amazing but horrible sight. The Ender Dude was swimming toward him in scuba gear.

Really?! This wasn't in the game! It was hardly fair, why should the Ender Dude get scuba gear too? Before he could finish the thought, the Ender Dude was upon him, tugging at his arm to pull him free. He pulled so hard SRG thought he would dislocate it. He could see his wristwatch between the Ender Dude's hands. He had thirteen minutes of air and counting. The Ender Dude kept pulling, and he slowly came free from the hatchway, just to slide into the full grip of the Ender Dude. This wasn't fair at all. He needed a plan and he needed one fast.

The Ender Dude grabbed SRG like a rag doll. The Boss Bass sank into the darkness of the hold and out of sight, leaving only a faint pink coloring to the water. The Ender Dude looked directly into SRG's eyes. He had a mask on his large face too, and an air regulator hose in his mouth, but through it all SRG could see that he was smiling. He tucked SRG under his arm and started swimming away from the ship. Having no idea where they were going, SRG struggled to get free. The Ender Dude just gripped him tighter. SRG couldn't believe how strong he was. He went limp to see if he could catch the Ender Dude off guard. But nothing he did made any difference. The Ender Dude had a death grip on him and wasn't letting go. SRG could barely make out the shipwreck now as he was dragged farther away from it. He could see his wristwatch, though—eight minutes and counting.

The Dragonwrigley was wedged tight against his body and his left arm was pinned. He slowly, carefully, steadily slid his right arm free and took hold of the sword's hilt. The Ender Dude was too close for him to get any purchase with the blade, and he couldn't swing it well underwater anyway. He thought about just letting it go and trying to come up with a better plan. Then he saw it—the Ender Dude's air regulator hose. It ran from the tanks on his back to his mouth.

The Ender Dude was swimming with confidence now. He had his prey firmly under control and wasn't paying any attention to SRG. He was large and in charge. SRG carefully slid the Dragonwrigley along his own body until the tip touched the air hose. He would only get one chance. Without warning he pushed as hard as he could. The blade sliced cleanly through the hose. Air bubbles poured profusely from the hose and created a cloud. The Ender Dude choked and coughed and jerked, dropping his grip on SRG as both hands came instinctively to his throat. He was reeling in the water and gasping for a breath, but only sucking water into his lungs. He swam hard for the surface. Without wasting time, SRG turned back toward the Sunken Jolly Roger. He couldn't see it yet, but he swam with purpose in what he thought was the right direction, kicking his fins as hard as he could. Time was running out.

The Ender Dude was coughing and gagging on the surface. Tannic ran by, taunting him and splashing him, but that was the best he could do without any real weapons. The Boss Bass paused only for a second to examine the Ender Dude. But even in his coughing fit, they had no interest in tangling with him.

The shipwreck came into view again, like a dark behemoth resting on the lake floor. SRG looked at his wristwatch. Five minutes left, at least if his watch was still working, and if there really had been thirty minutes of air. Of course, he'd been breathing rapidly several times already.

As he approached the bow of the ship he slowed down to study it. He should have just enough air if he could find the Rainbow Star quickly. He mentally ran through the pirate ship's anatomy. The very bottom level was the ballast deck. There might have been provisions and cargo there, but it was mostly large rocks used as ballast to hold the ship upright. The next deck up would be the orlop, or overlap deck. It would have some supplies and maybe ammunition. On top of that was the berth deck, with the crew's quarters, and then the gun deck, with gunwales that would allow the ship's cannons to be aimed at enemies. Then the main deck on top of that with the opening into the center hold that the Boss Bass had fallen into. The rear of the ship—the stern—would hold the Captain's quarters, and above those was the poop deck, the highest deck on the ship. The forecastle would be found at the front, or bow, of the ship. He'd learned all this while building a model ship in second grade. His thoughts were racing. There were too many places to check and not enough air. It was down to the wire. He wouldn't be able to look everywhere, so he'd have to use his best judgment and take his chances.

He reasoned that the Rainbow Star was most likely to be in the Captain's quarters at the stern. He swam to the door and pulled on it. It was stuck. He tugged on the latch and it gradually opened. The chamber inside was dark. He was a little scared. The Boss Bass should all be contained now, and he didn't really fear them as much anymore, and he'd pretty much disabled the Ender Dude, but still . . . swimming into a dark chamber of the unknown was scary. He wasn't afraid of the dark, but nothing in Rough World had been exactly like the video game, so he didn't know what to expect. He was getting used to expecting the unexpected. He gathered his courage and checked his watch. Two minutes. He swam carefully into the chamber, his senses on full alert. As his eyes adjusted to the dark, he explored the interior. He checked each of the cupboards but came up empty handed. The Rainbow Star wasn't there. Then he felt the tightness in his throat. He gasped for air. He looked at his wristwatch. Time's up. He'd taken a chance and guessed wrong. Now it was too late. He still had three Life Wedges, but it didn't much matter. He didn't have any air left.

With the last of the breath in his lungs, he kicked out to the main deck. His lungs were burning and he was losing his concentration. He felt his body growing weak. He kicked again, but it was no use. The dive had taken everything out of him, and he just couldn't move any more.

SRG felt himself sinking through the hatch, following the Boss Bass down into the darkness of the hold. It felt like floating down onto a soft pillow. Through his mask he could see a shaft of light coming down from the lake. But it was too late. He came to rest on his back on the floor of the hold.

His lungs were on fire. He had to take a breath, but it would be water he sucked into his lungs instead of air. He had a moment of panic, and then he felt peaceful. Where was Tannic now? Why hadn't he mown the lawn today? What would his parents think? He dropped his head to the floor and looked over to his left. He was lying next to the dead bass. *Perfect . . . I'll die right next to this beast I killed.* The fish was easily visible in spite of the darkness. It was lit up by light shining from underneath it. There was a whole rainbow of colors radiating out from it. The bass looked like a psychedelic dream. SRG reached out toward the Bass and the light, reached and reached and felt . . . something . . . and his world went suddenly black.

Chapter 6
Mount Parabora

The light was trying to blind him. He felt confused. Where was that intense light coming from? Where was he? His lungs were still burning, and he gasped for air. He took a deep breath, then another. He felt light-headed. Someone grabbed him around the waist and held him up. After a few more breaths his mind started to clear. He recognized Tannic, holding him upright, and a concerned Dr. Denton standing behind him. He recognized the lab. He tried to figure out what had happened.

"Oh, wow! I thought that was it! I can't tell you how happy I am to see you guys!" SRG blurted out. "You did a great job Tannic, it was my fault! I'm sorry."

"Your fault?" Tannic frowned in confusion. "What are you talking about? We're in Dr. Denton's lab. I'd say you did a good job, Compadre! All I did was run around distracting a bunch of fish."

"No, you don't understand. I ran out of time. I was attacked by a Boss Bass and then we were trapped in the hold door and then I was rescued by the Ender Dude and then he took me prisoner. And then I managed to escape him by cutting his air hose, but then I didn't have enough air left to get the Rainbow Star. I'm so sorry!"

"You're not making any sense, Compadre! You got the star, we're here in the lab. We completed Level 3!"

"Yes. You might be a little confused SRG, but you must have gotten the Rainbow Star, or you wouldn't be here. Open your hand," Dr. Denton suggested. SRG opened his left hand to find that he'd been tightly clutching a Rainbow Star. He looked at it in amazement.

"Now I remember. The light I saw under the Bass. I reached for it. I felt something. It must have been the star. I can't believe it," SRG mumbled.

"Woo-hoo! Three down, seven to go! We got this, Compadre!" shouted Tannic.

"Technically, that's correct," said Dr. Denton. "I've been doing some more thinking. Once you gain access to the inner chamber in the Evil Boss's office and defeat him with the Fortran Sword, I should be able to generate a power surge. You boys could get into the Transport Chamber and we could potentially send you home. We would just try to reverse the process and see what happens."

"That would be awesome Dr. Denton!" SRG said excitedly.

"Do you really think it's possible?" Tannic asked.

"Well, I'm not altogether positive," Dr. Denton answered, "but I believe it's worth a shot. Right now we still require seven more stars. You boys can undertake Level 4 as soon as you're ready. After that there's only one way to ascertain with certainty. We'll have to be tough!"

"Hey, you've got to be tough to live in the West!" SRG proclaimed.

"What?"

"Oh, it's just something my grandpa always says. 'You

have to be tough to live in the West.' I was thinking that you really have to be tough, period, to live in Rough World."

"Rough and tough, I'd say," Tannic added.

"Well, I'm just here to tell you that it does get rough sometimes and it always helps to be tough," Dr. Denton agreed. "Stay determined and focused on your goal. Never give up. That's pretty good advice for everything, if you ask me."

"Hey, my Grandpa says that a lot too!" SRG exclaimed.

"Says what?"

"'I'm just here to tell you,' . . . or 'I'm just telling you,' . . . or 'I'm just saying,'" SRG explained. "Hey, you know what, Dr. Denton? You kind of remind me of him a little bit too, now that I think about it."

"Is that a good thing or a bad thing?"

"Definitely a good thing. He's a scientist like you, and he's really smart too. He's always trying to help people. He's a good guy."

"Well, then, thank you, SRG. I am complimented. But right now, we have work to do. You boys need to complete Level 4. Of course, this is Rough World, so it will be harder than Level 3 was."

"Yeah, yeah, I know. The Mount Parabora level. We've completed it a bunch of times. We pretty much know what to expect, at least if it follows the game." SRG sighed. "But these levels don't exactly follow the game. We're never seen Minotaurs on the Sunken Jolly Roger level before. That caught us off guard. But we responded quickly enough. I guess we're pretty much ready for anything."

"I don't mind this level in the game, but I'm kind of afraid of heights, so I don't think I'm going to like doing it for real," Tannic confessed.

"Well, look at it this way, Tannic," Dr. Denton suggested. "You're not really afraid of heights, you're just afraid of hitting the ground! There's an important difference."

"Ha! I'm definitely afraid of hitting the ground. Thanks, Doc, that actually helps," Tannic replied. "I'll keep reminding myself of it! Although I still think I'm afraid of heights, and of falling, and of hitting the ground."

Doc and SRG laughed at his reasoning. "I'm more worried about the man-eating plants," SRG complained. "Those will be creepy in real life! The fish were bad, but it makes my skin crawl just thinking about being eaten by a plant."

"Not to mention the Wevern Boss Giant Dog," Tannic added.

"Well, you boys be safe. You've come this far, and I have faith in you. Do you have any other questions?"

"No, I think we know this level pretty well," SRG replied.

"Well, good luck then, boys. I'll be in the lab cheering you on and trying to figure out if my theory will get you back home."

"Thanks, Dr. Denton," they replied in unison.

With that the two heroes opened the door and stepped into the shadow of Mount Parabora.

The sun was low in the sky and it felt like early morning. There were just a few scattered high clouds and, it looked like another sunny day in Rough World. The vegetation was a jungle-like mixture of shrubs and other plants, ranging from light to dark green. It was thick but only knee-high to shoulder-high in most places. There was no canopy of tall trees.

The mountain loomed in the distance, dominating the horizon. Cliffs and platforms stood out prominently on its side, like chicken pox on a sick kid. Those would work like rungs on a ladder as the boys ascended from one to the next up the mountainside.

SRG looked down at his hands. He had the trusty Dragonwrigley in his right hand, but in his left was a new blade, somewhat lighter and smaller than the sword. It was a shiny and very sharp machete. He swung it a few times to get a feel for it. It felt good. He turned it over in his hand again and let out a low whistle. Made from expensive steel, not like the junk machetes you see so often, it was a fine example of what a machete can be. The blade was Damascus steel, hand-forged by pounding it with a hammer and grinding the edge on a fine stone until it was razor sharp. The grip was wrapped tightly in leather, and there was a generous guard separating the blade from the grip. That would keep SRG's hand from slipping onto the blade—and cutting his fingers off—when he swung it against hard objects. He shook his head in approval.

Tannic watched SRG get comfortable with the machete. It would be handy for blazing a trail through the thick jungle-like vegetation as they climbed platform by platform up the mountainside to the summit and the Guru Ender Dude. They'd have to cut their route up through the vegetation, looking out for man-eating plants. Of course, the cliffs seemed to be scattered everywhere on the mountainside so that climbing them looked nearly impossible. And if they didn't fall off, they'd still have to fight their way past the Wevern Boss Giant Dog. And somehow discover the meaning of life along the way, to give to the Guru Ender Dude. You only got three tries before he threw you off the summit to certain death. Every time they played the game, the meaning of life was a different phrase, but they'd only ever encountered five different phrases. With only three tries, their odds would three out of five, or slightly better than even, if they guessed.

"Looks like this could be a real cliffhanger, Compadre," Tannic offered.

"That's not funny, Good Buddy! I'm glad you can find humor in this, cause I really don't like this level. I don't even like it when we play it, so I'm sure I'm not going to like it in real life. Cliffs, man-eating plants, a giant man-eating dog, could it get much worse?"

"Sorry, just trying to lighten the mood. Besides, I'm the one who's afraid of heights."

"Listen to yourself! Didn't you learn anything from Dr. Denton? You're not afraid of heights, Tannic, you're afraid of hitting the ground!"

"Sorry again, you're right. I'll keep telling myself that. But is it okay to be afraid of cliffs in general?" Tannic pleaded.

"Yeah, I think that's okay."

"And don't forget about the Guru Ender Dude. I wonder what he looks like in real life. So, what's the plan, Compadre? Which route should we take? Where do we start this lovely adventure? How many Frenchmen can't be wrong?"

SRG laughed at the last question. It was a reference to a Groucho Marx line in an old black and white movie. The Marx Brothers were his grandpa's favorite comedy team, and SRG and Tannic had watched lots of their movies with him, even though they didn't always get the jokes and he sometimes had to explain them. But that didn't matter now. They were in Rough World, and there were no Marx Brothers here. SRG silently wished they were at home watching an old movie with his grandpa. He could almost smell the popcorn his grandma made. And they always got chocolate too.

That was her favorite.

He looked at Tannic, who was waiting patiently for him to respond. "I don't know. The routes to the summit change every time we play the game. I was thinking about starting with the closest platform above that small cliff." He pointed to the right. "Start small, get comfortable with the level, and then figure out which platform to work toward next. What do you think?"

"That sounds like a good plan. It will be good to get our footing before we hit the hard parts. Let's go, Compadre. You have to cut the vegetation, though. I can't even carry a machete, which really isn't fair, if you ask me. And I don't think running on water is going to help us here. Although it did help us in the mine, that and your quick thinking, so . . ."

"If I see any water for you to run on, I'll point it out. Maybe there's a waterfall or something. I'd trade you spots anytime if I could, Good Buddy, but I can't. So just keep your eyes and ears open to warn me about man-eating plants and dogs. That'll help a bunch."

"Oh, I don't think they'll really eat you, Compadre. You're a skinny, stinky 10-year-old boy. No, I'm afraid they'd prefer me. I'd taste much better! And I'm much better looking, too."

"Very funny! Right now you smell as bad as I do. I don't think they'll be choosy. I think they'll eat anything they can get their . . . teeth . . . into? Can plants have teeth? Just keep your senses on high alert!"

"That won't be a problem. The only option I have right now is high alert. Even my high alert is on high alert! Have you ever seen a Venus Fly Trap plant? They have teeth, big ones."

"Yeah, you're right. Great, these stupid plants probably

have teeth too," SRG spit out in disgust. Then he swung the machete at the chest-high greenery in front of him. To his surprise, it cut easily. The blade was sharp, all right. Still, he realized, hacking their way up the entire mountain was going to drain him physically. He was still worn out from the lake, and a little worried about whether he would have enough energy to fend off the plants or the dog. Regardless, he started swinging the machete in a rhythm, opening a narrow path. They made their way slowly toward the platform he'd picked out. They must have been a sight, SRG swinging the machete and Tannic, bringing up the rear, looking for any sign of danger in every direction as intensely as he could.

"You're doing good, Compadre," Tannic said.

"Thanks, but this is a chore. I'd rather be at home mowing the lawn. I'd even rather be yelled at by Mrs. Kibbitch right now."

"Yeah, me too. Funny how that's something we could look forward to."

"How many man-eating plants do we usually run into on this level? You remember?" SRG asked.

"Like five or six? But I never really kept track. It wasn't like they were going to really eat you, I mean like in real life or something."

"Yeah, me neither. But that sounds about right. In the game they look a bit different from the other plants. Like bigger leaves that just open up suddenly right before they devour you. I'll bet they do have teeth, Tannic. If you see anything that doesn't look right, let me know."

"Don't worry, I will. I hope we can recognize them. Hey, did we ever find a Heart Gem on this level? Do you remember?"

"Didn't we find a Heart Gem on one of the platforms one

time?"

"Yeah, that's what I was thinking. We could sure use one this time around."

They were about halfway to the first platform. It was just at the base of the mountain, and they'd still have ninety percent of the climb ahead of them when they got there. SRG was swinging the machete with his right hand and carrying the Dragonwrigley in his left, keeping it close by in case he needed it quickly. As he raised the machete again, the plant in front of him opened up and a huge mouth with row upon row of sharp fangs descended on them.

Some Random Guy jumped to the side just in time. Tannic didn't move fast enough, and before either of them knew it, half of his body was engulfed by the plant. Blood was flowing down his side. His legs kicked for a few seconds and went limp. The plant's mouth writhed around him, pulling him in further, and it seemed to swallow what was left.

Some Random Guy frantically swung the Dragonwrigley at the base of the plant, which now seemed stuffed and quite contented with its meal. It burped suddenly, and he chopped at it again, making slow but steady progress through the base. He remembered suddenly that it took eight strokes of the Dragonwrigley to kill the man-eating plants in the game. He swung with renewed vigor, swearing loudly at the plant as he hacked at it. At the eighth stroke, it stopped moving and slowly toppled over. Its mouth-like leaves flared open and deposited Tannic's unmoving body at his feet. One of the three Life Wedges above his head shone briefly and faded slowly away. Tannic stirred and opened his eyes. SRG had a strained look on his face. He was panting and sweating.

"Thanks, Compadre, you saved my life!"

SRG hesitated. "Actually, I didn't. You lost a life wedge.

I'm sorry, I should have screamed or something to warn you. I just jumped when it moved at me."

"It's okay. At least you were here to kill it. I was so focused on everything around us that I wasn't paying attention to what was in front of you. It won't happen again, I can promise you that."

"Well, there will probably be a few more next times. It's a long way to the summit. This is going to be harder than I first thought."

SRG looked at the dead man-eating plant. It didn't look much different from the rest of the plants on the mountainside. Its leaves were slightly larger, and maybe it was a darker green, but the differences were subtle. It might have been his imagination, or the light and shadows playing tricks on his eyes. In any event, it was going to be hard to spot the man-eating plants. They blended in well with the others. He would have to be much more careful. What if it had been him the plant swallowed? Would it eventually have spit him out, minus one Life Wedge? Or would that have been the end of him? This clearly wasn't the game. It was much worse and less predictable. It was as if the game was a guide to the real Rough World, but only a guide. Nothing was exactly the same, so they never knew quite what to expect. Worse still, they'd never gotten past Level 5. They had no idea what to expect after that. SRG stood silently, deep in his own thoughts. He just wanted to go home.

"Compadre? Compadre, snap out of it! I've been talking to you for a minute. Did you hear anything I said? You're scaring me. Are you okay?"

"Sorry, I was just lost in thought. I was wondering what else this level has in store for us. It's a bit overwhelming. I'm back now."

"Well, welcome back to Rough World. This is going to be a rough one, no pun intended. I was going to use a swear word, but I don't know which one would apply to our present situation."

"I think they all would. Are you ready? We should keep moving. We've got a long ways to go."

Some Random Guy stepped back onto the path and started swinging the machete again. Some of the plants were taller than others, but in general the foliage was about chest high, and it was thick enough that you couldn't see through it. Tannic was still on high alert, scanning in every direction, including the plants SRG was cutting through. The ground wasn't too steep yet, and they made steady progress.

After ten minutes they were standing atop the first platform. It was more of a flat embankment cut into the mountainside than an actual platform, and it ended in a cliff. SRG looked over the edge. It was forty or fifty feet down. Not enough that you would die for certain, but you'd more than likely break an arm or a leg if you fell. Maybe your neck, if you were really unlucky.

Tannic wouldn't go near the edge. He wouldn't even look in that direction. He preferred to keep his gaze focused on the hill ahead.

"Well, we're at the first platform," SRG announced. "Aside from one mishap, we're in pretty good shape. No sign of the Wevern Boss Giant Dog. Now we just need to make it to four more platforms, and we'll be at the summit. We got this. We just need to stay alert."

Tannic was clinging to the cut bank side of the platform, staring up the mountain. "Agreed," he replied. "Which one should we aim for next?" There were several platforms above them. They had to decide between three of them to reach the next level of the mountain.

"Are you feeling lucky, Good Buddy?" SRG asked. "I say let's take the direct route and climb for the one straight above us."

"Sounds as good as any of them. I like that thought. You lead the way."

So Some Random Guy stepped around Tannic and started working on the vegetation above the cut bank, heading directly uphill to the platform above them. It also happened to be the nearest platform. He developed a routine, rhythmically swinging the machete with his right hand and counterbalancing the movement with the heavier Dragonwrigley in his left hand. Sometimes he stuck the tip of the sword into the ground, using it like a walking stick to steady his balance as he climbed. Gradually, step by step, they worked their way up the mountainside. The terrain grew steeper, but they weren't having trouble climbing yet. The mountain appeared to be the steepest near the summit. The climb would get harder and harder. The cliffs would get taller and taller, and the platforms would get smaller and smaller.

Some Random Guy was about to swing at another plant when his senses told him something was wrong. Without thinking he jumped sideways. Tannic jumped the second he saw SRG move, and landed on top of him. The man-eating plant opened it leaves and chomped at them. Luckily they'd landed just out of its reach. The plant swung wildly back and forth, frantically chomping its razor-sharp teeth on the air as it tried to reach them.

"That was close!" Tannic shouted.

"Yeah, but you can get off of me now."

"Hold on, I'm having trouble standing." The ground was pretty steep under them, and Tannic was hunting for a foothold.

"Well, I'm lying on top of the Dragonwrigley and I need to get it free so I can cut this plant down to size. I don't like it biting at us. It's creepy!"

Then something weird happened. Slowly but steadily, the plant was getting closer to them with each bite.

"Look out, it's growing! It's going to get me in a couple of more bites," Tannic screamed. He rolled off of SRG and slid downhill. "Quick, kill it!"

The plant was straining now, trying to reach them. It was making a weird sound too, a sort of groaning mumble, as it stretched toward them.

SRG slid a couple of feet away from the beast and quickly rose to his feet. He swung the Dragonwrigley and caught the plant's open mouth mid-bite. It whimpered harshly and retreated. He attacked it repeatedly with the sword, stroke after stroke, until it finally fell down lifeless.

"Whew! That was another close call. Quick thinking, Compadre!"

"It was more of a reflex than anything else. Well, at least that's two down. Did we ever find more than one of them on the way to each platform?" SRG asked.

"I don't think so. But remember, this isn't the game. I wouldn't even be surprised if we ran into a bunch of Minotaurs."

"Yeah, I agree. We can't let our guard down. Let's keep our eyes peeled for any movement at all."

"Roger that, Compadre!"

So they continued up the mountain. When they looked up now, the cliff seemed much higher, and a platform atop it looked smaller. Some Random Guy kept whacking away at the vegetation as they worked their way up the left side of the cliff until they could clamber onto the platform. They didn't encounter another man-eating plant, or the Wevern Boss Giant Dog, to their relief. But they both knew it was just a matter of time. They'd never completed Level 4 without encountering the dog beast.

In the middle of the platform was a flat stone with something carved into it. SRG walked over to look at it, and Tannic inspected the cliff ahead.

"What does it say?" Tannic called back.

"Don't take anything for granted."

What do you mean? I'm not taking anything for granted. I just want to know what it says," Tannic argued.

"No, no. That's what the inscription says. Don't take anything for granted. That could be one of the meanings of life. I don't remember seeing it before. But it's pretty good advice, considering our current situation."

"You can say that again."

"It's pretty good advice, considering our current situation."

They both giggled for a moment. It seemed inappropriate, but sometimes laughing helps you cope with stressful situations. They stopped, and the air turned sober again. Tannic focused on the hillside, and Some Random Guy stepped back to the edge to survey the next level of platforms. The mountain was noticeably steeper here. The route to the platform on the right looked the easiest. The one to the left seemed the most challenging, and the one directly above looked to be about halfway in between. He glanced over at Tannic, who was still focused on looking up the hill.

"Any of the routes look better to you than the others?" SRG asked.

"Nope, they all look equally bad," Tannic replied

straight-faced.

"I like the look of the route to the right, but it gets much harder after that platform, and we'd have a lot more work cutting our way back to an easy route. I say let's just keep going straight up the hill for now. That work for you?"

"I'm fine with that, just as long as I don't have to look down."

"No problem. Just keep looking up, but please keep your eye out for the Wevern Boss Giant Dog. He could attack us from behind."

"In that case you'd hear me scream when he bit me on the backside."

"Okay, I guess that will have to do. Come on, let's go." Some Random Guy picked up the machete and the Dragonwrigley and nodded at Tannic. He started cutting at the brush above him clearing the path for their next ascent. Tannic stayed close to him, just out of the way of the machete. The ground was steeper here, and it was getting hard to stand up straight. SRG was still moving forward, but he was slowing down. The work was taking a toll on him. It was getting harder to keep his balance and swing the machete, and he was leaning on the Dragonwrigley for support more and more often. Tannic started humming to take his mind off the situation, placing each step carefully to maintain his balance. It was slow, monotonous going.

"You probably shouldn't be humming so loudly," SRG whispered. "You might draw the attention of the dog."

"Well, we have to face him sooner or later. It might be better to face him lower on the mountain where it's not so steep," Tannic whispered back.

"You might be right. But I'd rather just sneak past him if there's a chance."

"Yeah, like that would ever happen."

"You're probably right. Keep humming if it helps you. Can you hum something inspirational? Like 'I will survive?' That would at least make me feel better."

"I don't know it, but I'll make something up."

So they proceeded onward and upward, SRG swinging the machete and Tannic humming an unfamiliar tune, sometimes off key but always in rhythm. The sun was getting higher in the sky, the temperature was rising, and SRG was starting to sweat. The plants weren't tall enough to offer any shelter from the sun. So they just kept pace, one step after another, and constantly on edge, waiting for another man-eating plant, or worse still a man-eating wild dog beast.

Finally Some Random Guy could see the next platform through the bushes. The breeze picked up and the plant right in front of him swung around, and he jumped. Tannic jumped too, but it was a false alarm. It was just the wind. SRG regained his composure and cut the final few steps until they were both standing atop the platform. There was enough room for the two of them with very little to spare. In the center of the platform was another flat rock with an inscription. SRG picked it up and read it out loud to Tannic, who was looking up the hill.

"Life is meaningless. There is no meaning of life, just enjoy it."

"I don't remember that one from the game," Tannic replied.

"Me neither. Obviously this level doesn't exactly follow the game either. Anyway, the good news is we made it to another platform without getting eaten by a plant, and we didn't run into the dog."

"Yeah, but you know it's coming."

"Yeah . . ." SRG responded. "Time to pick our next route. What do you feel like this time?"

They both gazed toward the summit. They needed to get to two more platforms. They had four routes to choose from for the next one. The most direct route, above them, looked completely impassable. It was probably too steep to get up without mountain-climbing gear, which of course they didn't have.

Some Random Guy broke the silence. "I don't see how we can make it up the direct route. I think we should try the far right platform. It looks like the best route from here. It's kind of a ways away, but it looks like the most doable."

"I agree. The other two look too difficult."

"Can we rest for a minute? I'm getting a bit tired from all the chopping. I had no idea how much work that would be." Beads of sweat trickled down SRG's face.

"Sure, take your time. We need to be clear and sharp for the next ascent, Compadre." Tannic was still avoiding looking down.

Some Random Guy lay down on the platform. He was close enough to the edge to look down. The cliff was a couple of hundred feet high here, not something you'd ever want to fall off. You'd bounce a few times, hit hard, and surely die. He took a deep breath and looked at Tannic before closing his eyes. Tannic was adhering to the inner wall like a tight-fitting shirt. He was breathing fast and staring up the hill.

It was fifteen minutes or so before Some Random Guy stirred. Tannic hadn't moved. SRG stood and picked up the machete and the Dragonwrigley. He looked at Tannic and shook his head and stretched his shoulders. It was time to move on. He started into the jungle again, swinging the machete in a now-familiar rhythm. Tannic was glued to his back, his eyes as big as dinner plates. Step by step, bit by bit, they made their way toward the next platform.

Some Random Guy paused to catch his breath and wipe his brow. Sweat was dripping in his eyes and it burned. The sun was almost at its peak and was beating down mercilessly, and there wasn't enough breeze to cool them. The air smelled heavily of freshly cut vegetation, like new-mown grass. The smell jogged SRG's memory and he thought again about mowing the lawn and how he should be at home right now. He sighed and wiped his brow on his sleeve again.

"You okay, Compadre?"

"Yeah, I'm just a little tired, that's all. But I'll make it, don't worry about me."

"For the record, I'm worried about both of us."

"Yeah, me too, but let's just keep moving. You see anything suspicious—"

A plant behind Tannic seized him. Leaves open and teeth bared, it chomped down on Tannic's leg. There was no warning, and Tannic didn't have a chance to react. Later on, SRG would swear the plant roared just before it attacked.

"Help, Compadre! It's got my leg!"

SRG jumped on top of the plant and swung the Dragonwrigley at its stem just below its grip on Tannic's leg. Blood was appearing on Tannic's pant leg. The plant kept its hold on Tannic, and another leaf opened up and started to bite at SRG, He kept attacking with the sword, blow after blow, hacking at the plant like a logger chops at a tree. *Whack! Whack! Whack!*

"Hurry, Compadre, it hurts!"

"I'm trying! Hang on, Tannic!"

After four more good whacks, the plant let go and toppled over. Some Random Guy helped Tannic up. His leg was bleeding a little, but he'd be okay without bandages for now. It was just a close call, and they'd had no warning. At least Tannic hadn't lost another Life Wedge. But the encounter had put them both on edge.

Having no other choice, they continued up the path. They were slowed down a lot by the slope now, and there were more rocks between the plants that they had to climb over. It resembled an obstacle course more than a hiking path, and it was getting tougher with each step. They were exhausted when they climbed onto the next platform. It was slightly smaller than the last. There was another inscribed rock on the ground.

This time Tannic read it. "One man's imagination is another man's confusion."

"What is that supposed to mean?" SRG asked.

"I don't know. Another statement about the meaning of life? I don't remember that one from the game either. Do you?"

"No. It doesn't make much sense. Does it mean something one person thinks of doesn't necessarily make sense to somebody else?"

"Well, *that* doesn't make sense to me. So maybe that's the meaning of life." He sighed. "Anyway, we have a new phrase. This isn't looking good to me. I thought the phrases would be the same as in the game."

"Me too. But we can't do anything about that now." He looked up. "One more platform. We have three choices. Are you feeling lucky? Which way do we go?"

"I don't know. My leg hurts, and I want to go home."

"Me too, Good Buddy, but we need to pick a platform."

"Okay." Tannic pondered the platforms for a minute. "Well, the farthest one away looks the easiest. But it's also the farthest away. Do you have the strength to blaze the trail that far?"

"I'd rather not. How about this one?" He pointed directly above them. "It's steep, but I don't think it's as steep as the next one over."

"Yeah, that looks good to me. Are you ready?"

"Yeah, let's go, I want to get this level over with."

"Me too, Compadre."

Some Random Guy took the lead again. He was losing steam, but he gained confidence with every step he took toward the summit. Tannic was in his shadow once again, putting each step carefully in front of the last. It had been a long day, and this level was tiring for both of them. SRG stopped to wipe his brow and looked around. He could see for miles. The view from this high up was spectacular, and he wished he could have enjoyed it. He looked back at Tannic, who couldn't care less about the view. Tannic was doing his best to put on a brave face, but he hadn't looked down the mountain since before the first platform, and he wasn't going to look backwards now.

Some Random Guy was still looking at Tannic and didn't notice the plant ahead of him moving its leaves. The motion was almost imperceptible, like a seasoned predator advancing on its prey. When it struck, it struck without warning, clamping down hard on his left hand, the one holding the Dragonwrigley. He turned and screamed, pulling his arm back as hard as he could. But the more he tried to free it, the harder the plant gripped it. He was stuck, and so was the Dragonwrigley.

"Help me, Tannic!" SRG screamed.

"What can I do?"

"Help me get my left hand free so I can use the sword."

Tannic grabbed the leaves around SRG's hand, but as he did so another set of leaves rose up and moved toward him. He let go and jumped back reflexively. The plant continued to crush SRG's hand, and blood was starting to drip from his sleeve onto the Dragonwrigley. He had a death grip on the sword, but it was useless as he couldn't move his arm at all. Tannic watched in horror, helpless to save his friend. He yelled at the plant and called it names and threw a rock at it. Nothing deterred it. One of the Life Wedges above SRG's head illuminated brightly and then began to fade.

Another branch and set of leaves swung around and latched onto the top of SRG's head. He swung the machete in frustration. It connected with the plant and severed the leaf clean with one stroke, just like when he was cutting the pathway through the other plants. He swung again, this time next to his trapped left arm, and the leaf cleaved in two. The plant snarled aloud and then whimpered as it retreated. SRG advanced on it, this time swinging the machete instead of the Dragonwrigley. He was still bleeding from his left hand as he whacked at the plant until it was cut off at the ground. A blood-like green fluid oozed out of the freshly cut stump. The cut branches wriggled and squirmed on the ground.

Tannic ran up to him. "Wow! The machete cut that thing down in one stroke. The Dragonwrigley took eight. Brilliant thinking, Good Buddy! How did you figure that out? "

"I wish I could say I figured it out, but it was just a reflex. There was nothing else I could do. I just whacked at it in frustration. But now that I think about it, it makes sense. The machete's the special weapon for this level. It makes sense that it would have special powers. I should have tried it sooner. I mean, they may be man-eating plants, but they're plants just the same."

"Well, it was still good thinking, if you ask me. Are you okay? Your hand's bleeding. So's your head, but not that much."

"Yeah I'm fine. Let's just keep going."

The plant had stopped bleeding and a new shoot was already emerging. Some Random Guy and Tannic quickly cut their way beyond it and advanced up the hill. It was getting steeper, and SRG had to alternate between slashing the brush and using both hands to pull himself up a step. Then he would cut more brush, and climb another step. That slowed their progress a lot. Tannic stayed out of the way of the machete but close enough that SRG could feel his body heat. It was another fifteen slow minutes before SRG got his hand on the platform and wearily pulled himself up. In the middle there was another rock with an inscription. And on the other side of the rock, the Wevern Boss Giant Dog lay sleeping.

Tannic pulled himself up. They were only a few feet from the sleeping, man-eating dog beast. He carefully picked up the rock and they read the inscription silently. "Let sleeping dogs lie."

"No kidding," Tannic whispered into Some Random Guy's ear. "That thing is huge!"

"Shhhhh," SRG warned. But it was too late. The Wevern Boss Giant Dog opened one eye. It looked at them the way a dog looks at a bowl of dog food, or maybe the way a hungry kid eyes a cupcake at a birthday party. Actually it looked at them like they were biscuit wagons in a gravy train. It growled with a low rumbling sound and stood up. The hair on the back of its neck and down its spine stood up too, like on a Rhodesian Ridgeback. It snarled and bared its teeth. The dog was fully two feet taller than the boys. They were too scared to move. It growled again, eyeing them over from head to toe.

This is it, SRG thought. He switched the Dragonwrigley to his right hand and the machete to his left, and he charged. He swung the Dragonwrigley at the beast's neck with all his might. Nothing happened. Even the dog's fur was too thick and tough. The Dragonwrigley bounced off without doing any damage.

He swung again and again, but it was no use. The beast just stood there, like it was patiently waiting for SRG to stop. Tannic was certain he saw it smile. When SRG swung the blade directly at its face, the dog didn't even flinch. It just narrowed its eyes and bit down on the Dragonwrigley itself, ripping it from SRG's hand, and then turned its head and spit the sword over the cliff's edge. It grunted in satisfaction and wagged its tail for a second. It smiled and showed its teeth.

Then it growled again and turned back to SRG. He shot a panicked look at Tannic. There was still the machete, though. As the dog stepped toward him, he swung at its neck. But like the Dragonwrigley, it had no effect. He tried repeatedly, to no avail. Once again Tannic thought he saw the dog smile.

Without thinking, Tannic jumped forward and taunted the dog. He ran back and forth in front of the cliff's edge waving, shouting, and calling it names. It turned to him with surprise and then snarled. Tannic flung pebbles at it and teased it relentlessly as he danced backward closer to the cliff. The beast growled and finally had enough. It charged Tannic, and as it pounced he slipped backward off the edge and vanished.

The Wevern Boss Giant Dog followed him over. SRG watched its leap carry it far beyond the edge and down. It bounced off of the mountainside several times and cried out as it plunged to its death. He ran to the edge and looked over.

The dog's body was still in free fall, bouncing and ricocheting off the cliff walls. It hit the bottom hard, and he could just see its lifeless body piled up like a wrecked car. Tannic, though, was nowhere to be seen.

"Tannic! *Tannic!*"

"Down here, Compadre!"

SRG leaned out farther and looked down. Ten feet below him, Tannic was hanging precipitously from a small branch.

"Hang on, Good Buddy. I'll figure out how to get you back up here."

"I . . . I can't hang on much longer," Tannic panted, "and I'm afraid to move!"

"Can you reach another branch? Is there anything above you? Whatever you do, don't look down."

"Don't worry . . . I'm not about to do that . . . there is a small branch . . . just above—Hey! . . . there's a Heart Gem on it . . . if I can just reach it . . . little bit more . . ."

And then the branch Tannic was hanging from snapped, and he plunged down the cliff face. He bounced and fell head over heels. SRG tried to scream but he was so terrified he couldn't make a sound. Finally Tannic came to a stop right on top of the dead Wevern Boss Giant Dog. SRG saw a light glow over his head. He couldn't make it out at the distance, but he knew what it was. He just hoped Tannic still had another Life Wedge.

He shouted at the top of his lungs. "Tannic! Can you hear me?"

When Tannic opened his eyes, his first thought was *Wow! I fell all the way down from there? How did I survive? Hey, I survived!*

Then SRG shouted, and he replied, "I can hear you, Compadre! I'm still with you!"

"Good! Go to your left and you'll find our path! Climb back up! But try not to get eaten! You only have one Life Wedge left!" SRG yelled all that, his voice getting hoarse toward the end.

"What?"

"You only have . . . one . . . Life . . . Wedge . . . left!"

"Okay, I'll be careful! See you in a minute!"

Tannic all but ran up the hill. When he passed the newly growing man-eating plant, he was moving so fast that it didn't even have a chance to react. In a couple of minutes, he was standing on the platform again with SRG.

"Tannic! That was awesome! You saved our lives! How did you know there was a branch there?"

"I didn't. I was trying to taunt the dog over the edge, but I was going to jump aside at the last minute." He wasn't afraid to look over the edge anymore. He looked down at the spot he'd been hanging from. "The problem is, I slipped and went over it myself. Believe me, no way was I planning on jumping off."

"Well, it's just a good thing you still had two Life Wedges left. Otherwise . . . uh, hey, do you think we can reach the Heart Gem from here?"

He shook his head. "Forget about it. Let's get to the summit and take our chances with the Guru Ender Dude. Oh, wait. I have a present for you." He pulled the Dragonwrigley from behind him.

"Thanks! I forgot all about it."

"No worries. It was stuck in the beast. He actually fell on it and impaled himself. It was all I could do to pull it out."

"I was wondering what you were doing down there. Okay. We have the Dragonwrigley again, and we still have the machete. I have three Life Wedges left and you still have one. We have a fighting chance. Let's go."

They were close to the summit, and it looked like a straight shot. Some Random Guy whacked at the shrubs with a new sense of purpose, and in minutes they reached the peak and found the Guru Ender Dude sitting silently in the sunlight. He had a white robe, white hair, and a long white beard. He was a bit of a cliché, but they hadn't designed the game, so he was what he was. They approached him reverently. He appeared to be deep in thought. After a moment he raised his head and studied them without surprise.

"You have done well to reach the summit. What is the meaning of life? I will ask you three times, and you must choose wisely or you know the consequences. Please speak."

Some Random Guy and Tannic exchanged glances. They hadn't planned for this. They hadn't decided which phrase to say. SRG took a deep breath and guessed. "Life is meaningless. There is no meaning of life, just enjoy it."

"That is incorrect," the Guru answered calmly. "What is the meaning of life? Choose wisely." Some Random Guy noticed that the Guru had a Rainbow Star in his right hand. He looked toward Tannic, who had a sick look on his face.

"What do you want to try?" SRG whispered "Any bright ideas? Are you feeling lucky? What if it's not one of the inscriptions we found?" He looked back at the Guru, but the Guru didn't seem to mind them discussing their answer.

"Well, 'Let sleeping dogs lie' is pretty obvious, maybe too obvious if you ask me." Tannic frowned. "I mean, the dog was sleeping right next to the sign. That's not the meaning of life, it's just good advice. The first one was 'Don't take anything for granted.' I don't know, I say we go with the one about one guy's imagination. Whatever that was."

Some Random Guy took a deep breath and let it out

slowly. Tannic nodded at him, and the Guru looked on patiently. "One man's imagination is another man's confusion," SRG offered nervously.

The Guru studied them silently. The silence hung in the air like a bad fart. The tension was palpable. Some Random Guy looked at Tannic, who looked worried. Finally the Guru spoke. "You have chosen wisely, my son. Here is the Rainbow Star. Go in peace."

Some Random Guy sighed and his shoulders relaxed. He took a relieved step forward and received the Rainbow Star from the Guru. He admired the brilliant colors in his right hand. The next thing he knew, he and Tannic were standing in Dr. Denton's lab, and he was smiling at them.

Chapter 7

The Forever Forest

"You boys had me worried, especially when Tannic went over the cliff," exclaimed Doc. "Tannic, I thought you were afraid of heights!"

"Not afraid of heights, Doc," Tannic reminded him. "Just afraid of hitting the ground. Luckily I landed on a big soft cushion!"

"In any event, well played, boys, and well done!"

"I'm just tired, and I want to go home," Some Random Guy lamented. "I don't know how much more of this I can take."

"I understand," Dr. Denton replied. "But I've conducted further research on the topic, and I think the only possibility for getting you home is dependent on your finishing Level 10. Then I can test a hypothesis I'm working on. But you'll need to complete all ten levels for my plan to have any probability of success."

Some Random Guy sighed. "Okay, I know you're right, we just have to do this. Come on, Tannic. We've been to the Forever Forest before, but this time we need to nail it. I hate Level 5!"

"No worries, Compadre, we'll knock it off and be back

here before you can say Mrs. Kibbitch!"

That brought a laugh from the others. Then Dr. Denton pointed out the heat-seeking taser leaning against the door. It was the special weapon for Level 5, and would come in handy against the Weevil Beast, probably the worst enemy they had faced up to this point in the game.

Some Random Guy picked up the Taser. It was about the size of a handgun, but it had fancy-looking sights and a flashing LED in the middle. He carried it in his left hand and the Dragonwrigley in his right as Tannic opened the door and they stepped out of Dr. Denton's lab and into the Forever Forest. The door closed behind them with a metallic clang.

"This place still gives me the creeps," Tannic whispered. "I've never been a fan of the Forever Forest, even in the video game. I can't imagine what we're about to face."

"Yeah, me too. But we've done this before. We know what to do, at least in the game. So let's get it done. The sooner we start, the sooner we finish."

"After you, Compadre, but I have to point out one thing."

"What's that?" SRG asked.

"We've never actually completed Level 5. We don't know where the Rainbow Star is hidden, and we don't know anything about the Ender Dude. In a way, we *don't* know what to do."

"Well, he's got to be somewhere in here. We'll find him. We just need to keep from getting killed by the Weevil Beasts. We'll figure this out, Tannic. We've made it this far. Let's get it over with."

"You first, Compadre," Tannic whispered again. "If I remember correctly, you still have the weapons."

The Rough Forest, better known as the Forever Forest, was a dense jungle. The trees and bushes were every shade of green and ranged from waist high to well over forty feet. It seemed to be mid-morning. It was cool, even though there was no breeze on the forest floor, and it was definitely more comfortable than the direct sunlight. The canopy of tree branches provided plenty of shade, which was a nice change, but all the shadows and the thick plant life made it impossible to see more than a few feet. It was beautiful but haunting. All around their feet were vines that would tangle about their shins and make running all but impossible. Of course, the rest of the vegetation made moving faster than a slug's pace all but impossible anyway.

Some Random Guy and Tannic proceeded slowly, methodically, and with extreme caution. They took one step at a time, then cut the vegetation in front of them with the Dragonwrigley and took another. They headed toward what looked like the depths of the forest. Time seemed to move slowly, and it took ages to move just a few feet.

"No wonder they call it the Forever Forest. It takes forever to get anywhere," Tannic complained.

"Tell me about it. I'm the one who has to cut our way through this mass," SRG replied. "It's a lot easier in the game, I can tell you that much."

"You see anything yet that we need to worry about?" Tannic asked.

Some Random Guy paused and thought. "Not yet. I'm hoping there aren't man-eating plants in addition to the Weevil Beasts. But keep your eyes peeled for Minotaurs. There weren't any in the game, but that doesn't mean anything now. Stay alert for any movement or anything that looks out of place."

"You mean like that vine that's wrapped around your leg?" Tannic shrieked.

A vine had begun wrapping itself carefully around SRG's leg. It suddenly constricted and started dragging SRG into the bushes, toward a plant that had two large leaves lined with sharp fangs. The leaves formed a mouth, and it moved slowly toward SRG's head.

Tannic screamed, "Compadre! Use your sword!" But Some Random Guy didn't pay any attention. He didn't even struggle as he slid toward the plant's evil-looking mouth. It pulled SRG in with its long limbs just like a gigantic praying mantis.

"Use the Dragonwrigley!" Tannic screamed.

He grabbed the vine and began tugging, but it just dragged him along too. It started trying to wrap a vine around his arm. Some Random Guy looked lifeless now, offering no resistance, and he was close to the ugly mouth. A Life Wedge above SRG's head glowed briefly and began to fade. Tannic felt sick at the sight. It was all too familiar now, and he was tired of it. The plant carefully wrapped its leaves around SRG's head and chomped down. Tannic watched the Life Wedge disappear. He let go of the vine. It was too late, and he didn't want to join SRG in the plant's mouth. Suddenly the plant opened its mouth and Some Random Guy stood up and shook himself off.

"What happened? I felt like I was dreaming in slow motion!" SRG exclaimed.

"You just got eaten by that plant. You lost a Life Wedge. I kept yelling but you didn't respond. I tried to pull you loose but the vine started dragging me in too."

"I could hear you, but it was like you were a long way away in a tunnel. I couldn't tell what you were saying, and I felt all cozy, warm, and relaxed . . . It was weird."

"That must have been the vine. It did something to you,

liked drugged you or something." He shuddered. "Well, now we know that there are man-eating plants on this level."

"Yeah, we're going to have to be more careful about the vines. I thought they were harmless."

"I'm afraid nothing is harmless in Rough World, Compadre!"

They advanced slowly into the forest. It grew denser, darker, and more evil looking. Once SRG cut down a threatening vine directly in front of him. They stepped over it and went on.

The Weevil Beast was waiting for them somewhere in the jungle. It was a creature created by the Evil Boss to keep the poor people of the Jagged City from venturing into the forest and escaping his control. It had many legs and other appendages and a very menacing gigantic head that could swallow a person in a single gulp. Of course, its mouth was lined with razor-sharp teeth, so it would more often bite people in half, chew them up, and swallow the bits and pieces. It wouldn't take much imagination to understand how dangerous this creature was if you even saw a picture of it. It was scary enough in the game, and quite frankly just the thought of it scared Some Random Guy and Tannic to no end. But the odds were they'd have to face it sooner or later on their way to the Ender Dude. In the game, there was more than one Weevil Beast in the forest, though they knew by now that the real Rough World didn't follow the game exactly, so they couldn't be sure what to expect. They'd played Level 5 a few times, but they had never finished it, and they always lost all their Life Wedges to the Weevil Beast, so it seemed like their main nemesis here. Those memories were hanging over both of them like a little black cloud as they moved through the forest, although neither brought them up.

"Do you think we're going the right way?" Tannic asked, not wanting to think about the beast any more.

"Well, I'm trying to keep us in a straight line. I don't think we're going in a circle, or we'd have seen our own tracks at some—" Some Random Guy grew quiet. He was standing on what he'd thought was a fallen branch, but he felt it moving. He jumped back suddenly. Tannic screamed and jumped too.

"What was it?" Tannic asked.

"I don't know! I stepped on a vine or something and I swear it moved. Quiet. Listen for any movement," SRG insisted.

But it was completely quiet in the forest. There wasn't even the whisper of a breeze.

"I don't hear anything," Tannic said quietly.

"Me neither. It must have been my imagination. I'm kind of on edge. I can't help it."

"Me too, Compadre. But let's keep going. It was probably just a normal vine and it gave a little when you stepped on it."

"You're probably right. I mean, what else could it be?" Some Random Guy asked with a hint of sarcasm. That made Tannic smile. Then they both smiled.

Some Random Guy put his left foot cautiously forward, his right hand clutching the Dragonwrigley and the Taser held confidently in his left hand. He parted the brush with his left arm and moved forward again. The fallen branch was under his right foot again as he stepped down. He screamed. Tannic screamed and jumped too. This time the branch rose into the air until it was above them. It was attached to a larger branch, and the larger branch was attached to a large body, and at that point a giant head rose above the vegetation and glared at them with piercing eyes. It growled and opened its mouth wide, exposing rows of shiny razor-sharp teeth. It seemed to be smiling, like a 10-year-old kid holding a slice of his favorite cheese pizza, filled with anticipation of that first bite. SRG and Tannic stood stock-still, frozen with fear. It was moving toward them.

Some Random Guy came to his senses, dropped the Dragonwrigley, and raised the Taser in both hands. He fixed the sights on the beast's head and slowly squeezed the trigger. He was barely breathing and was totally focused on his shot. SRG had gone to the gun range with his dad lots of times and had developed a good slow squeeze for the trigger, as opposed to the sharp jerking motion that most people used. That would inevitably pull the sights off the target and result in a missed shot.

Time seemed to stand still. He didn't hear anything or see anything else but the Taser and the Weevil Beast. Suddenly the Taser barked and sparked brightly as it connected with the Weevil Beast's face. The creature stood there stunned, not moving. Its face was glowing faintly.

"Great shot, Compadre," Tannic said. "The Taser spoke once and the Weevil Beast heard its call. I think it said 'We own you, bitch!' Now what?"

"I don't know. In the game, one shot from the Taser kills it, but it's still just standing there. It doesn't look dead. Just frozen. I mean, the Taser's supposed to kill it. But the Weevil Beast always killed us first. It's not moving, but it's not dead either. At least I don't think so," SRG mumbled as he shook his head.

"Uh, this isn't the game, remember?" Tannic asked.

"Yeah, but what do we do now?"

"I don't know. Can we just walk on around it?"

"Maybe. You go first."

"Oh, no. You have the weapons, you go first, Compadre!"

"Oh, all right. Stay close."

"No worries, Compadre, I'm going to be like your second layer of skin!" And Tannic hugged Some Random Guy from behind.

"Ow! Give me a little room! You don't have to be that close."

They stepped cautiously around the Weevil Beast, never taking their eyes off of it. It just stood there frozen. It looked alive, just stunned. Really stunned. After they were past, they looked back at it. It was still facing the spot they'd been standing when SRG shot it with the Taser.

"So do you think it's dead? Or what?"

"I don't know. Maybe it takes more than one shot?"

"How many shots do you have?"

"I don't know that either. In the game you get three. Here it's anybody's guess, but I would think we have at least three. So we should have two left. Anyway, I guess we'll find out."

They were making their way through the dense undergrowth again, and the statue was lost to sight behind them.

"Maybe you should have cut his head off with the Dragonwrigley after you stunned him."

"Yeah, maybe so, Good Buddy, but it's too late now, and I'm not going back there. I want to get as far away from that creature as I can."

"Me too. I still don't like this level."

Some Random Guy swung the Dragonwrigley back and forth in a slow rhythm, like swinging a hammer on a chain gang. One step at a time, one branch, one vine, one step. Swing the sword back and forth, and then repeat. He paused for breath. Tannic was being unusually quiet, so SRG asked,

"How far do you think it is to the center of the forest?"

There was no answer.

"What's wrong, Good Buddy, cat got your tongue?"

He looked back at Tannic. Tannic was staring with glassy eyes and not responding. The lights were on but nobody was home. He looked like the Taser-stunned Weevil Beast.

"Tannic! Answer me! What's wrong?" SRG pleaded.

But Tannic just stood there. Then without warning he started to move to the left, but he was being dragged along. Some Random Guy saw the vine attached to his foot and quickly began swinging the Dragonwrigley at it, but he couldn't seem to cut through. Tannic was offering no resistance. SRG looked up and saw two large leaves forming a mouth lined with dagger-like teeth. It was opening wide as Tannic was drawn in by the vine. One of his Life Wedges shone and began fading away. SRG panicked and dropped the Dragonwrigley to aim the Taser. The plant was biting down on Tannic's head now, and the Life Wedge was gone. He set the sights on the plant and started to squeeze the trigger. But the plant moved at the instant the Taser fired. It barked as it hit Tannic right in the side of his head.

The plant glowed, dropped Tannic, and slowly lowered itself to the ground. It lay there motionless. Tannic stood up, a bit shaky. The glow from his head was disappearing, leaving a single Life Wedge behind. SRG had fired too late. Tannic had already lost one Life Wedge, and SRG had unintentionally taken another one from him. To make matters worse, he'd wasted a Taser shot. Now they might have only one shot left. It had all happened too fast, and the beast moved at just the wrong moment.

"Thanks, Compadre!" Tannic asked. "Hey, why the long face?"

"You were drugged and being dragged along by a man-eating plant. I tried to cut the vine with the Dragonwrigley but I couldn't cut through it. I tried and tried but it didn't work. The plant was about to eat you, and I panicked and shot it with the Taser."

"Wow! Great shot!"

"Well, not exactly . . ."

"What do you mean, Compadre? Oh, no, don't tell me . . ."

"Well, you remember when I accidently hit you with the fireball on Level 1?"

"Yeah, don't tell me. Please don't tell me."

"You see, the plant moved just as I was squeezing the trigger. It wasn't my fault. I accidently hit you with the Taser."

"I take back the compliment. And you wasted a Taser shot on me too. Perfect, just perfect," Tannic remarked in disgust.

"I know. I'm sorry. I just panicked when it had you in its mouth. I'm sorry. I was trying to save you. It's not easy, you know. I've never had to do anything like this in real life before." His lip trembled.

"Okay, I understand. I do appreciate you trying to rescue me. Now we're just in a more difficult spot. I only have one Life Wedge left, and we might only have one Taser blast left, and we haven't even gotten to the Ender Dude yet. We don't even know where he is or what he looks like. For all we know there could be another Weevil Beast on this level, and Minotaurs."

"Yeah, I know, we need to be really careful. Don't step on any vines. Let me know right away if you feel something on your leg."

"All right, let's go, I'm ready to get this level over with, one way or another."

"Don't say that, we've got to make it. We've just got to. We got this Tannic. We got this."

They continued in the same direction, now slower and more cautious than ever. Some Random Guy still chopped their path with the Dragonwrigley, keeping a tight grip on the Taser with his left hand, but he parted the vegetation every time before they took even a small step forward. The plant life was growing denser, the leaves on the bushes were getting larger, and it was getting darker and more difficult to see. The sun was still in the sky, but it was hard to tell through the thick greenery. They kept up their slow pace and rhythm.

It was an uneventful hour before they stopped to rest. They sat down amid the lush, dense growth. Some Random Guy was sweating, and they were both tired.

"This is really hard work," SRG admitted.

"Yeah, I'm really sorry I can't help you much."

"Just keep your eyes and ears open. That helps a bunch."

"We can't waste too much time," Tannic noted. "I don't like the dark to begin with. I'm sure I wouldn't like it in this forest."

There was maybe an hour of daylight left, and neither of them wanted to spend the night in the forest. There could be Weevil Wolves at night, or who knew what other creatures. They didn't want to find out.

"Alright, agreed. If you're ready, let's keep going."

"Lead onward, Compadre!"

Some Random Guy slashed through another wall of leaves. He stepped forward, Tannic close on his heels and looking in every direction. The vegetation was thinner here, and SRG could see between some of the plants now. A minute later, they stepped into something that was almost a clearing, though it was still covered in waist-high vegetation. There was no canopy of tall trees, though. It was about forty feet across.

"What do you think this is? Some kind of meadow?"

"I don't know. Are we in the middle of the center of nowhere?"

"You mean the center of the middle of nowhere!"

That made them both giggle. It wasn't a funny situation, but they were both too tired to be serious. They walked slowly to middle of the clearing. There was nothing remarkable about it at all. "I guess we keep moving," SRG said. "False alarm."

"Uh, Compadre, don't look now, but I don't think it's a false alarm. That tree over there on the edge just moved."

"Trees don't move."

"This one just did. I saw it. I swear. It moved."

"I don't see anything. Which one was it?" SRG turned around.

Tannic didn't have to answer his question. It was obvious he meant the tree with all of the jointed appendages and the two gigantic heads. It wasn't a tree at all, but the mother of all Weevil Beasts. And it was apparently the Ender Dude for this level. It held a Rainbow Star aloft in one of its talon-like claws.

It looked down and snarled at the two boys in a way that made their blood run cold. Well, one head snarled, the other growled instead, almost like two speakers that were slightly out of sync. Some Random Guy and Tannic turned to run at the same time but in opposite directions. They collided with each other and fell down in a tangle, and the beast pounced on them. It picked each of them up with a different appendage and hoisted one to each of its heads to study them carefully with its huge, snake-like eyes. They were afraid to move and afraid not to move. Then the beast lifted Tannic to its mouth, and he screamed.

Some Random Guy raised the Taser. He didn't dare drop the Dragonwrigley, so he was going to have to shoot with his left hand. He aimed as closely as he could at the eye on the head that was about to eat Tannic, and squeezed the trigger. The Taser barked. A bolt of energy shot toward the beast and hit it right next to the eye. For a moment the head lit up like a glow stick, and then it froze. The other head shrieked and darted toward the stunned one. SRG felt the grip on him loosen as the creature turned its attention to Tannic. He raised the Taser again, aimed, and squeezed slowly. But this time the Taser let out a pip-squeak of a bark and only a small stream of dancing laser light hit the other head, at the corner of the mouth. The head shrieked again and made an eerie crying sound, but it kept moving, apparently unaffected. SRG pulled the trigger again, but this time there was nothing. The Taser was depleted.

He dropped it to the ground, gripped the Dragonwrigley in both hands, and swung it hard at the appendage holding him. But it literally bounced off of the scaly, bark-like skin. He swung again and again, but it was no use. Then he remembered the fireballs and the crescents. He swung the sword and threw two fireballs at the beast's good head. All that did was irritate it. He fired a couple of crescents at it, which bounced back into the bushes on the ground.

The beast was slowly lowering Some Random Guy and loosening its grip as it focused more and more on its frozen head. Without warning, it let go of him entirely, and he dropped to the ground next to its foot with a thud. The fall knocked the breath out of him, and it took him a moment to recover. When he stood up, the beast's good head was about to close down on Tannic. He'd be shredded to bits with the first bite. The mouth looked like a great white shark on steroids.

Tannic only had one Life Wedge left. This was it. They'd never gotten past this point in the game, and here they were again, facing defeat or death. Some Random Guy swung the Dragonwrigley at the beast's foot in frustration. It had several irregular toes, with gross, disgusting nails dug into the earth. The blade sliced the nearest one clean off.

The beast let out a deafening scream. Green slime oozed from the wound. The Weevil Beast turned away from Tannic and focused intently on SRG. He swung again, with renewed enthusiasm, at the next toe. The Dragonwrigley cleaved another digit off of the beast's foot. It screamed again, and this time the ground shook. The head shot toward SRG as the Dragonwrigley cut the last toe from the foot, then it screamed again and flailed around in the air. Green slime was now gushing from its foot and puddling on the ground, around SRG's feet. It smelled like rotten eggs.

Tannic hung limply in the beast's claw. Some Random Guy was shouting some dirty words in his head, words he'd heard his grandpa utter more than once while salmon fishing in Alaska, but words he'd get in trouble for if he dared to say them out loud. He lifted the Dragonwrigley high over his head and was about to strike again. But abruptly the beast stopped screaming and went still. It stood perfectly lifeless for a moment, and time seemed to stop as SRG stood frozen too, staring up at it. Then the giant creature started to waver. It swayed back and forth, and finally toppled over. It crashed to the ground and lay still. Tannic was still motionless when Some Random Guy reached him.

"Tannic! Tannic!" SRG screamed. "Tannic! Are you okay?"

Tannic carefully opened one eye. "You rang, Compadre? Did you like the way I handled that critter? He won't mess with me anytime soon! I already had him right where I wanted him when you fired. I didn't need your help."

"Yeah, you really showed him." SRG grinned. "Who would have thought that his toes were his only weakness. I think he bled to death. That green stuff was disgusting. It smelled horrible."

Some Random Guy helped Tannic out of the beast's claw, and they walked over to the one that held the Rainbow Star. "Go ahead and pick it up, it's your turn," SRG told Tannic. "You've earned it."

"With pleasure!" Tannic replied. He grabbed the brightly colored star and clenched it tightly in his hand.

Chapter 8

The Abandoned Plains

And just like that they were standing in Dr. Denton's lab again, survivors against the odds once more, triumphant but tired. They'd finally defeated Level 5, and this time it had been for real. More importantly they were still very much alive.

"I don't know how much more of this I can take!" exclaimed Dr. Denton. "You boys all but gave me a heart attack on that level. I thought you were goners when the Weevil Beast had you. I didn't see any way out. That was very clever of you, SRG. How did you know its weakness was its toes?"

"I didn't," SRG replied. "I was just mad, and its toes were the closest thing to me."

"Oh, well then . . ." Dr. Denton pondered.

They were quiet for a few minutes. Some Random Guy spoke to break the silence. "Now what?" he asked. "What comes next?"

"Well, we're on to Level 6," Dr. Denton responded.

"*We're* on to Level 6? Who's we, Dr. Denton?"

"Hey, we're all in this together. I'm doing all I can to help you boys. I'm on your team," Dr. Denton affirmed.

"Yeah," Tannic agreed. "We're a team. And a damned

good one if you ask me!"

"Tannic, you just said damn!" SRG scolded him.

"Yeah? After what we've been through today, I'm going to say whatever I feel like!"

"Well, don't let Dad hear you. He'll think you've been hanging around Grandpa, and then we'll all get in trouble. Including Grandpa," SRG added.

Dr. Denton laughed. "Okay, boys, let's forget that and focus on the task at hand. Level 6 is up next, and it's no picnic. What do you guys know about it?"

"Uh . . . there's something we should probably tell you, Dr. Denton."

"What's that?"

"Well, we've never actually finished Level 5 before. So we don't know anything about any of the rest of the levels. I mean, we didn't even know how to beat Level 5. We just got lucky."

"Don't underestimate yourselves, boys. That was more than luck, there was some major intuition at play. I think you have a real feel for this game. You've defied the odds so far. You have a talent for it."

"But I was just mad and frustrated! And his toes were just in the wrong place at the wrong time," Some Random Guy protested.

"Well, I could show you some other examples. Do you want to watch any highlights from Level 5?" Doc asked.

"No!" SRG replied sharply. "That beast was the worst thing we've ever faced. I never want to see that level again. If we manage to get home, I don't think I'll ever even play this game again." He sighed. "I'd give anything to go home right now. Any activity through the reverse screen, Doc? Has anybody been home?"

"No, there hasn't been any activity at all. But I'll keep an eye open."

"Okay. So what's next? Please tell us it gets better."

"I'm afraid I don't have good news for you there. The levels will keep getting harder and more dangerous. Now let's see. Level 6. This region is called the Abandoned Plains," Dr. Denton began. "They were abandoned for a reason, and that isn't good news either. They're filled with Boss Bison, Plains Minotaurs, also known as Bisotaurs, and then there is the Slagebrush—that's a plant that stings you and creates an itchy rash—and the Ender Dude is a great Grizzly Bear."

"The Boss Bison are like regular bison, but bigger and meaner. They can run much faster than you. If they stampede, they can pretty much flatten a city or whatever's in front of them. They're incredibly strong and have a great sense of smell. You'll want to avoid them as completely as possible. The Dragonwrigley won't be much use—strictly a numbers thing. There are simply far too many of them, they run in vast herds and you won't be able to stop them with a sword."

"The Plains Minotaurs are bison versions of the Minotaurs you've already seen, they're also much stronger. You'll understand why they're referred to as Bisotaurs. They're meaner, too. They'll tear you limb from limb. I don't know if they have a weakness. Maybe their eyesight. They're fewer in number than the Boss Bison, so your odds with the Dragonwrigley will be more favorable."

"The Slagebrush is poisonous. It won't kill you, but you might wish it did. You will develop an agonizing, almost debilitating rash. It's like poison oak, only much worse. And there won't be any Tec-Nu products to help you out. If you come in contact with it, you'll just have to tough it out." He paused, thinking. "I don't know if it affects the other creatures. Hmm."

"Anyway, the Ender Dude is, roughly speaking, a supercharged Grizzly Bear on steroids. Except that he also wears the Rainbow Star on a collar and never sleeps. That may explain his distemper. He is severely sleep deprived. Like most bears, he has an incredible sense of smell but very poor eyesight. Incidentally he may charge you and then stand up at the last second to get a good look at you. Grizzly Bears have a tendency to do that. Nobody's quite sure why, but it's probably a combination of charging you to see what you do and stopping to get a better sense of what you look like. On account of their poor eyesight. They may even stand up just to put on a display and frighten you off without a confrontation. That won't be the case with the Ender Dude, though. He isn't afraid of anything—he's the 'king of the mountain' on this level, so to speak. The top of the food chain, the apex predator. Nevertheless, he does have bear instincts so he may behave like them. He probably can't help it. If he does stand up in front of you, that's your opportunity to shoot him. Oh, that reminds me. As with the other Ender Dudes, I'm not sure how effective the Dragonwrigley will be against him. Your special weapon on this level will be a bow and arrow. It's a simple re-curve bow, nothing fancy, but the arrows are very effective on the local enemies. You just need to be careful to shoot them in the chest. Anyhow, that might be your best bet against the Ender Dude."

"Whew! That was a lot of information, but that's about it. Oh, wait, one last thing. The Slagebrush looks like normal sagebrush, except the flowers are white instead of yellow. So, yellow sagebrush flowers are safe, white flowers are bad. That's about all I can give you. And I guess it goes without saying, but please be careful out there."

"That is a lot of information Doc, but thanks. You really are a great help. I don't know what we'd do without you. I've shot a re-curve bow a couple of times with my grandpa, so I'm at least familiar with them. Hopefully I can shoot well enough to get us through." Some Random Guy turned to his best friend, who seemed overwhelmed by all the information. SRG nodded and said, "Come on Tannic, let's go get that bear!"

"Uh, let's get the Rainbow Star. I don't really want to get the bear. I hate bears! I don't want to meet one!"

"I don't think we have any choice. We have to face the Ender Dude to get the star, and he's a Grizzly Bear. So just take a deep breath and focus."

Some Random Guy and Tannic walked to the door. SRG picked up the bow and the quiver of arrows, looped the quiver over his shoulder, and picked up the Dragonwrigley with his free hand. He paused and looked back at Doc, the lab, and the reverse screen, taking it all in one more time. Then he nodded silently again at Tannic, lowered his shoulder, and walked through the door, from the warmth and safety of the lab into the great unknown of the Abandoned Plains. He set off at a brisk pace.

"Wait up, Compadre. You in a hurry?"

"Sorry. I'm just a little anxious. We've never been to this level before. The enemies sounded pretty serious and I didn't want to tell Doc, but I'm not really that good with a bow and arrow. I mean, I've shot one. I'm just not very good at it. So I'll do my best, but I'm scared."

"I'm not," Tannic replied.

"Not what?"

"Not scared."

"Yeah, me neither."

"You just said you were scared."

"I lied. I was just trying to make you feel better in case you were really scared."

"Yeah right. Well, I think you're lying now, but I appreciate it. Come on, we can do this. You'll make the shot. I have faith in you. And I watched you when you used a bow and arrow with your grandpa, remember? You weren't that bad."

"That was at a target, not a charging Grizzly Bear. But thanks. I'll do my best."

The plains seemed completely vacant. There were low rolling hills and a few ravines. Some of the ravines had sharp rocky edges, almost cliff-like, interrupting their walls. Those small cliffs held a few juniper trees but were otherwise pretty bare. They were high enough that falling from them would result in broken bones and maybe death. Other ravines were just gentle slopes with broad flat mesas in between them. The sun was just rising, and there were some clouds scattered against the blue background. It felt like midmorning, and it was comfortable now but it felt like the kind of day that would be warm later. A gentle breeze was kicking up a little dust into the air, which felt pretty dry already.

The level was well named. It reminded Some Random Guy of pictures of the Great Plains he'd seen in geography class. At first glance, it looked harmless, but it was fraught with dangers. They had no illusions about that fact, though. They were in enemy territory.

The boys wandered forward, keeping a steady pace. They looked in every direction, anxious about Boss Bison, Bisotaurs, and the Ender Dude. But there were just scattered juniper trees and sparse, low-growing grass punctuated with the occasional sagebrush plant. The sagebrush was in bloom, and all the blossoms were yellow. They actually smelled like the sagebrush from home. The fragrant smell caught Some Random Guy off guard, and he found himself longing for the times he went fishing with his grandpa in the Steen's Mountains. The sagebrush and juniper instantly took him back there. He was lost in another place and time when he was jolted into the present by a thundering gallop. A Bisotaur was rushing at them. Tannic was shouting in his ear. The Bisotaur had its head lowered, and it was charging straight toward them. Time seemed to shift into slow motion as SRG raised the Dragonwrigley and launched a couple of fireballs followed by two crescents. The Bisotaur caught the fireballs and crescents all in its throat and went down hard, driving its head into the dirt and coming to a stop nose-first at SRG's feet. A cloud of dust came with it, and Tannic sneezed twice.

"That was close! I didn't think you were ever going to shoot!" exclaimed Tannic as he wiped his nose on his sleeve. "What were you doing there, Compadre?"

"Sorry. I was kind of daydreaming. I guess after all we've been through this place seemed pretty low-key, and I let my guard down and forgot where we were. It was the smell of the sagebrush and the juniper. It reminded me of trips to the Steen's Mountains. Sorry about that."

"I don't think we have the luxury of daydreaming, Compadre. We need to stay focused. That was a close one, and he came out of nowhere."

"Don't worry, Good Buddy. I won't let it happen again. It won't happen again. We've just been through a lot today. I'll stay focused, I promise."

"Well, next time around we might not be so lucky! Good thing it was just a Bisotaur and not a herd of Boss Bison."

"Listen to you—*just a Bisotaur*! Yesterday that would have scared the life out of us. We'd be on the edge of the couch screaming like little girls!" SRG sighed. "But you're right. It was *just* a Bisotaur. How fast life changes, huh? Come on, Tannic, let's keep moving. I want to get this level over with."

They moved in unison, walking across the plains. An hour passed and they didn't meet anything, although they were on edge the whole time. They were studying the horizon, looking for Bison and Bisotaurs. Some Random Guy looked over his shoulder every couple of minutes to check their back trail. He didn't want something sneaking up on them from behind.

The sun had risen to the middle of the sky, and it was getting warm. The breeze helped, but there wasn't really any shade, and they hadn't seen any water. Both of them were feeling the heat and had dry throats. SRG was sweating and starting to get a sunburn. That was going to be hard to explain when he got home. If he ever got home. He forced himself not to think about that. He needed to keep moving forward. Forward to the end of the level, forward to the end of the game, forward to home. Home. *Home, sweet home!* He was slipping into another daydream when a loud roar brought him back to the here and now.

He and Tannic looked in the direction of the noise. There appeared to be a dust storm on the far horizon. Dirt was boiling into the air and rushing across the plains, hugging the ground. They looked at each other quizzically, then they both realized. It wasn't a dust storm. It was a herd of Boss Bison, and they were headed straight toward them. The roar kept getting louder, and the ruckus was drawing closer. At the speed it was approaching, they had only minutes before it overtook them—and maybe consumed them.

"What do we do now?" Tannic spoke loudly over the thunder. "Do you think they're charging us? How could they have seen us? There must be a hundred of them or more!"

"I don't think they know we're here. They must be charging for some other reason. I think we should find a spot to hide and let them pass. Not a tree, though, not if they can level a city. A hole in the ground that they'll run past. I saw something like that on an old western movie. Hurry, let's move!"

They ran to the closest ravine. It wasn't deep. A lip jutted over its edge, and directly below it was a small indentation, not quite a cave but large enough for both of them to crawl into. The lip protruded over them and provided some cover. They pressed in tight like they had in the mine shaft on Level 2. Tannic was in back and Some Random Guy squeezed in front of him, the ever-present Dragonwrigley in his right hand and the re-curve bow in his left. He tucked his chin to his chest, and they both held their breath.

The stampede was getting closer by the second, and the ground started to rumble and shake. After a minute, the noise was so loud they couldn't have heard each other speak even if they had tried. The first of the huge bison appeared on the opposite side of the ravine and jumped off the edge, followed by too many more to count. They were coming straight toward the boys, but they jumped up and over them to get to the top of the ridge and continue on. The ground shook around them. The air was thick with dust, and SRG and Tannic were having trouble breathing. The dust obscured the sun and it got dark inside their hollow. Tannic sneezed constantly. The stampede lasted for a few minutes, and then just as fast as it had started it was over. The noise dwindled to a low rumble and then nothing. The dust hung in the air for a few minutes and slowly settled down and dissipated. Tannic sneezed one last time. They were both covered with dirt. They crawled out of the depression and began dusting themselves off.

"Wow, that was something! Good thinking back there, Compadre."

"Yeah, we were just lucky there was a place to hide. If there hadn't been, I don't think we'd be having this conversation. I think we'd have been squashed like everything else in their path."

They looked in the direction the stampede had come from and then the direction it had gone. All the juniper trees, sagebrush, and grass were flattened as if a steam roller had gone over them. The soil looked like it had been tilled. Wisps of dust still hung in the air. Tannic took a deep breath and wiped his nose again.

"Well, we have a clear path to walk if we want. Do you think that's safe?" he asked.

"What are the odds of two herds of Boss Bison stampeding down the same track?" SRG answered with another question.

"I don't know. I don't know anything anymore, Compadre. I just think it would be easier walking. What do you think?"

"Yeah, what have we got to lose? Except a few Life Wedges."

"Good one, but that's not really funny."

"Sorry," SRG said. "I think you're right. Let's walk in the path they created and let's walk away from them. How does that sound?"

"I like that plan."

The boys started down the churned up path of the

stampede toward wherever the bison had come from. The stampede itself was out of sight. They passed through one ravine after another. As they approached a much deeper one, Some Random Guy stopped to listen for any sign of danger. He approached the edge slowly, stopping with each step to look at the ravine as it slowly came into view. If there was anything lurking in it below, he wanted to duck before it saw him. It was a classic predator tactic. See your prey before it sees you, and you have the element of surprise on your side. He was learning to act like a predator. Tannic crept along behind him like his shadow.

"I don't see anything. I think it's clear. But it seems really quiet, almost too quiet, you know what I mean? Do you hear anything?" SRG whispered.

"No, Compadre, I don't hear anything at all. I think that's a good sign."

"It feels eerie to me, kind of unsettling."

"I think you're just getting jumpy."

"Maybe I am, but with good cause, I'd say."

"Yeah, you're right. Let's look to see if there's any cover in there. I could use a few minutes of rest. It's hot out here."

"Okay. I didn't see anything down there, but just approach the edge slowly so you can see into it before something down there sees you."

Tannic walked slowly to the ravine and very slowly crept up to the edge, stopping to look for danger before moving on. Just before he reached at the edge, he heard something. He froze, then slowly leaned forward and peered down. A few yards below them, there were a bunch of Bisotaurs. Some Random Guy hadn't gotten close enough to see them. They appeared to be digging into the hillside with pick axes and shovels. They hadn't noticed Tannic, and he slowly retreated to a curious SRG and lay down next to him in the sagebrush.

"What is it? Why did you stop?" Some Random Guy whispered.

"Bisotaurs, digging into the hillside down in the ravine. I'm surprised you didn't hear them."

"Did they see you?"

"I don't think so. I—"

But the words were barely out of Tannic's mouth when the first Bisotaur hopped over the edge and charged towards them. SRG raised the Dragonwrigley and began firing furiously at the beast, and then there was another and another. Within a few seconds there were too many for him to hold off. He was slowing their charge, but the Bisotaurs had them outnumbered. It was just a matter of time before they closed the distance and overwhelmed the boys.

Tannic made a break for the ravine, running as fast as he could. SRG thought for a second that he was being abandoned on the Abandoned Plains, but Tannic was trying to draw a few of the Minotaurs away to divide and conquer them. He ran straight at the edge of the ravine and leaped without looking.

He landed smack dab in the growth of sagebrush. They broke his fall, but as he picked himself up he thought something was out of place. Then he saw it. All of the flowers were white. He felt a sudden surge of panic followed by a tingling sensation that spread over his body. Within seconds it was a ravenous burning sensation. He felt like he was on fire. He felt like his skin was burning off.

As he stood up, reeling in agony, about half the Bisotaurs followed him over the ridge, and they too jumped without looking. They all landed in the Slagebrush patch with him. They immediately started baying and moaning, grabbing at their arms and legs. They were writhing on the ground, twisting and turning in agony. They no longer cared about Tannic. They were cursed with the same affliction he was. And they seemed even more affected by it. They were rolling about, screaming in pain, seemingly unable even to stand.

In the meantime, Tannic worked up his fortitude, stood up, and crawled back up the ravine and over the edge. His body was still burning, and it was all he could do to command it to keep moving. He wanted to lie down on the ground and die. But he kept going and arrived just in time to see Some Random Guy fighting the last two Bisotaurs. One was on each side of him, and he was having trouble keeping them both at bay. Tannic yelled to draw their attention, but it was no use. They were completely focused on their prey.

Some Random Guy was trapped, and they were slowly, methodically closing in on him. If he attacked one, the other would be on him before he could respond. He swung the Dragonwrigley at the closest Bisotaur and then spun around to swing it at the other, and then swung around again to the front. He couldn't keep this up. The Bisotaur in front sensed his weakness and made its move. It dove at SRG with its axe. SRG responded by swinging the sword. The Dragonwrigley came down hard on its skull, but the hilt caught on the pick axe handle, and they were both flung out of Some Random Guy's reach. The Bisotaur behind him darted in and SRG spun around, grabbed an arrow, nocked it in the bowstring, drew back, and released just as the creature reached him. The arrow sank completely into the Bisotaur at point blank range. The broad arrowhead ripped into its chest and the arrow blew right through.

Tannic watched the red-stained arrow fly out of the Bisotaur's back and disappear into the sagebrush. The

Bisotaur, unfazed and seemingly unaware of the hole in its chest and the blood pouring out of it, smiled at the now-unarmed SRG and lunged toward him. And kept lunging, right to the hardpan headfirst. It landed on its face in the dirt, graveyard dead. It kicked twice and lay still. Some Random Guy let out a long sigh. For the moment he forgot about the Dragonwrigley. He was relieved to see his friend.

"You okay?" he asked Tannic.

Tannic had been so shocked by what he'd just witnessed that he'd entirely forgotten about his rash and pain. It returned with a vengeance. He doubled over in agony, moaning as he hit the ground.

"Tannic, are you okay? What happened?" SRG asked.

"Slagebrush . . ." he moaned.

Some Random Guy rushed over to Tannic and saw the flaming rash on his arms. They were swelling up, and his skin was bright red and bumpy.

"Help me, Compadre! I'm on fire!"

"I don't know what to do! Doc said he didn't know what would cure it. I'll do anything, but I don't know what will help! Maybe it will go away in a little bit," he offered weakly.

Tannic rolled over and groaned again. "Well, at least those Bisotaurs are worse off than me. They can't even stand up. You should have seen them." His face lit up with a grin. "That makes me feel a little better."

Some Random Guy walked over to the dead Minotaur and pried his sword loose of the axe handle. He turned it over. It was in one piece and appeared to be none the worse for wear. "We should get out of here, and then I can look you over and try to figure out what to do next. Can you walk?"

"I'll do my best. But I have to tell you, this hurts really bad. I don't think I've ever felt this much pain before." He pushed himself to his feet with a grimace.

They made their way through the ravine and climbed the far ridge onto the plain. Then they continued across the plain under the noon sun. It made Tannic feel even hotter than he already was. He collapsed once and Some Random Guy carefully helped him back up. They walked in silence to the next ravine.

Some Random Guy was deep in thought, worried about his friend and not certain what to do. He'd realized that the Slagebrush wasn't fatal, and Tannic hadn't lost a Life Wedge, but he didn't want to point it out. It wouldn't be much of a consolation, and he could see how badly Tannic was suffering. A lone juniper tree stood proudly at the edge of the ravine, surrounded by flat rocks. They sat down in the shade beneath to rest. Some Random Guy wiped his brow, still deep in thought, and wished for a cool breeze. Tannic mindlessly picked a few juniper berries and was rolling them around in his hand like prayer beads, trying to take his mind off the terrible pain. Suddenly he stopped. He looked at SRG.

"Compadre, look . . ."

"Look at what?" SRG asked.

"The juniper berries—where they touched my skin the rash is going away. Look!"

"That's amazing! It is! Quick, let's get more berries!"

They picked a couple of handfuls of berries, mashed them with their hands and applied them like a poultice to Tannic's rash. Within minutes redness was dissipating and Tannic's skin was returning to normal. The pain was going away too. Tannic took a deep breath and let it out. They both looked on in amazement as his rash vanished.

"Well, that's good to know. Even Dr. Denton didn't know about that," SRG noted. "But I guess he does now."

"Yeah, he's watching us. I'll bet that surprised him," Tannic added.

Some Random Guy grinned. "I'm just glad you're feeling better. Let me know when you feel up to moving, Good Buddy. We still have to find that star."

"I'm ready now. I feel like a new man. It's unbelievable. I was in so much pain and then suddenly the berries just cleared it up. I'm ready, let's go."

The two partners left the shade of the juniper tree and walked down into the draw. They climbed over a few rocks and avoided all the sagebrush. Just as they were starting up the opposite side, Some Random Guy became aware of a low roar that was getting ever-so-slowly louder. They looked back in the direction the Boss Bison stampede had gone. A dust cloud was visible on the horizon. The stampede appeared to be heading back their way, directly down the path it had gone in the first place. They looked at each other in amazement.

"*What are the odds?* That's what you said, right, Compadre?"

"Ok, I guess the odds are pretty high. Quick, look for a spot to hide. We need another depression or a cave to crawl into."

They scanned both sides of the ravine, but there was nothing to be found. The only apparent refuge was another lone juniper tree atop the ridge. Some Random Guy grabbed Tannic's shoulder and pointed at it.

"We'll have to climb up there and hope for the best."

"Don't waste any time, then. That stampede is coming fast."

Some Random Guy and Tannic scrambled up the hillside and climbed the tree.

Juniper trees are not very tall, but they are thick and bushy. They're also prickly and hard on your hands if you're not wearing gloves. In short, they are difficult to climb. But when you're climbing for your life, things like that don't matter, and those things didn't stop Some Random Guy and Tannic. Within a minute they were as high up the tree as you could get and running out of tree to still climb. And they weren't a second too soon. The first bison appeared and ran right under the tree and off the edge into the next ravine. The entire herd soon followed. A virtual sea of Boss Bison parted as it flowed underneath the tree. The ground shook and the tree shook. Some Random Guy and Tannic held on for dear life. A cloud of dust accompanied the moving mass. It enveloped the tree, and Tannic sneezed again. SRG had the Dragonwrigley firmly gripped in his right hand as he watched the bison race past below. He had slung the bow over his shoulder next to the quiver so that he could climb. After a few minutes, the last of the bison passed under the tree. The stampede seemed to be over. The ground stopped shaking, and the dust cloud started to thin out, so they made their way down the trunk. SRG dropped to the ground and landed just before Tannic.

"Another close one, huh, Compadre?"

"Yeah, the power of those beasts is amazing. I've never seen anything like it. I've read about stampedes, but I've never seen one, and they are much more powerful to witness at close range than you could ever—"

"Compadre!" Tannic interrupted.

"What now?"

"Behind you!"

Some Random Guy turned to see that the last Boss Bison had stopped and was sniffing the air. Without notice it charged straight toward them. It had evidently smelled them, and it was closing in fast. It looked much huger from ground level. SRG scrambled to pull the bow over his head, but the string caught on his collar. He struggled but couldn't get it loose. The Boss Bison lowered its head and then tossed it, making its massive sharp horns flash in the sun, the same way he would toss SRG like a wet rag if he hooked him.

Tannic yelled and waved his arms to draw the beast's attention, but it ignored him. Some Random Guy pulled up the Dragonwrigley and sent a volley of fireballs at it. They hit their target, but had no effect other than making the bison angrier. He then launched a flurry of crescents, and the bison's thick hair seemed to stop them from penetrating. It was close now. Tannic stood watching the scene in horror. With no other options, Some Random Guy let the sword fall, dropped to one knee, grabbed the bow again, and tugged hard. He used both hands to pull with all his strength. This time it came loose. He quickly raised it, nocked an arrow, and drew. He was so focused that time again seemed to stand still. He let the arrow fly at point blank range for the beast's chest. There was a loud *splat* as the broad head hit the bison and penetrated its thick fur. The arrow sank until only half the shaft was sticking out.

The bison stopped in its tracks. It retreated slowly toward the ravine. It stopped just short of the edge and lay down. For a few minutes nothing more happened. Tannic and Some Random Guy looked at each other and sighed. Neither of them spoke. Then the bison let out a loud, mournful death bellow. The eerie sound echoed across the canyon.

"Wow! That was spooky!" Tannic said.

"Yeah, they do that when they're dying, they let out this loud bellow. I don't know why."

"Maybe it's to let the rest of the herd know they're dying."

"I don't know, but—"

The distant thunder of the stampede went quiet much too quickly. At the sound of the bellow, the rest of the herd had stopped. They milled around a little bit and pawed the ground. Then they turned and came charging right back. With no time to spare, Some Random Guy and Tannic scrambled back up the tree they'd just come down. The entire herd was back in a flash. This time they crowded around the tree, pawing at the ground, grunting, bellowing, and throwing their heads in the air. The boys were at the top of the tree again, hanging on for dear life. The whole herd was directly below them and angry.

"What do we do now?" Tannic whispered.

"We be very quiet," SRG whispered back.

The herd of bison continued to mill about under the juniper tree, agitated and looking for revenge. Some Random Guy and Tannic sat very still, trying to wait them out, hoping they would eventually leave. Nothing changed for almost an hour. And not only were the bison dangerous, they didn't smell so good either. Their stench filled the air. They almost made the Minotaurs smell like a spring day. Then, slowly but surely, the bison began leaving, one by one, in the direction they'd last come from. In a few minutes the entire herd was gone.

That was the good news. The bad news was the reason they were leaving. Some Random Guy and Tannic were about to climb down when the scene developing below froze them in place. From the previous direction of the stampede, the Ender Dude Grizzly Bear was walking on all fours straight toward the tree. He was sauntering along with the air of casual indifference only top predators can project. He stopped periodically and lifted his nose in the air before continuing on. He was also large and in charge. This was his level and he owned it and everything in it. He was the master of this domain.

The gentle breeze was blowing directly from the boys to the bear. Even over the stench of the bison, he could smell them, and he was steadily closing the gap. He approached the tree with caution and looked up. He seemed to stare directly at the boys, but then he turned his head back and forth as if he couldn't see what he was looking for. He growled and sniffed loudly. Strings of drool hung from his mouth. Tannic had a panicked look on his face. Some Random Guy was focused on the bear. It was much bigger than he'd imagined, and it was only fifteen feet below them. He could see the collar with the Rainbow Star. He slowly nocked an arrow and looked for an opening, but he couldn't get a clear shot. The branches were too thick. Then the bear did the unexpected. He stood up and put on a display. Again Some Random Guy tried to get a shot at the bear, but it was no use. Then the bear put his paws on the trunk and started shaking the tree and roaring loudly. It was an awesome display of power, something the boys would have marveled at had they not been the object of the bear's rage, and also scared to death. A raging beast was right below them and their only refuge was the juniper tree. They hung on for their lives as the bear continued to roar and shake the tree.

Some Random Guy couldn't hold onto the tree and both weapons at the same time. First he lost his grip on the bow. It rattled down through the branches, hit the bear on the head, and bounced to the ground at his feet. The loss of the bow sent a cold shiver up SRG's spine. It would all depend on the Dragonwrigley now. He'd have to take his chances. But that option was suddenly no longer an option. SRG lost his grip on the sword as he tried to cling to the shaking tree. He watched in horror as it bounced from limb to limb and hit the ground. The bear didn't even glance at it. He just kept roaring and shaking the trunk. Tannic looked at Some Random Guy in panic. His eyes were huge. He tried to shout, but he was too scared to even speak. SRG felt panicky as well. It was now all they could do just to stay in the tree. They were without weapons, and the bear was huge and powerful. The outlook was bleak and getting bleaker.

Suddenly, the bear stopped rocking the tree. For a moment Some Random Guy and Tannic thought they'd survived another close call. Their sense of relief faded as the bear began pushing steadily on the tree trunk. He hadn't just been shaking the tree. He had been methodically loosening the roots. SRG felt the tree slowly starting to give. At any minute it would go, and then they would be on the ground, unarmed, face to face with the biggest grizzly he'd ever seen. There was no way they would win that fight.

The tree gave its last creak and then it was over. They started accelerating toward the ground. Some Random Guy hit first, and Tannic landed almost on top of him. They scrambled to their feet as the bear approached and stood over them. They were trapped and helpless. The bear roared and snapped his jaws as he turned his head back and forth again, shaking the Rainbow Star that hung prominently from his collar. They could feel his breath and prepared for the worst.

"I'm sorry, Tannic!" SRG shouted over the bear's roar. "It's all my fault. I should have obeyed my mom and not played the game! We wouldn't be in this mess!"

"No, it's my fault, I talked you into it! Goodbye,

Compadre!"

"Goodbye, Good Buddy!"

The bear opened his mouth wide and grabbed Tannic in his jaws. His mouth was so large he could have eaten them both at the same time, but he picked Tannic first. Then he pinned Some Random Guy to the ground with his other paw. His claws had to be a foot long, and they began to cut into SRG's chest. He could feel the wetness of his own blood on his shirt. He struggled but couldn't get free. The bear was too large and far too strong. Tannic screamed, and then the bear froze. Some Random Guy felt him flinch and felt his paw move. Then he watched an arrow emerge from the monster's chest. It sprayed blood on him as it exited the bear. Tannic was still dangling from the bear's great mouth. SRG didn't understand what had happened. It didn't make any sense. He looked in the direction the arrow had come from. Dr. Denton was standing there with an empty bow and a satisfied look on his face. SRG was about to speak when Dr. Denton pixelated and just faded away. The next thing he knew, the bear came crashing down hard on top of him. Tannic was thrown free and landed next to SRG, who was still pinned under the massive paw. They both looked at each other in amazement, not really understanding what was going on.

Some Random Guy came to his senses. "Quick, Tannic, grab the Rainbow Star!"

"I can't reach it," Tannic replied.

Some Random Guy squirmed and inched his way toward the bear's chest. He stretched his right hand out as far as he could and grabbed onto the collar. He pulled himself closer and finally he could reach the star. He clutched it tightly, and a wave of relief rushed over him.

"No problem, I've got it," he replied.

Then, before you could say "Gentle Ben," they were standing next to a smiling Dr. Denton in his lab.

Chapter 9

The Great Fire Lake

"What was that?" Some Random Guy asked. "What happened out there? I swear I saw you shoot the Ender Dude! Then you just disappeared."

"Well, lucky for you boys I was digging around in the programming, looking to find you a way home, and discovered a hole that let me write myself into the level. I was following the bear when he discovered you boys in the tree, and when he started shaking you out of it I stalked in closer. I saw that you didn't have any weapons, so I fired. Luckily for all of us I aimed well. I've only shot a bow and arrow a few times. Anyway, he was so focused on you guys that he never even knew I was there."

"We were so focused on him that we never knew you were there either," Some Random Guy added.

"Well, I made the shot, but then the program wouldn't let me stay any longer. I was suddenly back here in the lab. But I knew you'd be okay after the bear was dead."

"Yeah, I saw you leave! It was weird, you just kind of broke up and faded away. I didn't know what was going on. But you saved our lives out there! When I dropped both of the weapons, I thought we were in a bad spot. Then when he tipped the tree over I thought it was game over for sure. Then you showed up in the nick of time! That was quick thinking and good shooting. Thank you, Doc!"

"Hey, I said we were a team, and I am doing my best to help you boys. I found the programming hole by accident, and I just acted on my instincts when you boys were in trouble. By the way, how did you know to use juniper berries to combat the Slagebrush?"

"We didn't. Tannic discovered it by accident. He was just playing with the berries, and they made the rash disappear. So that was just another dose of luck. But we really appreciate you saving our lives, Doc!"

"Yes, we do!" Tannic agreed.

"Well, I'm not sure I'll be able to help you like that again. You never know. One man's imagination is another man's confusion. But that little adventure is behind us now. Are you ready for another one? I don't think you're going to like Level 7, but it is what it is."

"I'm pretty sure you're right, Doc," SRG agreed. "We're not going to like any level from here on. But you have my curiosity. What's Level 7? I'm almost afraid to ask!"

"Level 7 is the Great Fire Lake. It's an accurate name. The lake is literally on fire. The surface of the water burns day and night. The actual physics is hard to explain, but basically the lake consists of the fifth phase of water—which, it turns out, is flammable."

"Wait a minute! Five phases of water? I thought there were only three: solid, liquid, and gas. Those are ice, liquid water, and steam, right? We learned that in science class. So you have me going, what am I missing here?"

"Actually that's what we used to believe. But it turns out that water has several properties that can't be explained with three phases. Personally, I think there's quite a lot about water that we just don't understand yet. It may seem like a pretty simple material, but it's a lot more complex than you realize, and three phases just can't explain all of water's physical properties and behavior, so a fourth phase has recently been described. The fourth phase is what's happening when water slips by itself in a stream. For instance, think about a water pipe. Now, we actually know that the water contacting the wall of the pipe isn't moving, but the water in the center of the pipe is moving along quite rapidly. We understand the idea of a liquid having a current—or a fluid flow, we call it—but this is something different. The water molecules *dissociate* and slip past each other, so that one molecule can remain stationary while the other one moves along the interface between them. That's the fourth phase of water. I know it's a little hard to understand, but there just isn't any other explanation."

Some Random Guy and Tannic nodded slowly, still a little puzzled, and he continued.

"Now in Rough World, we've discovered a fifth phase of water. In the fourth phase, the *molecules* are only loosely bound to each other, and that allows for the slippage, so to speak. Now, the hydrogen and oxygen *atoms* that make up each water molecule are also loosely bound together, and in the fifth phase of water that bond is so loose that the hydrogen atom can ignite—it can catch fire, basically. Hydrogen is flammable, and if you burn hydrogen in the presence of oxygen it actually produces water. Well, this is the reverse chemical reaction. Here the hydrogen atoms in the water are burning away and leaving the oxygen atoms behind. The Great Fire Lake is basically a lake of water in the fifth phase. It burns water to produce oxygen. Does that explanation make sense?"

"I think I understand. Wow, Doc, you're really smart," Some Random Guy affirmed.

"Yeah, Doc, you're probably the smartest person I've ever met," Tannic added.

"Well, thanks, boys. I appreciate your confidence, but it's not that novel a concept. There are probably more phases of water we haven't discovered yet. But for now, we just need to worry about the fifth phase of water. It won't burn you the way normal fire does, even though it is a real fire. So you can swim in the lake without getting burnt. And there's plenty of oxygen being produced as the water burns, so you won't have any trouble breathing. That's about all I can tell you."

"How about running on the lake? Do you think that will be possible?" Tannic asked.

"I don't know about that one, Tannic. It is real fire, after all. I guess you'll just have to give it a try and see what happens. The lake surface is still water. It's just on fire."

"And it's not a fire you can put out with water, right Doc?"

They all laughed.

"Good one, Tannic. Anyway, that's what I know about the lake, but it's really just the background for the level. The Ender Dude on this level is Captain Killbeard. He's a liar and a scoundrel and probably the black-hearted-est pirate that ever sailed the Seven Seas. To put it mildly, he's one bad dude. Captain Killbeard keeps the Rainbow Star hidden in his wooden leg. The leg is hollow—most people don't know that, but I'm certain that's where you'll find it. He also has a crew of five pirates protecting him, the Hearty Crew of Five. They're pretty dishonest even as pirates go. I wouldn't even trust them to honor a parlay and take you to

Captain Killbeard. "Parlay" was a right in the original Pirata Codex—the Code of the Pirate Brethren—that allowed any person to invoke temporary protection from attacks and be brought before an enemy captain to negotiate. You could ask for a parlay, but I wouldn't count on the Hearty Crew to honor it. Captain Killbeard used to have two crews, but his old ship, the Sloop John B, sank in the middle of the Great Fire Lake. Most pirates can't swim, so the Laurel Crew drowned. You'd think pirates would learn to swim, considering they spend most of their lives on the water. But that's beside the point. Anyway, it was a fine mess they all got into, and now he only has the Hearty Crew left."

"So is there anything else we need to worry about?" Some Random Guy asked.

"There are a number of new enemies you'll be facing too. First, there are the voice-activated Trap Birds. When they hear your voice, they attack. They sting you, and you lose a Life Wedge. So you'll have to keep your talking to a minimum. Every time you speak another flock of Trap Birds will come your way. Oh, and the lake also has Tree Boss Bass in it. They look like logs drifting in the water, but they're as bad as any of the Boss Bass you've seen so far," Doc continued.

"Any recommendations on what we should do?" Tannic asked.

"Well, as for strategy, I can give you one pointer. Captain Killbeard's treasure chest is still in his sunken ship at the bottom of the lake. There are three items in it that he desperately desires but can't retrieve because he can't swim. These are bags of gold coins, rubies, and emeralds. If you can recover all three, he will gladly trade the Rainbow Star for them. I think. Of course, you'll still have to get past the

Hearty Crew to even see him. Oh, and . . . he will probably want your special weapon for this level too, the Skull and Crossbones sword."

"I was going to ask if I get a special weapon on this level," SRG interrupted.

"Yes, you do. When you meet Captain Killbeard, I think it's okay to give him the Skulls and Crossbones sword too. You won't be needing it again. As soon as you have your hands on the Rainbow Star you will be safely back here with me. However, he has been known to cheat. I'd recommend you give his wooden leg a good whack with the Skull and Crossbones sword to expose the Rainbow Star. That should slow him down a little and discourage any notions he has of cheating you out of the star. And once you have that, it doesn't really matter what he ends up with."

"Now then, I suppose that's a lot of information to absorb," he finished. "Any questions?"

"Yeah, I have a couple," SRG said. "What does the Skull and Crossbones sword do? And do I get some sort of scuba gear, like on Level 3? Otherwise how am I supposed to dive down and get the treasures? And how do I find the Sloop John B when I'm down there?" SRG asked.

"I'm sorry, I forgot to tell you. The Skull and Crossbones sword is just as effective underwater as above. Do you remember how awkward the Dragonwrigley was underwater, and how the fireballs and crescents didn't really work? Well, the Skull and Crossbones sword actually gets lighter underwater—especially in the fifth phase of water. And here's the other good news. Remember, water is made up of hydrogen and oxygen atoms, and when it burns, it releases the oxygen, so you'll be in an oxygen-rich environment. The air on the surface of the lake will be very high in oxygen. If you take a couple of deep breaths before you dive, you should be able to stay under for about one to two minutes."

"I'm not exactly sure where the ship is, I just know it's at the bottom. A couple of dives should give you enough time to retrieve the items once you've located it. The treasure chest itself will be much too heavy for you to pull to the surface, so you'll have to unlock it and take the three bags. But to complicate matters, the chest can only be unlocked with the Skull and Crossbones sword itself. The key is hidden in the handle somehow. I'm not sure how. I've looked it over carefully and I'm not sure how it works. You'll have to figure it out when you're down there examining the lock. But whatever you do, don't lose that sword! Ultimately, it's your key to the Rainbow Star too."

"I think I got it, Doc. It sounds like a real challenge, but I'm sure Tannic and I will figure it out. I've never met a real pirate before. And the fifth phase of water, that should be interesting. Who's going to believe that? I mean, not that we're looking forward to it. I mean who's going to believe any of this? But you've been a great help, Doc. Hopefully we'll see you soon. Come on, Tannic. If you're ready, let's go."

"I was just thinking, Compadre. Can't we stay here with Doc? It's really nice in his lab. Are there any rules against that?"

"Maybe not for you, but I want to go home, and this is the only chance I have of getting there. Come on," Some Random Guy prodded. "We can do this. We've gotten this far. Wait, what's that sound? Do you hear that? It sounds like a quitter! Do I hear a quitter?" SRG asked sarcastically.

"There is no quit in me, and you know it. I was just asking. Anyway, we both want to go home. Let's get this over with."

The Skull and Crossbones sword was leaning against the door. Some Random Guy picked it up with his left hand. He kept a tight grip on the Dragonwrigley with his right hand. He wasn't about to lose it again. He was getting more ambidextrous as the game went along, carrying the Dragonwrigley in his right hand and whatever special weapon the level offered in his left. Now he'd be carrying two swords at once. He examined the special weapon closely and swung it through the air a few times. It actually felt pretty good with his left arm. The sword had great balance and was lighter than the Dragonwrigley. It wasn't awkward at all. The handle wasn't much different from the Dragonwrigley's, and he didn't see an obvious key pattern, but he was sure he'd figure it out once he saw the lock. Of course, diving and holding his breath at the same time would make it all more complicated. He was glad he'd taken all of those years of swimming lessons and at least felt at home in the water. In fact, he loved to swim. He could have been a fish. This was different, though. He wasn't swimming for fun. He was more or less swimming to save his life. He hefted the two swords, relieved that he wouldn't have to carry them both up Mount Parabora or across the Abandoned Plains, and nodded to Tannic. They disappeared into the mist of Level 7.

"This place is creepy. I don't like all the mist and smoke," Tannic whispered. "It feels kind of eerie, too. Like it's haunted, maybe."

"Yeah, it gives me the creeps too," SRG responded. "It's definitely spooky. And it's hard to see anything."

"So what's the plan, Compadre?" Tannic asked.

"Well, I think we should find the Great Fire Lake to start with. It's probably in the middle of the level. I think if we just follow the mist and smoke to its source, we'll get there."

With that, they set off through the gloom.

After a few minutes, SRG added, "Oh, Doc didn't mention it, but I'm going to assume there are Minotaurs of some kind, and maybe man-eating plants too. And who knows what's in the lake. I just hope the Tree Boss Bass and the Chomp Cheap Carp don't breathe fire."

"I should be able to distract them if I can run on the lake. I'll give it a try. While I'm doing that you can dive to the ship and retrieve the treasure. It sounds pretty simple to me." He frowned. "But we've thought that before and been wrong, haven't we Compadre?"

"Yeah, we sure have. Look," he pointed through a thinner patch in the fog. "That's the lake. The flames are coming directly from the surface. That's amazing. Nobody will ever believe this. I wonder if you can still run on the fifth phase of water."

"I guess we're about to find out."

The lake was shrouded in mist and smoke, like a blanket of thick fog hugging the ground. They could see a hundred feet at most. Flames were dancing about three feet high on the water as far as they could see. They undulated in brilliant blues, reds, and yellows. But the surface of the lake itself was calm. There wasn't even a gentle breeze stirring it. The air was dead still except for the flicker of the flames. They reminded SRG of the crackling scented candles his grandma lit in her kitchen, or gas logs burning in a fireplace. There were no signs of life, but they both felt the effects of the oxygen-rich air. In spite of the gloom, the air had a clean crisp smell to it, and they felt downright perky.

"Wow, I suddenly feel energetic. Do you?" Some Random Guy asked.

"Yeah, I do too. That's weird, but it's just like Doc said.

The air is really rich. I feel great! What should we do now?"

"First you should test your special ability. See if you can run through the flames."

"Okay. Hold your breath, here goes nothing." Tannic took a run at the lake and was soon dashing smoothly through the flames. The fire and the fifth phase of water didn't seem to make a difference. He made a strange sight, though, running over the water with flames licking him up to his waist, like a weird apparition passing through the fire and smoke. The flames parted briefly as he ran along and then merged back together in his wake.

He hadn't gone far when some Tree Boss Bass came to the surface and started following him. They left a wide wake in the water that parted the flames behind them as well. Tannic hadn't noticed them yet.

"Look out, Tannic! Behind you!" SRG yelled.

Tannic glanced back and smiled. He slowed down a bit so the bass could catch up to him. Then he ran alternately fast and slow, toying with the fish that were pursuing him furiously. He'd let them almost catch his heels, and then he'd run faster and they'd fall behind. He was shouting and singing, thoroughly enjoying the moment, and almost didn't notice the Chomp Cheap Carp on a collision course in front of him. He screamed and turned hard just in time to avoid their mouths. The schools of carp and bass collided with a big splash on the surface. Tannic headed straight for the shore but looked back. The water was roiling, and he was sure there was a fight going on. He didn't have a clue which fish would win. But he yelled to SRG and pointed excitedly at the fish.

A flock of voice-activated Trap Birds heard Some Random Guy and Tannic yelling back and forth. A dozen of them came flying out of the brush and homed in on the voices. They shot straight toward SRG, coming in low from behind. He heard their wing-beats at the last second and reflexively ducked just in time to avoid being stung. As the birds turned and circled back toward him, he raised both swords and swinging them in turn. The Skull and Crossbones sword didn't do anything special, unfortunately. No special effects, no flames, no fireballs, no crescents. But it kept the birds away on one side while the Dragonwrigley set them on fire. Fireball after fireball connected, frying the birds into smoking carcasses that dropped to the ground. Each time he swung more birds fell. They were persistent and kept attacking him until he had killed them all. There were dead birds laying everywhere. His uncle Billy Bob would have described it as a "rat killin".

"Whew! That was close!" Tannic said with relief. He spoke quietly in case there were more Trap Birds.

"Yeah, well you got a bit careless out there, too. That was too close for comfort!"

"Oh, I had no problem running on the water, and the flames didn't burn me. In fact they had no effect whatsoever. I couldn't even feel any heat. I just got a little overconfident is all. I wasn't expecting that carp to show up." He grinned. "But if that's the sum of it, I can handle the fish for sure. Now that I know what's out there. As long as that's all that's out there."

"Yeah, let's hope that's it. We don't need any more surprises. You can distract the fish while I dive for the treasure. It's worked before. We can make it work again."

Tannic walked over to where Some Random Guy was standing and kicked a dead bird out of the way. They sat down to study the lake and contemplate their next moves.

They were so deep in thought that they didn't hear the Minotaur sneaking up on them from behind. It wasn't an ordinary Minotaur, either. It was a Pirate Minotaur. It was much bigger than a usual Minotaur, probably twice as big. It also had tattoos, an eye patch, and a beard with dreadlocks and beads. It quietly drew its long sword as it snuck closer. It held a cutlass between its teeth, too. It was ready for a rumble. There was a murderous look in its one good eye, and it was focused on the boys.

"Hey, look at that weird shadow," Tannic observed. The shadow was growing slowly in front of them.

"Yeah, that's strange. It kind of looks like a Minotaur," SRG noted.

Then the shadow moved faster. Some Random Guy and Tannic turned around just in time to jump out of the way of the shiny sword blade that was coming right at them. The Minotaur's sword clanged loudly against the rock. Tannic ran out onto the lake without thinking. SRG stood up with a sword in each hand. The Minotaur was recovering from its miss and towered over him. SRG swung his swords one after the other. They gave him good balance and felt like nunchucks in his hands. He'd never actually handled nunchucks, but he thought that was how they would feel.

Some Random Guy took a couple of swipes at the Minotaur, who dodged back. Then he swung the Dragonwrigley at it and launched two fireballs. They caught the Minotaur in the neck but had no effect. He fired a burst of crescents, and they hit their target too, but they did little to deter the creature. The Minotaur smiled and stepped toward SRG. He raised his own sword, studied SRG with his good eye, then pulled the cutlass out of his mouth and laughed. It was a frightful sight, and SRG's heart was pounding in his ears. He swung again, but this time the Minotaur caught the blade on his own and knocked it out of SRG's hand. The Dragonwrigley sailed through the air and plunged into the lake, the flames parting around it as it splashed into the black water and then coming back together behind it.

Some Random Guy shifted the Skull and Crossbones to his right hand and backed up to the water's edge. The Minotaur was larger than any he'd seen. He was completely outsized by it. It laughed again, let out a menacing roar and then charged SRG, slicing the air with its long sword. SRG backed into the lake. He swung the sword aggressively, but it was going to be useless here.

Tannic ran by, being chased through the flames by a school of bass and a large carp, all of them snapping at him. SRG looked at the Minotaur, then back at the lake and the flames. He didn't have a choice. He dove into the water and started swimming toward the middle of the lake. The Minotaur roared and pursued him, but gave up when the water reached its waist. Like all Minotaurs, it couldn't swim— and being a pirate didn't help either. It cursed in pirate talk, turned around in disgust, and walked out of the lake and into the smoke and mist and gradually disappeared.

SRG took a look around him. He didn't see any dangerous fish. The sword was light in his hand as he swam. The flames flickered constantly around him, but they didn't seem to pose a problem. He could breathe just fine and he still felt energetic. The flames actually parted with each stroke he took and then fused together behind him. The water was surprisingly warm, like a hot bath even. He reckoned the fire must have kept the water heated. He could hear Tannic shouting in the distance and the ruckus of the fish in his wake. He swam for a few more minutes, then took a couple of deep breaths, looked around, and dove below the surface.

While the water appeared almost black from above, the flames actually provided some light and let him see fairly clearly below. He looked down, but he couldn't see the ship. He decided to continue under the surface to get a feel for how long he could stay under before surfacing for more oxygen-enriched air. His lungs felt light, and he estimated that he had swum for about two minutes or so before he felt the need for a breath. He'd never been able to stay underwater that long. It was amazing. As he broke the surface, the flames parted, and he took in a couple of full gasps of air. He dove again and swam until he was around the center of the lake. He kept looking below for Captain Killbeard's ship, but nothing materialized. He could make out a pretty smooth mud bottom with only a little debris and a few sunken logs. It looked like an ordinary lakebed. Eventually, after a few more dives and breaths, he made out a large, dark object beneath him. A mast took shape as he got closer, and then he could see the outline of a boat. It had to be the Sloop John B. It was dark and looked like it had settled upright in the mud. It was covered with a layer of silt, but it didn't have vegetation or anything else growing on it.

Tannic was still yelling and running from a school of man-eating fish. Some Random Guy could just hear him over the low rumble of the crackling flames. He took a couple of big gulps of air and dove straight down, the sword in his left hand leading the way. It took some hard kicks, but he reached the deck. He grabbed the railing and looked for the hatch that led to the ship's hold. The treasure chest should be there. He half-pulled and half-kicked his way to the center of the deck. He was feeling fine on his air supply.

He stuck his head through the hatch. It was dark in the

hold, and he could just make out a couple of dark objects. He was trying to figure out what he was looking at when one of them started moving towards him. By the time he realized something was wrong, the dark object had turned into a Chomp Cheap Carp swimming at him with its teeth bared.

The sight struck him as funny for a moment as he realized that carp shouldn't have teeth. He just couldn't get over the paradox. In the real world, they're bottom feeders with large, sucker-like mouths. But not in Rough World. Here they had teeth that would rival a Great White Shark. He pulled his head back just in time and the carp missed. It turned around to make another pass. He pulled the Skull and Crossbones sword up, and it moved swiftly and gracefully through the fifth-phase water. He swung it, and a laser beam sliced the carp nearly in half. It hung in the water for a second and then slowly descended into the depths, drifting back and forth like a leaf as it sank. It left a trail like a ribbon of red water wafting above it.

The Skull and Crossbones sword did have some additional powers, it seemed, but evidently they only worked under water. Some Random Guy supposed that could come in mighty handy later. But for now, he was out of breath and had to resurface. He kicked hard and swam toward the colored light above him.

After he caught his breath, Some Random Guy took a few slow, deliberate, deep breaths and slipped below the surface again. He made his way back to the hatch, grabbed the frame, and looked inside again. His eyes adjusted slowly, and he saw the treasure chest. He pulled himself through and swam into the hold. In a few moments he laid his hands on the chest.

He wiped off a light layer of silt, which clouded the

water a bit. The chest had a large lock that was rusty but looked intact. As the water cleared, he held the sword handle up to the lock. The keyhole was far too small for any part of the sword's hilt. He turned the sword over and over again, studying it from every angle, but there was no way it would fit. And there wasn't any other obvious way to use the handle as a key.

He was running out of air and would have to resurface soon. SRG was frustrated. He hadn't expected it to be so hard to figure out. He hit the lock a couple of times with the pommel, but it didn't budge. He backed up and swung the whole blade at the lock, again with no result. Then he swung it and fired a laser beam. The beam bounced off of the lock and lit up the cloudy water, but nothing else happened.

His lungs were starting to burn. He decided to leave the sword behind this time. He could get to the surface and back much faster using both hands. He dropped the sword, and it settled against the chest as he rose to the light above.

Some Random Guy poked his head out into the flames and breathed deeply. The oxygen tasted sweet. He looked around for Tannic, but not seeing his friend anywhere, he dove again. This time he swam straight to the treasure chest and picked up the sword. There was a key sticking out of the pommel. It had a skull emblem on its head, which SRG remembered seeing on the butt of the sword before. He stared at the key in surprise. It hadn't been there before. But now it was staring back at him. When the sword hit the floor, it must have tripped a switch or something that exposed the key. He wanted to shout, but he was under water. He pumped his fist anyway, then took the key and slid it into the lock. He tried to turn it, but to his dismay it wouldn't move. He pulled it back out and looked closer. It could fit into the lock in two ways, so he turned it over and reinserted it. This time it twisted easily, and there was an audible click as the latch released.

He pried the lock open and removed it from the chest. Then he carefully lifted the heavy lid. Three woven bags lay inside. He grabbed them in his left hand. They were heavier than he expected, but he managed to pull them up. He clutched the sword in his right hand, and kicked hard for the surface. His lungs were starting to burn again. Seconds later he broke the surface and the flames parted around him. He treaded water as he caught his breath. He could hear Tannic's commotion in the distance, but he couldn't see him. He also couldn't see the edge of the lake anymore. He ducked under and looked at the lake bottom to re-orient himself, and started swimming in what he thought was the right direction. He had only one other thing on his mind now, and that was the Dragonwrigley.

Swimming with three bags of gems in one hand and a sword in the other is not easy. Some Random Guy struggled along at the surface, and it took him a long time to reach the shore. When the lake was shallow enough, he staggered out of the water and tossed the three bags to the bank. The place looked familiar, sort of. He was fairly sure it was the spot where he'd confronted the Minotaur. He laid the sword down and opened the bags one at a time. They contained the gold coins, rubies, and emeralds that Doc had described. He had everything he needed for Captain Killbeard. Now he had just two problems. He needed to find Tannic and he needed to find the Dragonwrigley.

He'd be lost without the sword, and he had a sudden panicked thought that it might be like trying to find a needle in a haystack. But he had to try. Carrying the bags back into the lake wasn't an option. There was no way he could retrieve the Dragonwrigley and carry the Skull and Crossbones sword and the bags all at the same time. There was a risk leaving the bags on the shore and having a Minotaur find them, but he had to take the chance. He tried his best to hide them under a bush, and content that they were sufficiently camouflaged, he turned back to the water. SRG kicked off his shoes and stashed them under a bush close to the three bags. After being in the water a few times, he realized he could swim better without them. He wasn't sure if he should take the Skull and Crossbones with him, though, or leave it with the bags. Finally his instincts took over and he carried it with him into the water. He swam to about the distance where he'd last seen the Dragonwrigley and started scanning below the surface. The lake was only about fifteen feet deep here, and he could see the bottom clearly. He swam in circles, moving farther and farther out, all the while looking for a sign of the sword. Suddenly Tannic appeared out of nowhere, churning the surface of the lake and parting the flames, with a school of fish in hot pursuit.

As they passed by, one of the carp noticed Some Random Guy and came straight at him, snapping its jaws and exposing its razor-sharp teeth. He was grateful for the Skull and Crossbones sword as he swung it at the carp. The laser beam caught the big fish broadside, and again the sword had performed its duty. The carp was cut nearly in half and wriggled as it sank below, trailing a thread of red water.

But the commotion only attracted more of the fish chasing Tannic, and they were now turning back to attack SRG. He started swinging the sword wildly, stopping as many of the fish as possible, but there were just too many. Tannic ran in front of Some Random Guy to draw the fish away, but they would not to be deterred. They were focused on SRG now. The school of fish had him surrounded like a pack of wolves. He spun around as best he could in the water, slashing the sword continually to keep them at bay and firing laser beams when he could. He was careful not to fire in Tannic's direction. He'd taken two Life Wedges from his friend already, and he really didn't want to take another.

He felt a tug on his right leg. One of the bass had attached itself to his foot. He swung at it as another fish bit his left shoulder. They were closing in. He cut the fish off of his foot. Then without warning, the fish scattered. Even the one on his shoulder let go and swam away. Something was wrong.

Some Random Guy looked around but didn't see anything. Then he looked down and saw a huge shadow moving past his own on the lake floor. It was the biggest fish he'd seen yet, easily three times the size of the carp. It swam slowly, studying him with large eyes. It seemed to be patiently stalking him without a care in the world. A shiver of fear ran up Some Random Guy's spine at the prospect of being the fish's next meal.

Something shiny gleamed on the fish's back. As it got closer he realized he was looking at the Dragonwrigley sticking out of its back. The sword must have stuck the fish when it sank tip-first into the lake. The fish didn't seem to mind it, but it would be a real challenge for SRG to get it back.

"Tannic! Help me! I need you!" Some Random Guy yelled.

Tannic appeared the through the flames, jogging towards SRG. "You rang, Compadre?"

"Yes! I need you to attract a gigantic fish here so I can get my sword back from it. The Dragonwrigley is stuck in it!"

Tannic looked curious. "How did your sword get stuck in a fish? What did you do?"

"Long story. Just get this guy's attention before he eats me!"

Tannic started splashing the surface with his hands and taunting the fish. It turned toward him. He paused and waited as it swam cautiously toward him. It was huge and getting bigger by the moment as it drew closer. Some Random Guy swam behind the fish, trying to catch up without making noise. The fish hadn't noticed him and was intent on Tannic. SRG needed a few more seconds to reach the Dragonwrigley. Tannic was ready to run, and SRG could tell that the fish was about to strike. He kicked hard and reached out. Tannic started running, and the fish sped up to chase him. SRG closed the fingers of his right hand around the hilt of the Dragonwrigley. He clenched it tightly.

Some Random Guy was holding onto the sword handle with all of his strength. Tannic was running as fast as he could, and the fish was swimming even faster. It seemed to be unaware of its passenger. SRG's fingers were slipping, and he didn't know how much longer he could hold on, when the blade finally pulled free. He slowed to a stop and started swimming back to the shore. It was a labor with the two swords but he was glad to have the Dragonwrigley back. He was unaware of the small smile on his face.

Tannic drew the giant fish in a circle and arrived back as SRG made it to the shore. He ran up onto the bank and collapsed next to him. "What was *that*?" he asked.

"It was the biggest fish I've ever seen, and I hope I never see another one. It looked like a Great White Shark. I thought it was going to eat me whole. I'll probably have nightmares for months."

"Me too, I think."

"Nightmares? You don't sleep!"

"Yeah, but it will scare me at night even if I'm awake!"

"Okay, I understand that!"

"So where are we? Did you get the goods?"

"Yep. They're in the bags there under the bush next to my shoes. The lock was harder to figure out than I thought it would be, but I managed. So we're ready to find Captain Killbeard."

"How do we do that? Do you know where he is?"

"I don't know. But I have a suspicion he's also looking for us. And I just had a chilling thought. If his Hearty Crew finds us and beats us, they'll just take the items and we'll never get the Rainbow Star."

"I don't mean to be contrary, Compadre, but if they defeat us, we won't need the star. You know what I mean?"

"Huh. Yeah, you're right." SRG half smiled. "But we didn't come this far to lose now. What do you say? Let's go kick some pirate butt and take their booty! Set the sails and load the cannons!"

"Arr, matey! Let's hoist the Jolly Roger! We're going to defeat this level and the next one and then the one after that, and then we're going home!"

It didn't really matter which way they went, as they'd walk the whole lakeshore eventually. They set out walking clockwise around the lake. SRG carried the swords, and Tannic carried the bags of booty. The gold coins were heavy, but the emeralds and rubies were much lighter. The shore was lined intermittently with trees, and the flames off the lake cast a strange light on them. The colors almost made them look like Christmas trees. The lake itself looked like a magical and inviting place, as if it was pretending not to be full of man-eating fish. The light, smoky mist drifted among the trees and beyond, as far as they could see. Hopefully they would spot the Hearty Crew before the pirates spotted them.

"What's our plan when we find these guys?"

"I don't know. I'd rather avoid them. But if we have to fight them I'll start swinging the swords and try to take out the leader first. We'll just have to be spontaneous. You try to distract any of them you can. That's all I can think of."

The two boys walked slowly and carefully along the lake's edge, sneaking in and out of the trees. Some Random Guy was wet, Tannic was pretty dry, but they were both warm. They just needed to stay on alert for the Hearty Crew of Five. The smoky mist made it hard to see very far, so they would take a few steps, look around, then proceed. After a while they got used to the process. Take a few steps, stop and look, repeat. They'd used this maneuver on a few of the levels now, and it was starting to feel like business as usual.

They continued this way until a pirate stepped unannounced from the trees directly in front of them. They were so surprised by him that they didn't notice the other pirates stepping quietly from the trees all around them.

The pirate barked at them. "Who are ye and what do ye want?"

"We've come to see Captain Killbeard," Some Random Guy shakily responded. "Can you tell us how to find him?"

"Have ye, now? Ye've got no business with the good captain, and he doesn't want to see ye's anyway!" the pirate insisted.

"He will when he finds out what we're bringing him. And he'll be happy that you brought us to him. We would like to invoke our right to a parlay," Some Random Guy spoke louder with more confidence. He thought the parlay would get their attention.

"Hah! Ye've been watching too many movies. We don't honor parlays here in Rough World. In fact, us pirates don't honor anything at all! Aarrgh! Ye miserable scurvy knaves, we'll just take whatever ye have for the captain and be off with yer heads."

It was then that Tannic and Some Random Guy realized they had company. The other four pirates were closing in behind them. SRG made one last plea. He drew the Dragonwrigley and tried to sound dangerous. "We mean you no harm. We're not seeking trouble. If you let us see your Captain for a parlay, we'll let you all live."

"Har, har, har . . ." He earned a laugh from all the pirates as they closed in on the boys. Then the leader spoke again. "A couple of little boys will let us live, will they? We'll just see about that. Har, har! Slap leather, boys! Let's see what ye've got! Har, har!"

His laughter cut off as the first crescent took him in the throat. He doubled over and fell forward dead, blood spurting out around the blade jutting from his neck. He kicked once and then didn't move. Some Random Guy spun around to face the other pirates. They looked less confident now, not moving forward or backward, just frozen in their tracks trying to size up the situation. They were dead silent. They looked puzzled and confused. SRG was deciding which one to take out next when Tannic did something unexpected. Without warning, he started screaming and ran toward the pirates. Then he stopped and started performing tai chi moves. The pirates shifted back a couple of steps. His boldness had taken them off guard. He kept shouting and moving in a dance-like rhythm, staring at them with wild eyes.

"What's up with 'im? 'E's bloody crazy!" one of the

pirates shouted.

"No, he be possessed!" another one added. "It be witch-craft! Look out!"

While the pirates were distracted by Tannic's display, Some Random Guy swung the Dragonwrigley and released a flurry of fireballs and crescents. Two pirates fell dead as they were drawing their swords, and at the sight of their fallen mates the other two turned and ran into the woods.

"Pirates! Huh! More like a tea party of little girls, I'd say!" Tannic boasted.

"That was brilliant, Tannic! Where did that come from? They thought you were crazy! For a second there, I did too! I thought you were going to get yourself killed. But it was brilliant. Where did that come from?"

"I don't know. It looked like they weren't going to give us a parlay, so I figured we had nothing to lose. *Always fear the man who has nothing to lose, Compadre!*"

"Well said, Good Buddy! Desperate times call for desperate measures. Anyway, I guess we'll have to find the good Captain Killbeard ourselves now."

"What about those other two pirates?"

"Something tells me we won't be seeing them again. Maybe they ran back to the captain. I guess Captain Killbeard now has a Hearty Crew of Two. Or a Cowardly Crew of Two, if you ask me."

Some Random Guy and Tannic continued searching around the lake. They were a little more relaxed but still alert. They walked along without talking. SRG seemed to be in deep thought while Tannic was just quiet. After a time they came upon a well-used trail leading away from the lake and directly into the timber. SRG pointed up the trail with the Dragonwrigley and looked back at Tannic. Tannic nodded in agreement. This trail had to lead to Captain Killbeard. And to the Rainbow Star.

A few yards into the woods, Some Random Guy stopped and whispered back, "Are you ready? Do you need a break?"

"I'm good to go, Compadre. How about you?"

"Oh, I could use a rest, but let's get this over with. We can rest for a bit once we're back in the lab."

"You're pretty confident that we'll get back."

"Well, I figure we've been through the worst of this level. And Captain Killbeard really wants this treasure. I think we've got leverage. And we haven't lost any Life Wedges yet. I think that's a first. I'm feeling pretty good about our chances now."

"What's to prevent him from just taking the bags?"

"Oh, I don't know. Maybe a couple of 'little boys' and a Dragonwrigley? What do you think about that? Har, har! Come on Tannic, let's go meet this good captain! I want a parlay!"

Some Random Guy stretched his body and swiped both swords through the air, and they walked on. The vegetation grew denser and the forest got darker and quieter. It was an eerie place, with its ever-present mist and smoke. It reminded SRG of early November mornings at home, when the fog would hug the ground like a flat cloud and lie there all day without burning off. The heavy mist accumulated on the leaves and branches, and dropped water on them as they brushed by. SRG's clothes had started to dry out, but the mist and the water would keep them damp at best. Tannic's clothes were getting damp now too.

Half an hour in, the forest opened up and exposed a deep ravine. Its sides were steep, and sharp rocks like shards of glass stuck out of them all the way to the bottom. Some

Random Guy had never seen rocks like these. They had jagged edges and looked like they would tear your clothes and cut your hands if you touched them.

The air was clear in the canyon and a wrecked ship was sitting upright at the bottom. A Jolly Roger flapped gently in the breeze atop its main mast. Tattered remnants of sails hung about the masts, but the flag looked new. The ship looked otherwise abandoned, but Some Random Guy reckoned it was the headquarters of Captain Killbeard. He looked at Tannic and nodded. Tannic nodded back and smiled. Tannic led the way as they started their slow descent into the canyon. The rocks were as jagged as they looked. They tore the boys' clothes, they got slivers in their hands every time they grabbed rocks to balance themselves. SRG had the worst of it, shifting the two swords back and forth in his hands and awkwardly trying to climb down without falling. Tannic had tied two bags together and slung them around neck. He had the third bag in one hand and used the other for balance.

Dark clouds had been rapidly gathering above them as they descended. Suddenly with a loud crack, and a flash, thunder broke over their heads and made them flinch. They both paused, clinging to the rocks, and looked up. Again the thunder boomed loudly, directly overhead, with a flash of blinding lightning. Then the rain came, heavy and pounding in huge drops. It was so fierce that it was like standing in a shower. Some Random Guy and Tannic were drenched immediately.

"Perfect. Just perfect," Tannic complained.

SRG looked up at the angry sky. "Really? It has to rain *now*? Right while we're halfway down the cliff? And my clothes were just starting to dry! You know, I'm really starting to hate lightning and thunder. That's the whole reason we're here in the first place!"

"Come on, Compadre, we'd better hurry," Tannic urged. "The rocks are getting slick. It's going to get harder and harder to climb the longer it rains."

"You don't think we might be struck by lightning, do you?"

"Hey, what's the worst that could happen? You lose a Life Wedge? I'm not worried about the lightning."

"Yeah, well you're not carrying two lightning rods. Maybe you're right. We'd probably only lose a Life Wedge. I just hate the thought of being struck by lightning. It can't possibly feel good."

"I don't think anybody's ever described what it feels like. Everything would happen so fast you wouldn't know what hit you."

Some Random Guy nodded in agreement and wiped the water from his face. They climbed on in silence, slipping here and there on the rocks. At one point SRG lost his hold and landed on his butt. The rocks tore his pants and his leg was bleeding. He couldn't feel it, but a red stain appeared on his soaking wet pant leg. His shoes were starting to fill with water from raindrops running down his legs.

"Are you okay?" Tannic asked.

"Yeah. My leg is bleeding a little but I'm okay. The only thing I hurt was my pride!"

Near the bottom, the rocks abruptly gave way to sand. They were soaking wet, and the sand was slippery too, so they sat down and poured the water out of their shoes.

The bottom of the canyon looked like a deserted river-bed. Ahead of them, protruding halfway out of the sand, was the wrecked ship. It must have been stranded high and dry at some point. It sat upright in the sea of sand like a sphinx.

It was an odd sight. The ship boards were worn and some were missing. Most of the paint had peeled off long ago, leaving the wood faded and rough. The gunwales were open but there didn't appear to be any cannons left. Nothing but tattered and faded fabric remained of the sails. Even the riggings were torn and hanging in pieces. They flapped in the wind. It was still raining hard. The boys were completely soaked as they approached the ship. Even close up it seemed deserted.

"Ahoy! Captain Killbeard, are you in there?" Some Random Guy called out. There was no response, so he repeated his greeting louder.

Eventually a mean-looking pirate peered over the railing. He was covered in tattoos of skulls and crossbones. One showed a skull with a single rose. It reminded SRG of a story his grandpa had told him, but he dismissed the thought and studied the pirate.

Killbeard's eyes were black and shiny, while his teeth were yellow and brown, at least the ones he still had. He wore a captain's hat with a long plume, and his face ended in a scraggly, braided beard. His shirt was striped in faded red and white, his pants were sky blue with a yellow stripe down the outside of each leg, and he wore a purple sash for a belt. A cutlass and a dagger were tucked into it. Overall, his clothes were dirty and tattered. And altogether he was an intimidating and ghastly sight.

On his right foot he wore a black shoe with a tarnished silver buckle. And from his left knee down he sported a wooden leg that tapered to a smooth, round knob.

"Who are ye and what's yer business? What do ye want of the good cap'n?" he growled.

"We've come to see Captain Killbeard. We would like

a parlay. We have some items to trade. Are you Captain Killbeard?"

"Nobody gets to see the captain, not nobody, not no-how. I'll handle whate'er business ye have with him. Climb up the ladder and I'll take a look at yer goods."

With that the pirate tossed a rope ladder over the railing. SRG struggled a bit to climb with the two swords, so he tucked the Dragonwrigley down the back of his shirt and into his belt. He kept the Skull and Crossbones in his left hand. Tannic helped steady the rope as he climbed, then scrambled up behind him carrying the three bags.

Once they were both on deck, the pirate stepped back and drew his sword. He glared at them with his black eyes. "That will be far enough, lads. Now let's see what ye have to trade. Hurry up! Be quick about it!"

Tannic tossed the bags to the deck at the pirate's feet. Well, at his one foot. He bent down carefully, keeping his eyes on SRG and Tannic, and flipped one open before looking down. His eyes betrayed him, though, and lit up when he saw what was inside. He gasped first, and then tried to act casually not interested. While he was staring at the booty like a long-lost friend, SRG slowly pulled the Dragonwrigley from his back.

"How did ye get these? They come from the Sloop John B at the bottom of the Great Fire Lake!" the pirate exclaimed. "These be my—eh, I mean they belong to the good Captain Killbeard."

"We swam across the Great Fire Lake and dove down to retrieve them," Some Random Guy said casually. "It wasn't that hard. If you wanted them so bad why didn't you go after them yourself?"

"Ye don't know? Why do ye think we make pirates walk

the plank? Har, har! Pirates can't swim! And I'm a pirate!"

"Pirates can't swim?" Some Random Guy couldn't resist poking fun. "That would seem to come in pretty handy for you. Especially when you're forced to walk the plank. If I were a pirate, I'd learn how to swim."

"Aargh, well . . . obviously yer not. Now what is it ye seek from the cap'n?"

"We'd like a parlay with him. We've come for the Rainbow Star, and we were told Captain Killbeard would trade for the items in these bags."

"Ah, were ye now? And what else have ye got to trade?"

"We have this Skull and Crossbones sword we could trade as well," Some Random Guy answered confidently. He was feeling good about their position.

"Well, be quick about it then, boy. Let me see it. Toss it over here."

Some Random Guy dropped the sword to the deck and kicked it to the pirate, who picked it up and admired the fine work of the blade and hilt. He made a couple of quick cuts through the air, feeling its balance. It looked like an old friend in his hand. He tucked it carefully into his belt. It seemed to belong there.

"I'm sorry to say that I have bad news for ye, boys. I'll be keeping these items, but I don't—eh, the good Captain . . . he doesn't have the Rainbow Star. So ye won't be getting the item ye seek. And this parlay is over. But lest ye think yer trip was wasted, I won't be making ye leave empty-handed. I'll teach you a valuable lesson instead."

"What lesson would that be?" Some Random Guy asked with an edge in his voice. He was irritated. He looked over at Tannic, who was frowning as well.

"Har! Never trust a pirate!"

Captain Killbeard laughed through his brown teeth and turned to walk away.

Some Random Guy leaped forward and swung the Dragonwrigley hard against the pirate's wooden leg. The wood made a crunching sound as it cracked and shattered. Splinters shot everywhere on the deck, the pirate lost his balance and fell, as the Rainbow Star rattled out of the hollow wooden shaft and onto the deck.

Killbeard, Some Random Guy and Tannic froze for a moment as they stared at the brilliant radiating star sitting in the middle of them. Simultaneously they all dove for it. Tannic got there first. He wrapped his fingers around it.

Chapter 10

The Egerian Castle

"Hi, Doc! It's great to be back. You were right about Captain Killbeard. He tried to cheat us. He's a scoundrel" Some Random Guy declared. "A one-legged scoundrel now. He'll be needing to carve himself a new leg."

"He truly is a scoundrel. You should have whacked his leg the second you got on deck, but you did get the Rainbow Star!" Doc replied excitedly. "That's all that counts!"

"I've never met a real pirate before. That was pretty cool, even if he did try to cheat us!" Tannic added.

"I've never met one either, but I'm glad to have that level behind us. Anything happening through the reverse screen, Doc?" SRG asked.

"Nothing. It appears that no one is home yet. I think you're still in the clear. And you boys have been amazing out there. You didn't lose a single Life Wedge on that level. The levels really are getting harder, but I swear you boys are getting better with each one. You're a great team!"

"*We're* a great team, remember, Doc? You're a part of our team now. We couldn't do this without your help. So what's up next?" Tannic asked.

"Well, Level 8 is the Egerian Castle at edge of the

Jagged City. This castle is modeled on the Eger Castle in Hungary, which is famous for the battle that was fought there in 1552. The Turks were expanding their empire—the Ottoman Empire—and invading European countries to their north. But when they reached the Eger Castle, two thousand Egerians withstood an army of sixty thousand Turks for five weeks and finally defeated them. It was a truly remarkable feat. It's one of the greatest stories of an underdog prevailing against insurmountable odds."

"Anyway, maybe you can guess the bad news. The castle is very hard to penetrate, and that's what you have to do next. First, the moat that surrounds the castle is filled with Tritons. Tritons have human bodies from the waist up and fish bodies from the waist down. Think of mermaids, except these mermaids are warriors, and they are mean. They're more like mermaids crossed with Minotaurs crossed with Great While Sharks. That's only the beginning of it. Once you get past the Tritons, the outer wall of the castle is solid rock, nearly a hundred feet tall and about twelve feet thick. There are four rotundas, one at each corner of the castle—"

"Wait," Some Random Guy interrupted, "we have to cross the moat and then climb the wall?"

"I'm afraid so. And all while the Egerians may be shooting arrows and bolts at you. It would be best if you made it in without being noticed, but I'm not sure that's possible. In any case, if you make it over the outer wall, the inside is just like most castles. There's a large courtyard with several buildings. There's also a real dungeon, with a torture master and an executioner. The Ender Dude is also an executioner, but he resides in one of the rotundas. I don't know which one," he finished.

"Anything else, Doc?" SRG asked.

"Your special weapon is, well, not exactly a weapon. You'll have a camouflage cloak. It looks exactly like the rocks the castle is made of. Wear it while you're climbing the wall and whenever else you need to disappear. You'll blend into the wall or a pile of rocks equally well. It should be very useful."

"Anything else?" SRG asked again.

"Umm, no . . . not really. Hmm," Doc stammered.

"Are you okay, Doc? You've got a strange look on your face and you're acting kind of funny."

"Uh, no. No. I'm fine, really. I'm fine."

"No you're not. Something's wrong. What's up, Doc? You can tell us."

"Well . . ." Doc hesitated.

"Well what?"

"Well, it's not really about the castle. It's just . . . only one team of players has ever made it this far in the game, and the main player died on this level. They executed him in the dungeon by cutting off his head with his own Dragonwrigley. You remember I cautioned you about the Dragonwrigley at the beginning?"

Some Random Guy's voice got stuck in his throat. He leaned against the wall and tried to swallow. He felt sick. Tannic had a worried look. The reality of Rough World was sinking in for both of them.

Doc continued. "Are you going to be okay? I'm sorry I told you about that. I shouldn't have. You didn't need to know that."

"No. Thanks, Doc. Really. We do need to know that." Some Random Guy sighed. "It's just that I'm only ten years old. So far today I've faced Minotaurs, man-eating fish, man-eating plants, pirates, beasts of every description . . . I've had to fight for my life, literally. Tannic too. Ten-year-olds aren't supposed to have to do that. I really don't like this game anymore. I want to quit. I just want to go home," he lamented.

"I'm sorry to say it's not a game anymore, boys. It really is Rough World you're in now. I wish I knew how to stop this and send you home, but I still think our best bet is to finish all ten levels if we can and try my idea with the Transport Chamber. I'm sorry. I wish there was something else I could do."

"It's okay, Doc. You're doing your best. We appreciate it." Some Random Guy perked up and summoned his courage. "Come on, Tannic. Let's go do something 60,000 Turks couldn't do. Let's go take Eger Castle. We got this."

"I'm right behind you, Compadre!" Tannic replied.

Some Random Guy took the camouflage cloak from the hook next to the door and tossed it over his shoulder. Tannic laughed briefly when his friend turned into a pile of rocks with a head, but SRG was staring at the Dragonwrigley in his right hand. He was getting used to having it. It felt comfortable in his hand. If he ever did get home, he was going to feel naked without it. But he didn't figure he could show up to Oak Grove School carrying a deadly sword, especially one that shot fireballs and razor-sharp crescents. Although that might come in handy on the playground sometimes. Mainly it seemed weird to him that carrying the sword didn't seem weird anymore. He paused and studied the sharp double edges. It really was a double edged sword, in the sense that it could kill him too. He vowed under his breath that he wouldn't let any enemy take it from him, ever. That wasn't an option. His life had changed so much in just one random day. He took one last look at Dr. Denton and opened the door. Tannic was his shadow as they disappeared into Level 8.

"Be careful, boys," Dr. Denton whispered to himself. "Be careful out there." He had a worried look on his face as the door closed.

The castle stood at the top of a large rock obelisk. It stood out like a sore thumb. You couldn't miss it. It would be an uplifting sight if you didn't have to swim the moat and climb the wall. The Minotaurs guarding the castle were just visible pacing back and forth atop the wall. Some Random Guy and Tannic looked up at them and then back down at the moat.

"You can see now why the Turks didn't take the castle."

"You can say that again. So, what's the plan, Compadre?" Tannic asked.

"Why do I always have to come up with the plan? Why don't you decide?"

"I don't know, maybe because you have the weapons. Plus you're good at planning things. You're always thinking ahead. You do a good job of being logical and intuitive. Your plans have gotten us this far. So as far as I'm concerned, you should keep coming up with the plans. Besides, you heard Doc, nobody's ever gotten past this level. And I trust your ideas more than mine."

Some Random Guy sighed. "Okay. I have been thinking. Your running-on-water skill has been working well for us, and I think we should keep using what's working. The obvious thing is for you to get the attention of the Tritons while I swim the moat. Hopefully you can run faster than they can swim. They sound pretty creepy. Once I'm across, I scale the wall. Then I'll have to figure out which rotunda has the Ender Dude and the Rainbow Star. I'll sneak past the guards, scale the rotunda, take out the Ender Dude, capture the star, and we'll be back in Dr. Denton's lab in no time. How does that sound?"

"It sounds great. But it also sounds too easy, and these levels keep getting harder. If that doesn't work, what's Plan B?"

"I don't have one. I guess if I get caught you'll have to scale the wall and give it a go."

"Uh, one problem, Compadre. I'm still afraid of heights."

"No you're not, remember? You're afraid of hitting the ground. In this case you'd be hitting the water in the moat instead. That wouldn't be so bad. You'd just have to be up and running quickly so the Tritons don't get you."

"Uh, I still don't think that's a good plan. That wall scares me just looking at it. I don't think I can do it."

"Okay, then. I guess I can't see you climbing that wall either. So we'll just need to make the first plan work. I'll make sure I don't get caught."

Some Random Guy and Tannic crept through the waist-high vegetation to the moat. The sun was high above the horizon and it was approaching midday, but most of the sky was covered with dark clouds, giving a gloomy feel to the day. They peered into the moat. Tritons were swimming around at random, apparently not paying attention to anything. Their human halves protruded from the surface while their fish halves propelled them along below. They looked relaxed. They weren't swimming very fast, and they each left a small wake behind them, creating an irregular wave pattern in the moat. They were much bigger than SRG had expected. They were easily eight feet long and must have weighed a few hundred pounds each. Judging by the size of their fins and tails, they must be able to swim fast, certainly much faster than a human could. And judging by their well-muscled arms and hands, they could probably tear a person apart without much effort. SRG really didn't like the look of them. Tannic was trying to judge how fast they'd be able to swim. He felt anxious but didn't want to worry SRG. At least the Tritons hadn't noticed the boys yet.

"Well, here goes nothing," Tannic spoke under his breath as he approached the water. "Good luck, Compadre. Be careful!"

"You know it, Good Buddy. You too. Give them a run for their money." He was going to say "Give them hell," but he figured he shouldn't get used to swearing too easily. At least not yet. Talk like that would get him in trouble at home, and he was still holding out hope of getting home again before the day was over.

Tannic ran onto the water and did a few circles to catch the attention of the Tritons. It didn't take much. As soon as they saw him, they went after him with surprising speed, and left a wide wake behind them as they chased him out of sight around the corner.

Once they were gone, Some Random Guy slipped into the water and swam the fifty feet across the moat. It wasn't far, but he needed to be climbing the wall by the time Tannic rounded the moat with the Tritons on his heels. The Dragonwrigley and the cloak slowed him down a bit, but he kicked for all he was worth. As he neared the wall he heard Tannic shouting insults at the Tritons. He would reappear any second now. SRG kicked hard again and pulled himself out of the water just as Tannic came in sight. Tannic's ability was truly impressive. Even the Tritons couldn't catch him, and he was clearly just toying with them. SRG wondered how far they would have gotten in the game—the real Rough World, rather—if Tannic didn't have this skill. As the Tritons disappeared again he looked up at the wall.

The commotion in the moat had attracted the attention

of the Minotaur guards. They were looking over the edge watching Tannic and the Tritons. It must have been quite a sight from that height, a boy running on the water and being chased by fish-men. But it wasn't long before arrows began raining down. The guards still hadn't spotted Some Random Guy on the wall, but now Tannic would need to avoid both the Tritons and the arrows. He was running in a random fly pattern and doing his best to make himself a difficult target.

Some Random Guy pulled the cloak up over his shoulders and started his ascent. The rocks were irregular in shape and offered pretty good handholds and footholds. They were a bit slick and there was some scattered moss, so it wasn't easy. But he moved methodically, looking for a handhold and pulling himself up, looking for another handhold and repeating. He had tucked the Dragonwrigley into his belt. Climbing took both hands, and the going was still slow. Every few steps he looked down, and he could see that he was getting higher on the wall. Every few minutes Tannic came running by, trailed by the Tritons and a rain of arrows. SRG was thankful at least that he wasn't afraid of heights. Not yet anyway. He continued upward, one step and one rock at a time. The cloak was keeping him pretty well concealed. From above he must have looked like an irregular rock protruding from the wall. The guards hadn't noticed him yet.

He knew he was getting close when he could hear the Minotaurs' voices and feel the vibrations of their bowstrings and the whiz of arrows flying past him. He slowed down and moved very carefully. He didn't want to be discovered now. For his part Tannic kept running to distract the castle Minotaur guards while SRG penetrated the castle. He planned to continue doing that until SRG had the star.

Some Random Guy finally put his right hand on the top

of the wall. Then he waited until Tannic and the Tritons went by again below. The guards were apparently following the action clockwise around the wall, running along and shooting arrows and bolts down at Tannic. SRG took a deep breath, wished himself luck, and lifted himself up onto the ledge.

It was no wonder the Turks had been defeated. He knew the wall was twelve feet thick, but he hadn't really thought about what that looked like. It was amazing. *This castle must be almost indestructible.*

He held his breath and lay still with the cloak covering him as the Minotaurs ran by again. When they were gone, he crawled to the inner edge and jumped down three feet to the courtyard. He quickly surveyed his surroundings. There were the four doors, one in each of the corners under the rotundas. There were a few scattered buildings, but all-in-all it was pretty plain looking. There were maybe twenty Minotaurs in the yard. Aside from the eight that were chasing the action in the moat, there were several patrolling the walls and a few others just milling or standing around. He needed to move.

The closest rotunda was to his right. He would check it out first. He took a few slow steps and stopped, listening. None of the Minotaurs seemed to notice him. So he moved a few more feet and stopped again, cautiously peeking out of the cloak to see if he was still undetected. The next time he stopped, he heard two Minotaurs approaching from behind. He froze and listened as they casually strode by. After a moment he slowly let out his breath and glanced out. They had moved on. After a few more cycles of creeping and stopping, he heard the Minotaurs approaching again. He froze and took shallow breaths. He stared down at his feet and tried to become a pile of rocks.

One of the Minotaurs stumbled into him. It hurt, and SRG let out a noise from the pain.

The Minotaur grunted. "Did you hear something?"

"No. Did you?" the second Minotaur responded.

"I think I just heard that pile of rocks squeal."

"Rocks don't squeal. Hey, what's this pile of rocks doing here, anyway? It wasn't here this morning."

"I don't know. Let's toss them over the edge. We'll see if we can hit that invader with them."

The first Minotaur grabbed the rocks and the cloak came off Some Random Guy, who was squatting on the ground.

"Well, well. What do we have here?" The Minotaurs grabbed SRG's arms before he could draw the Dragonwrigley. "We've caught another one. Let's take him to the castle guard master." And they carried and dragged SRG across the courtyard to the smallest building. All the other Minotaurs stopped what they were doing and crowded around to watch. It was a real novelty to see an intruder inside the castle walls.

Inside the building was the Minotaur in charge of the patrols. The Minotaurs held SRG up, one on each arm. The castle guard master looked him over curiously. "This is the second one we've caught this month. And they've both been carrying the same sword." He addressed SRG. "Who are you and why did you break into our castle?"

Some Random Guy didn't know what to say. He certainly didn't think the Minotaurs would understand his situation. *Rough World is just a video game. Somehow I ended up in it for real. I'm trying to collect Rainbow Stars so I can go home. To the real world.* For the moment Rough World felt real enough. So he just stared at the floor and offered no response. He could hear his heart pounding.

"Oh, a quiet one, eh? We'll coax some answers out of you soon enough. Now won't we, boys?" The other Minotaurs laughed raucously. "This looks like a job for the Dungeon Master! Take him away! We'll soon find out who he is and why he's here!"

The Minotaurs picked him up and took him back across the courtyard. He felt like he was going to puke. The thought suddenly struck him as funny. He couldn't even remember the last time he ate. It must have been breakfast, at home. That seemed like years ago. Home, he just wanted to go home. He just wanted to wake up from this nightmare in his own bed. He struggled to free himself, but the Minotaurs had a death grip on him. And they had the Dragonwrigley. They dragged him through another door.

It was eighty steep steps down into the dark abyss to get to the dungeon. Some Random Guy was scared stiff. It was like descending into a black hole. The dungeon was damp, musty-smelling, and foreboding. It was dark, but by the time they reached the bottom his eyes had adjusted. There were four empty cells along the right wall. They looked well used. Along the left wall were strange contraptions that didn't look like anything from the school playground. There was a stockade, with holes cut for your head and hands as they locked you into a block of wood for a period of time. And there was another, giant wooden block in the center of the room. Next to it a small open fire was burning, and next to that stood a huge Minotaur with a leather helmet and mask on his head. His horns poked through the helmet. He was heavily muscled and smelled of campfire smoke, mold, dirt and, well, Minotaur. The air in the dungeon felt heavy.

Meanwhile, back in the moat, Tannic was having a few problems of his own. The Tritons had gotten tired of chasing him and had decided to divide and conquer. He'd been too busy to notice that there were only three left, and now, as he approached the spot where he'd entered the moat, he saw the other three round the corner in front of him. In a few seconds they would all collide, and that would be a disaster for him.

There was a rock a few feet up the wall that looked like a decent handhold. He ran as fast as he could and jumped. He just managed to grab it with both hands. He also managed to scrape his chin on the wall. He was just out of reach of the Tritons on the wall. They were jumping and doing their best to grab him, but each attempt fell short. He wanted to stick his tongue out at them but thought better of it. Tannic looked up the wall from his perch. He had no choice. He couldn't stay there longer and risk being spotted. He couldn't go back down. The Tritons were gathered below waiting for him to fall, like a pack of cats watching an injured bird. They smelled blood, and they weren't going anywhere. He needed to climb and climb fast.

The Minotaurs that had been shooting at him were no longer on the wall. Tannic didn't know it, but they had all turned their attention to Some Random Guy when he had been captured. Tannic took a deep breath, cast one last look at the Tritons below, and started climbing. He told himself that he was no longer afraid of heights, just of hitting the ground, and kept putting one hand in front of the other. He concentrated on reaching the top of the wall. There was no reason to look down again. He clung tightly to each rock and just kept putting one hand in front of the other and one foot in front of the other.

And it took a while, but he finally put his hand over the top. Slowly, carefully, he pulled himself up. He lay on the top of the wall for a few seconds surveying the yard. There were only a few Minotaurs and they didn't seem to notice him. Some Random Guy was nowhere to be seen, so he slid down the inside wall and landed softly on the ground.

In front of him was a strangely familiar looking pile of rocks. It took him a second to realize what it was. Something must have gone wrong for Some Random Guy. The cloak shouldn't be lying there.

Tannic crawled to the cloak and slipped it over himself. Now he had cover. He heard a moan, almost a scream, coming from the distance. He wasn't certain, but it sounded like SRG. Tannic surveyed the yard and decided to check the rotunda to his right, as it was the closest one to him. It was maybe forty feet away. He moved slowly and tried to keep a steady pace. The Minotaurs didn't seem to notice the rock pile edging slowly along the wall, pausing every now and then and then moving again. He heard more low screams in the distance, but he couldn't tell their source, so he focused on the rotunda. It took him a few minutes to reach the door. He stepped inside before taking off the cloak and hanging it on a rock. It was a bit cumbersome and he wouldn't need it climbing the stairs in the rotunda. The door was small and it would be a tight squeeze for a Minotaur. It was almost a tight squeeze for him.

The interior of the rotunda was just a tight spiral of stone steps with an inner and outer wall. He climbed about fifteen steps and stopped. It was getting darker, and the walls seemed to be closing in on him. He'd never felt claustrophobia before, but he'd never been in this situation either. He felt panicky, and he was breathing rapidly. *Add claustrophobia to my fear of heights*, he thought as he scrambled back to the door and the fresh air. Then there was another scream, only this time he heard his name: "Tannic! Help me!" He recognized his best friend's voice this time.

Tannic felt like he'd been punched in the gut. He started back up the stairway with determination, but he just couldn't do it. He had another panic attack. The walls were closing in on him. And then the realization hit him. The stairway was almost too small for him, it was much too small for a Minotaur to negotiate comfortably, and the Ender Dude would be much larger than a regular Minotaur. He'd never fit in this stairway. He was in the wrong rotunda.

Tannic ran down to the door, pulled the cloak over himself and stepped back into the yard. He took a quick survey. Two of the other rotundas had doorways the same size as the one he was in. The last one, the one to his right had a huge doorway, easily big enough to accommodate the Ender Dude. It was too obvious.

It was about a hundred feet away. The buildings would provide good cover from the Minotaurs. He clutched the cloak tightly as he heard another pained scream. It was definitely Some Random Guy, and whatever was happening, he didn't have much time left to find the Rainbow Star. He was in the clear, so he broke into a run. He was breathing hard when he reached the door. His heart was pounding. He stepped inside and knew he was in the right place. This one had a different kind of staircase, though. Instead of rock, it was just a series of wooden planks jutting out of the exterior wall. There was no inside wall and no railing, and you could see daylight through the gaps between the stairs. There were stairs that led up and also down. From where he stood at the courtyard level, it was thirty feet or so up to the top of the rotunda, but looking down it must have been eighty feet or more all the way down inside of the rotunda to the base of the castle wall near the moat. His heart stopped as he looked down. He had no choice. He didn't know what was happening with Some Random Guy, something had gone wrong. He instinctively knew it depended on him now to get the Rainbow Star. Everything was on his shoulders.

He tentatively put his foot on the first step. This wasn't going to be easy. He would have to look down into the open space just to put his foot down safely on each step. As he climbed, his fear of heights would come into play. He forced those thoughts away and focused on taking one step at a time. He heard another distant scream. *Hang on, Compadre,* he thought, *I'm coming!*

Some Random Guy didn't like where he was, and he didn't like being locked in the stockade. It hurt his arms and neck, and it wasn't long before he was very uncomfortable. But he didn't answer any of the executioner's questions. What was the point? They'd never understand, and they wouldn't believe what they didn't understand. For the first time in Rough World he felt hopeless.

But the rack came next, and it was more painful than the stockade. The stockade was just a warm-up, apparently. He was slung over a large barrel, his hands tied to one spot and his feet tied to a rope wound around the barrel. When the executioner turned the handle on the barrel it rotated, tightening the rope at his ankles, and began to stretch him. It didn't take much before he felt like he was going to be ripped in half. His shoulders hurt and his ankles hurt. He had heard about the waterboarding controversy on the news at home, and he wasn't sure what that was all about, but this was torture. He couldn't imagine worse. And just when he thought he would pass out, the executioner relaxed the pressure and started questioning him again. Still, he remained silent, except to scream when he was in pain. He screamed for Tannic, but that was useless. He knew Tannic was in the moat fending off the Tritons. He was on his own now, and he was in a really bad spot. The story about the previous player being killed in this dungeon with his own Dragonwrigley came back to him. He sighed dejectedly. He was resigned to his fate. Then came the red-hot steel.

Tannic worked his way up the staircase. He wanted to run back down and hug the ground, but he knew everything depended on him now. So he kept on going, one deliberate, careful step at a time. He kept his right hand on the wall, holding onto every rock he found. He looked down only long enough to see the next step, and he tried to focus on the step, not on the growing depth spiraling down the center of the rotunda. It was a long way down. If he fell, he'd have enough time to think about it on the way down. His heart was racing. He kept telling himself he wasn't afraid of heights. It was like a mantra that kept repeating in his head. Every time he heard Some Random Guy scream in the distance, his resolve grew stronger. He would do this. He would reach the top. He would defeat the Executioner Ender Dude. He would get the Rainbow Star. He would not let his friend down. Not now. One more step, one more look, one more step. Not ever. Stay focused. Repeat.

The Executioner Minotaur pulled a branding iron out of the fire. Some Random Guy could see the red glow from the tip. He could feel its heat while it was still a few feet away. The Executioner brought it slowly toward his chest.

"Still have nothing to say? Who is Tannic? Why are you here? Maybe this will get you to speak!" But as he brought the iron forward, SRG only screamed again, half out of reflex, half out of fear.

Tannic was almost at the top. The platform was just

above him. There were windows set radially around the exterior wall. They lit the interior brightly. *The view must be spectacular*, he thought. *At least if you aren't afraid of heights.* And then he saw the Executioner Ender Dude. He was standing at the farthest window from the stairs, staring out. He seemed to be preoccupied. The Rainbow Star was on a shelf next to him.

Without thinking, Tannic took the last few steps and emerged onto the platform unannounced. The Ender Dude saw him now. He turned to face him, looking on with curiosity or amusement, Tannic couldn't tell which. He quickly realized that he wouldn't be able to reach the star before the Ender Dude reached him. He thought for a second and waited for the Ender Dude to charge him. He didn't have to wait long. The Ender Dude hurtled across the platform with his arms extended. Tannic dropped and rolled to the inner edge. He waited a split second, then let himself fall just as the Ender Dude reached for him. He went over the edge, but it was too late for the Ender Dude to stop his charge. He went right over too.

It was a long way to the ground down the middle of the rotunda, all the way to the base of the outer castle wall. The Ender Dude would have enough time to think about it on the way down. Tannic had grabbed the first step with one hand as he rolled off the platform. Now he hung in space watching the Ender Dude plummet downward, bouncing off of a few stairs and disappearing into the darkness. Tannic finally heard him piling up on the ground below with a loud crash. He felt a bolt of fear pulse through his body. Tannic took a deep breath and swung his second hand onto the step. He struggled to pull his leg up. He didn't dare look down now. He just needed to get back onto the platform, and the

Rainbow Star was his. He grunted and swung his leg higher.

The Executioner Minotaur had run out of patience. The red hot iron hadn't gotten Some Random Guy to speak either. There was an audience of Minotaurs in the dungeon now, and at his signal two of them hauled SRG off of the rack and dragged him to the large block of wood in the middle of the room. One Minotaur held each arm as they forced his head and neck down to the block. The Executioner Minotaur took the Dragonwrigley in both hands and hoisted it over his head.

"Any last words?" he asked Some Random Guy. Then he looked around. "Good one, huh boys?" His entire audience burst into laughter, then began cheering him on. SRG closed his eyes. He didn't want to see what was coming. Life Wedges didn't matter now. He thought of home, his parents, and his brothers. He just wanted to be in his own bed. He was anticipating the feel of the sword on his neck. He hoped it would be over quickly. He wanted to cry but he couldn't. He didn't know what to do, and his mind was racing. He was out of options. He screamed "Tannic!" one last time. Then he waited for it.

"What, Compadre?" Tannic answered.

Some Random Guy opened his eyes in disbelief. Had Tannic died too? But he hadn't felt anything yet. Was he dead? No, they were in Dr. Denton's lab. Doc was smiling at them.

"What happened?" SRG asked wearily.

"Well, I don't know about you, but I got the Rainbow Star!" Tannic bragged.

"I can't tell you how happy that makes me!" Some Random Guy replied. He gave Tannic a bear hug.

"I can't tell you how happy—and relieved—it makes

me," Dr. Denton added. "You boys are going to be the death of me. I don't know how much more I can take. I thought you were a goner for sure. I didn't think Tannic would make it in time. I need to sit down, I'm shaking."

"Me too," SRG said. His knees suddenly got weak and buckled from under him.

"Make that three of us," Tannic added, and they all laughed in relief. There wasn't anything funny, but there was no point in crying, so they laughed instead.

"Any activity at home?" SRG asked.

"Not a thing," Dr. Denton replied. "Now it's on to Level 9."

Chapter 11
The Valley of the Caves

"So tell us about Level 9," Some Random Guy said softly as he regained his composure.

"Well, nobody's ever made it this far, so I don't have any firsthand experience to share with you. But I'll tell you what I do know," Dr. Denton explained. "Level 9 is the Valley of the Caves. There are roughly three hundred caves here that the people of Rough World use to hide from the Evil Boss and his henchmen outside the Jagged City. However, the Evil Boss has found some of the caves and set booby traps inside them. One cave—and only one, but unfortunately I don't know which one—leads to the Jagged City. That cave also hides the Cave Ender Dude and the Rainbow Star. The rest of the caves, those that aren't booby trapped, will either have citizens from Rough World hiding in them or will be deserted. The people won't be able to help you much at all, I'm afraid, unless they can tell you which cave leads to the Jagged City. But they probably won't know and wouldn't tell you even if they did. Got it?"

"Your special weapon for this level is a laser headlamp. Pressing the switch once turns the headlamp on and off. Pressing it twice in succession turns on a laser beam that will cut through almost anything. Be *very* careful where you look when the laser is on. It will slice whatever you're looking at in half. And that's about all I know. The headlamp is hanging next to the door. You should have about a couple of hours of battery life. Do you need anything else?"

"I don't think there's much else we *could* ask for, Doc. Are there Minotaurs or other man-eating things here?" SRG asked.

"I really don't know. But I think you should assume there are," Doc answered.

"Okay, I figured as much. We'll be on the lookout for anything dangerous. We're really happy to have you on our team, Doc. Come on Tannic. Eight down, two to go. We can do this."

"I'm right behind you, Compadre."

And the two boys stepped out of Dr. Denton's lab and into the Valley of the Caves.

The valley was lush and beautiful, with plants and trees in fifty shades of green. There were random paths crisscrossing it, some that looked well used and others that hadn't seen foot traffic in a long while, overgrown by the grass and shrubs. The valley wasn't deep or wide, just long. You could walk from one side of the valley to the other in about five minutes, but it might take an hour or more to reach the upper end of it. The entrances to the caves weren't readily apparent. It took Tannic and Some Random Guy some careful looking to make out any at all. Most of them were capped off with a wall and a door and had thick greenery growing over them, making them almost invisible. They were well camouflaged, but once you knew what to look for, they became more and more apparent. And there were three hundred or more, but only one led to the Rainbow Star.

Some Random Guy checked his grip on the Dragon wrigley. It looked much better in his hand than above his head in the executioner's hand. That was a close call. He reflexively felt at his neck. It was still attached to his head. He swallowed and brought his mind back to the present problem. They had to find the cave to the Jagged City. Dr. Denton hadn't been much help this time, they didn't have any clues, but they couldn't afford to test every cave. The math didn't pencil out. They'd have to rely on their wits and on luck.

"Which cave should we start with, Compadre?" Tannic asked.

"Well, we can't just look at random. Some of them are booby trapped, and we don't have enough Life Wedges to make that work. Do you have any ideas?"

"Well, we could go into each cave alone. That way we could check out six caves and make five mistakes, instead of three caves if we both go in. It would sort of double our Life Wedges."

"Going it alone didn't work out so well at the Egerian Castle."

"What do you mean? We got the Rainbow Star!"

"Yeah, and I came real close to getting killed with my own sword."

"Oh, sorry. Well, we need to start somewhere. I think we should just take our chances and pick a cave and investigate it. See what we're up against. But I do think one of us should go in first in case it's a trap."

"Are you feeling lucky? Do you want to pick the first cave?"

"No way, Compadre, you pick. I trust your instincts."

"Okay then, I say we start with . . . that one." Some Random Guy pointed to a cave two hundred yards away and halfway up the right valley wall. It was as good a starting point as any.

They walked up the center of the valley. The sun was shining and the air was fresh. It would have been a pleasant place if it didn't hold such bad odds for them. The path to their cave looked like it had seen some recent use. The opening was about ten feet across, but it had been walled over with planks, and there was a heavy wooden door in the middle. The door had a large latch for a padlock, but there was no lock. Some Random Guy pulled the handle. The door creaked as it swung slowly open.

The cave was dark. SRG turned his headlamp on to light his way. He gripped the Dragonwrigley tightly in his right hand, probing ahead and led the way with it, preparing for the unexpected. But nothing happened. A few cobwebs hung from the wall, and there was some broken, dusty furniture. The air smelled stale and musty. There were shelves on one wall, but they were mostly bare. A few empty cans and boxes littered the floor randomly. If the cave had ever been used, it wasn't recently. SRG called out to Tannic to join him. Together they followed his headlamp beam another fifty feet into the hill, where the cave came to an abrupt end.

"Well, that was a dead end," Some Random Guy stated the obvious.

"Yeah, but we didn't get hurt either. At least not yet. I didn't see anything that looked like a booby trap."

"Me neither." He shrugged. "Let's pick another cave to explore. At least we eliminated one from the list."

"Kind of like Formula 409," Tannic added.

"What's that supposed to mean?" SRG asked.

"The cleaning solution, Formula 409. It got its name because it was the 409th attempt that finally worked," Tannic explained.

"Who did you learn that from?"

"Who do you think? Your grandpa."

"Too bad we only get six tries between us. Actually five. Well, maybe only four if we're both going to survive. We need to actually figure it out, or else get really lucky. Formula 409," SRG shook his head and chuckled.

Satisfied that the cave held no answers for them, they emerged back into the sunlight. The sky was blue and cloudless, and there was a gentle breeze carrying a clean scent from the plants. Some Random Guy led the way back to the main path. They turned right and proceeded deeper into the valley, looking carefully at the paths that led to the individual caves, but there was nothing hinting at where they should go next. Tannic suggested they try a cave on the opposite hillside. SRG agreed, and they climbed the path in that direction.

This entrance was capped with rocks and stones and sported a hefty steel door. It too had a large latch but no lock. There was lettering on the door that reminded Some Random Guy of Egyptian hieroglyphics he'd seen in schoolbooks, but neither he nor Tannic could make sense of it, so he opened the door and peered inside. The cave was dark and musty. Layers of dust covered the inside. It didn't look inhabited either.

"Hello. Anybody home?" SRG cried out. There was no response so he stepped inside. He heard an odd sound and turned to Tannic. "What was that?"

Before Tannic could answer, the tripwire triggered the improvised exploding device, and there was a loud blast. Tannic was blown back from the door. He picked himself up and ran to help Some Random Guy. He found his friend lying lifeless on the cave floor. Tannic watched as a Life Wedge briefly flared up, illuminating the cave, and then slowly faded away.

"What happened? What was that?" SRG asked as Tannic helped him up.

"Booby trap. A bomb or something. You lost a Life Wedge, Compadre."

"Wow, I don't remember anything. I guess we can conclude that this isn't the tunnel we're looking for."

"So how do we know what to look out for next time?" Tannic asked.

"Well, I'm thinking. It seems like if a path looks really worn, it could mean people from the Jagged City have been using it recently. If it doesn't look worn down, maybe the cave is booby trapped and that's why people aren't using it. What do you think?"

"What if the Evil Boss's secret police make it look like it's been used a lot, so that people won't think it's a trap?"

"Yeah. That makes sense. I don't know. It's kind of overwhelming."

"Do you think the hieroglyphics meant it was a trap? It could have been a warning."

"I don't know. Let's pick a cave that looks like it hasn't been used too much *or* too little. How does that sound?"

"That sounds about right to me, Compadre. Not too much, not too little, one that's just right. Lead on, Goldilocks."

Some Random Guy laughed. "You crack me up, Tannic. I don't know how you can keep your sense of humor at a time like this. At least it cheers me up. Thanks!"

So they walked farther up the valley, inspecting caves and pathways and deciding to go in and then changing their minds. Some of the paths were well worn and some of them were grown over from lack of use. Finally they found a path that looked just right. They were feeling pretty confident by the time they reached the cave. It had been blocked with corrugated sheet metal, and it had a metal door. The metal showed some rust, and the upper half of the entrance was covered in leaves and branches. They looked vaguely familiar. Some Random Guy cleared the plants out of the way with the Dragonwrigley. There was a heavy metal latch on the door, and this time there was a big padlock hanging from it.

"That looks like a problem," Tannic said. "We don't have any keys."

"Yeah, but it might be a good sign. Maybe this cave isn't booby-trapped," SRG responded. As he lifted the lock, it popped open in his hand. "Maybe that's a good sign too?" he added. "Maybe not?"

Tannic just shrugged. So Some Random Guy opened the door and peered inside. He didn't see any signs of life. He also didn't see a trip wire, which he was now looking for. He stepped carefully inside and looked farther into the cave. It was as deserted as the first two caves. "Let's go, Tannic," he called out.

There was no response.

He walked back and stepped through the door. The plant's tendrils were wrapped around Tannic, and it was dragging him up the wall. One of his Life Wedges was dimming quickly.

SRG drew the Dragonwrigley and hacked at the plant. It took a few swipes to cut Tannic free, and the plant made a whimpering sound as it retreated, green goo oozing from the freshly cut stump. He helped Tannic up.

"That wasn't good. Now you're down to two Life Wedges

too. I should have recognized that plant, but I wasn't even looking for man-eating plants. I guess we need to expect anything and everything from the Evil Boss on this level. So I guess be on the lookout for anything suspicious at all."

"Thanks, Compadre! It had me before I could even yell. Next time I'll stick closer to you."

"If you did that, you'd have lost a Life Wedge along with me from that bomb."

"Oh. Uh, good thinking. Now what do we do?"

"I don't know Tannic. I'm tired of this stupid place and I want to go home!" SRG cried.

"Don't give up, Compadre! We've come too far to quit now. We only have two levels left. We can do this. We've got to."

Some Random Guy wiped his brow. "Yeah, I know. You're right. I'm just getting tired of this. Let's pick another cave. This isn't the one we're looking for. How about you pick the next one?"

"Okay, how about the one right next door? What are the odds that two caves next to each other are both traps?"

The neighboring cave had a wooden front, a wooden door and latch, and no lock. No vegetation was hanging over the door, and there were no hieroglyphics. Some Random Guy slowly opened the door and shined his headlamp inside. It looked like it had been used recently, but it was empty now. There wasn't much dust, and there were food and other supplies on the shelf. They crept carefully inside, slowly and deliberately placing one foot in front of the other. SRG was looking for trip wires. There was a cup on the table. SRG touched it. It was still warm. He shot an odd look at Tannic.

"Shhh. I think somebody's here," he whispered. "That cup is warm. Somebody was just using it."

"That's scary. I have a bad feeling about this. Let's get out of here."

"No, we can't. Let's go farther in and see who it is. If it's a Minotaur it would have charged us already," Some Random Guy reasoned.

He put the cup down carefully and they walked slowly forward, deeper into the belly of the cave and farther from safety. There were large crates and boxes strewn randomly about on the dirt floor. It looked like a hoarder's storage unit. At the end of the cave, hiding behind a box next to the wall, was a small girl. She looked at them anxiously. She was shaking.

"Are . . . are you going to hurt me?" she asked.

"No, no!" replied Some Random Guy. "We're trying to find the cave to the Jagged City. Maybe you can help us. Do you know where it is?"

"No. My parents might know. They left me here to hide yesterday."

"When will they be back?" SRG asked.

"I don't know. Maybe tomorrow? They didn't tell me. I thought maybe you were them when you were outside. But I didn't recognize the voices, so I ran here to hide like my parents taught me."

Tannic looked at Some Random Guy. "This isn't the right cave either. We should just go back outside and leave her alone."

"Yeah. We still have work to do." They walked back into the door. The small girl followed them back to the table and picked up her cup. She watched them leave.

"Now what, Compadre?" Tannic asked.

"Let's pick a cave. Which one do you like?"

Tannic pointed at an opening across the valley.

The path to the cave looked used, but not well used. The opening was filled with rocks, and it had a metal door. There was no lock, just a small latch and handle. There was no vegetation over the door. The moment Some Random Guy lifted the handle, two Minotaurs charged out.

The first knocked SRG down and grabbed Tannic. It lifted Tannic over its head in both hands. The second Minotaur was on SRG before he could draw the Dragonwrigley. The sword got tangled in his belt underneath him, and when the Minotaur picked him up he lost his grip and the sword clattered to the ground. He looked over at Tannic and watched one of his remaining Life Wedges illuminate and start fading away.

"The headlamp, Compadre, the headlamp!" Tannic screamed.

In the commotion Some Random Guy had completely forgotten about the headlamp. With his free hand he pushed the switch twice. A laser beam shot forth. He looked at the Minotaur holding Tannic, and with a careful head movement cut the beast in half in a cascade of smoke and bright flashes. The Minotaur fell to the ground in two sizzling pieces, taking Tannic with it. It smelled like grilled steak. The Minotaur holding Some Random Guy paused, but didn't know what to do next. SRG slowly turned his head to look at the creature, and the laser cut a path clean through it. Before he could react, SRG was falling to the ground with its body. He fumbled to turn the switch off as he fell.

"Sorry, Tannic! I completely forgot about it in the confusion." He reached down and helped his friend up. Then he picked up the Dragonwrigley. "That was a close one. You're down to one Life Wedge now. This isn't working! We don't have enough Life Wedges to find the right cave this way.

There are just too many of them!"

"I agree, Compadre. So let's sit down and figure this thing out logically. There must be a way to solve it. What do we know so far?"

"Okay. Well, I think we're looking for a cave that doesn't have too much activity. But it has to have some sign of activity, or else it's deserted. I don't think the type of wall and door matters, or whether it's locked or not. I don't think the hieroglyphics make a difference. That's about it. Well, I do know we need a cave with no trip wires, man-eating plants, or Minotaurs."

"Okay, how about this. Let's say you wanted to dig a tunnel from the Valley of the Caves all the way to the Jagged City. Where would you start?"

Some Random Guy thought about it. "I'd start as close to the Jagged City as possible so I wouldn't have to dig too far."

"So would I," Tannic agreed. "I say we go back to the other end of the valley and look for the cave closest to the city."

"That would be the first cave. Do you think it could be that obvious?"

"Do you have any better ideas?"

"Nope. Let's go. What have we got to lose? I mean, besides some Life Wedges."

"That's not funny, Compadre!"

So the two boys hiked back down to where they started. The first cave was on the right side of the valley, not far from the bottom. The path to the entrance looked moderately used. The entrance was sealed with big wooden planks, and there was a heavy metal door. On the door were a large latch and a very large padlock. Some Random Guy and Tannic looked at each other curiously.

SRG picked up the lock, but this time it stayed closed. It was locked solid.

"Perfect. Now what?"

"I don't know. Try the Dragonwrigley," Tannic suggested. "Can you pick the lock?"

Some Random Guy poked the sword's tip around in the keyhole, but nothing happened. The tip was too big and the keyhole was too small. It was frustrating. He stepped back and whacked the lock with the sword, but nothing happened. He shot some fireballs at it, but again nothing happened. They didn't have a way to get in.

"Wait a minute, Compadre!" Tannic exclaimed. "The weapon, the headlamp laser beam. Doc said it would cut anything in half!"

"Good thinking, Tannic! Stand back." Some Random Guy carefully aimed the laser at the lock and pushed the switch twice. The beam made a loud sizzling noise and smoke as it cut through the lock and part of the metal door. The lock fell to the ground smoking. SRG carefully turned the laser off before looking at his friend.

"We're in, Tannic! Let's go!"

"Not so fast, Compadre. Let's go, but let's go carefully. This still might not be it, and it could be booby trapped, and there could be Minotaurs. And if it is the right cave, there's an Ender Dude inside. Let's proceed with caution."

"You're right, what was I thinking?"

Some Random Guy gently nudged open the door. This cave was dark too, but it immediately smelled different, as if there was a source of fresh air. He hollered, "Anybody home?" and heard a faint echo.

"Did you hear that? That was an echo, Tannic. This

tunnel is longer than the others. I can feel it. This must be it!"

"Yeah, I heard it too. Let's just be careful. I'm down to one Life Wedge."

"Okay, good plan. Follow me and stay close. If we go down, we go down together."

Some Random Guy and Tannic moved slowly into the belly of the cave. The headlamp lit up the cave enough for them to see fairly well. This cave was longer than the others, but there wasn't much in it. It looked deserted. It certainly didn't look like a place anybody had been hiding out in. There was no furniture or food and no boxes strewn on the floor. They continued down the tunnel, and eventually it turned to the right and started to climb slightly. It was dead quiet. At the top of the rise they found a door. This end of the tunnel was finished off with a rock wall and a metal door. There was a small metal latch and no lock. Some Random Guy and Tannic looked at each other. Tannic shrugged and made a face. A huge Minotaur jumped out of the shadows.

He had to be the Ender Dude. He held the Rainbow Star in his left hand. He grunted and swept Tannic up in his right. Tannic went limp. The Ender Dude had caught them both off guard, and Some Random Guy had jumped reflexively and dropped the Dragonwrigley. Now he stepped back and stared at the towering Minotaur. It was far bigger than any ordinary Minotaur, and the Dragonwrigley wouldn't have been any use. SRG's mind was racing as he watched the beast lift Tannic over its head. Then he saw Tannic's lone remaining Life Wedge. SRG confidently pushed the headlamp switch twice. The laser beam flashed on. He carefully aimed it at the Ender Dude's left forearm. In a flash of light, smoke, and the smell of burnt Minotaur, the hand fell to the ground, still clutching the brilliantly radiating Rainbow Star. The Ender

Dude just stood there in disbelief, staring at the smoking stump that had been his left arm a minute ago. He still held Tannic in his right hand.

Some Random Guy darted forward and picked up the Rainbow Star. As he did, the Ender Dude pixilated and disappeared and Tannic dropped to the floor. The metal door creaked open slowly to reveal a brightly lit room.

"Hello boys!" Dr. Denton cheered. They opened the door fully and stepped into the lab. "So which cave was it?"

"Can you believe it? It was the first cave in the valley, the one closest to the city," Some Random Guy replied.

"How did you figure it out?" Doc asked.

"Actually, Tannic did. He figured that if we wanted to dig a tunnel, we'd start as close to the city as possible so we wouldn't have to dig as far. And it turns out that's exactly what the citizens of the Jagged City did. It was too obvious, but it was the one."

"And the Ender Dude totally caught us off guard," Tannic added. "I don't know where he came from. I didn't even see the star's light until he stepped out of the darkness."

"Well, that was great thinking, boys. I'm proud of you both! Now there's only one level left. Are you ready?"

"Yeah, Doc, tell us about Level 10."

Chapter 12
The Jagged City

"I'm afraid I won't be much help on Level 10, either," Doc started. "From what I understand, it consists mainly of urban warfare in the Jagged City itself. There are two rivals gangs of teenage Minotaurs terrorizing the citizens. The gang warfare is probably how the Minotaurs get their training for the other levels. I'm going to guess it's a very dangerous level. The gangs are the "Shirts" and the "Skins." The Rainbow Star is currently held by the Shirts—they wear red shirts, of course. Their nickname is the "Minute Hours." A little play on words I would presume. The Ender Dude is also a member of that gang. Their part of the city is pretty rough even by Rough World standards. It's mostly slums. There are a lot of abandoned buildings, broken windows, graffiti, and vacant lots. It's not the sort of place you visit by choice. The citizens of the Jagged City avoid it at all costs."

"That doesn't sound like someplace I want to go either," Tannic responded.

"The worst thing you have to look out for is the asphalt trap. It's like quicksand, but it's asphalt. It looks like normal asphalt, but as you walk across it you sink in and don't stop sinking until you're completely gone. They call it

"Quickphalt." Your special weapon will be a grappling hook and rope. If you get caught in the Quickphalt it might be your only escape."

"Is that all?" SRG asked.

"That's about it," Doc continued. "I'll keep an eye on you and try to time my own plans so that I can create a diversion at the power plant and get that power surge ready for you when you need it. If you survive the gangs and capture the Rainbow Star, you'll end up back here in the lab, but I'll already be gone. The Fortran Sword will be leaning against the door for you. That's the strongest weapon in Rough World, and you can defeat any enemy with it. When you go through the door with the sword, it will open onto the hallway outside the Evil Boss's office. Put the ten Rainbow Stars into the notches in the wall, and the door will open. With the Fortran in your hands, I don't really think the Evil Boss will offer any resistance. He's just a bully, and most bullies are cowards at heart."

The Transport Chamber is at the back of his office and looks like an elevator. Get inside and close the door, and I'll make sure the power is surging at the right time. With any luck, you boys will be on your way home. I'm sorry to say that if everything goes according to plan, I won't be seeing you again. I've grown fond of you two, and you've inspired me with your courage. No team of players has ever made it this far before. I'm proud of both of you! But I really do want to see you safely back home. Good luck!"

"Thank you so much for your help, Dr. Denton. It was wonderful to meet you, and we would never have made it this far if it hadn't been for you. We'll never forget you, right Tannic?"

"That's right. We'll never forget you or what you've

done for us. You are the man with the plan!"

"And if your plan doesn't work, and we don't get transported home, I'm guessing we will see you again," Some Random Guy added. "Is that right?"

"Probably. But let's do everything in our power to get you guys home."

Some Random Guy looked at Tannic, and they both walked over and gave Doc a farewell hug. Then they walked to the door in unison. SRG picked up the grappling hook and coiled the rope over his shoulder. He tightened his grip on the Dragonwrigley and nodded at Tannic. One last glance at the reverse screen still didn't show anyone in the family room. They took one last look at Doc standing in his lab. They opened the door and stepped into the middle of the Jagged City and urban warfare.

* * *

The assistant ran nervously into the Evil Boss's office. He was a Minotaur sharply dressed in a three-piece suit and tie. He was immaculately groomed for a Minotaur and also well spoken. "Mr. Eville, sir, we have a situation."

"And what exactly would that be?" Mr. Eville grunted. The Evil Boss was short and heavy-set. He had a square jaw and a mean square face. His nose looked like a dog's who had chased one too many parked cars. His hair was thinning on top and sprouted in little black tufts above his ears. They almost looked like little horns. He also wore a three-piece suit, a navy blue one, and a red necktie. The collar of his starched white shirt was tight around his almost non-existent neck.

"It's from Level 10, sir. The two boys discovered the tunnel on Level 9 and have just entered the Jagged City!"

"What!? I thought the executioner took care of them on

level 8! Why am I just learning about this?" he demanded.

"Well, we thought so too, sir. But the accomplice managed to retrieve the Rainbow Star just as the executioner was about to eliminate player number one."

"This is unacceptable! You know the risks! I should have been informed of this sooner. No player has ever made it to Level 9 before, much less Level 10! Contact the Ender Dude on Level 10 immediately! These two must be stopped before they get the last Rainbow Star," he screamed. "I will not be compromised now!" Suddenly he smiled evilly. "But if these two little snots do think they can march in here and defeat me, I'll have a little surprise of my own for them. Now go and take care of this! I pay you to solve problems like this!"

"Yes sir," was all the assistant could muster. He turned and walked stiffly out of the office.

* * *

The sky was overcast above the Jagged City. It was grey and gloomy. The air carried a faint haze and smelled like industrial pollution. The streets were empty of people, and the buildings were run down. Many displayed broken windows, faded paint, and business signs that looked like archeological relics. The occasional vehicle carcass was parked on the street. Most of them appeared to have been destroyed by fire and were sitting wheel-less on their hubs. Some Random Guy and Tannic walked cautiously up the street, but there was no sign of life.

"What's our plan, Compadre?" Tannic asked as usual.

"I have no idea. I need to get a feel for the city. Did Dr. Denton say where the headquarters of the Minute Hours gang was? I don't remember him mentioning that."

"I don't think he did. I'm guessing they're on one side of this urban mess and the Skins are on the other, and they fight over the turf in between. Does that sound about right?"

SRG nodded. "That would make sense."

They both heard the din behind them at the same time and turned in time to see a dozen shirtless Minotaurs coming up the street. Some Random Guy and Tannic ducked into a burned-out brick building without being seen. They watched in silence as the gang marched by. They were carrying axes, picks, clubs, and swords. It was an odd assortment of weapons and individuals.

"Whew!" SRG whispered. "There's too many of them to fight with just the Dragonwrigley."

"Yeah, we'd just be outnumbered. I think we can safely assume the Minute Hours are at least as many in number. Probably more, since they control the Rainbow Star."

"Good thinking. We're going to have to find the Minute Hours' headquarters and figure out how to sneak in and capture the star."

"That should be easy!" Tannic smiled.

"Yeah, right," Some Random Guy answered with an edge in his voice. "Let's follow these guys and see where they go. Maybe it'll give us a clue. What do you think?"

"I'm right behind you," Tannic whispered. "You go first."

"You know, just once it would be nice if you went first. The Dragonwrigley won't be much help. Neither will the grappling hook. So I don't think it'll matter if you go first. You know, if we ever play this game again, it'll be your turn to be the player. And you're going first all of the time and I'm following you!"

"Really, Compadre? If we survive this mess, will you ever want to play the game again?"

"Ha, no! If we get out of this alive, I never want to hear the words 'Rough World' again, much less play the stupid game!"

"So you're going first, then?" Tannic asked.

Some Random Guy sighed. "Yeah, I'm going first . . . like always."

He made a mental note as they snuck along behind the gang. If he somehow changed his mind, and he and Tannic actually did play Rough World again, he would make sure that Tannic went first, carrying the weapons and leading the way. It would be his turn.

While he was thinking about this, the gang turned up a street to the left and marched on, like they were on a mission to get somewhere. Tannic and Some Random Guy followed as close as they dared. They weren't prepared for the sight that met them as they rounded the corner. They ducked into an alleyway to hide and watch the show.

Coming from the opposite direction was another group of teenaged Minotaurs, all clad in bright red shirts. The Ender Dude wasn't with them—presumably he was back at their headquarters guarding the last Rainbow Star. The gangs were evenly matched in numbers and similarly armed. The battle started without warning and rapidly became a huge melee. It looked like a free-for-all in a bar room brawl.

After a minute, Some Random Guy whispered, "Something doesn't feel right. This doesn't look like two rival gangs who hate each other fighting over turf and bragging rights. And the Rainbow Star."

Tannic saw that he was right. There was a loud ruckus, and dust was being thrown in the air as they attacked each other. Somehow, though, it didn't look real. Nobody died. No one was even injured. The clash had the feeling of a training exercise. In fact, it almost looked like the two gangs were sparring partners. The fight resembled a carefully choreographed dance. They were putting on a show.

As if to drive that point home, a Minute Hour knocked a Skin to the ground. He could easily have finished him off, but instead he extended a hand to help him up, and they went back to sparring. It was unnerving behavior to watch in Minotaurs, who were usually so ruthless.

"Yeah, this just seems weird," Tannic said. "I think if we got in a fight with them, they'd all suddenly be on the same team. All of them against me and you."

"I was just thinking the same thing. And it means that we can't take advantage of their rivalry. We'll need a way to draw them all out, not just half of them, and distract them while we grab the Rainbow Star."

"You mean I get to be bait while you get the star? Isn't that what you mean?"

"I was just thinking, that's all. I can't fight one gang, much less two. And I don't want to fight at all, really."

"Okay, so what's your plan?" Tannic asked.

"I don't have one yet. But I think we should follow the Minute Hours and see if they lead us to their headquarters," Some Random Guy whispered. "Maybe we can come up with something once we see what we're dealing with."

"Sounds good to me. How long do you think they'll keep this charade up?"

"I don't know. We'll just have to wait it out."

The Minute Hours and the Skins were fully engaged in their battle, even if it was the polite sparring kind. They were occupying most of the street now, battling each other one on one. If there were traffic, they would have been blocking it, but there wasn't any traffic in this part of the city. It looked like taxis wouldn't even come here, and they hadn't seen anybody else on the streets. The only sign of life was the two

Minotaur gangs.

* * *

Mr. Eville leaned back in his leather chair and propped his feet up on his desk. He surveyed his office, his domain. He was the Evil Boss and this was his high command post and his favorite place in all of Rough World. In this inner chamber he was lord and ruler over everybody and everything. The room had oversized dark walnut furniture and intricate dark walnut paneling on the walls. His favorite things were in the room, his mementos of victories past. The photos on the walls all pictures of him, and there were assorted awards that he had mostly given to himself. The carpet was thick and plush and the room was quiet. He puffed gently on his cigar, savored the smoke, and then slowly exhaled with pleasure. He loved this place.

The only flaw in his masterpiece was the Transport Chamber door in the far corner. It was a necessary part of his existence and a daily reminder of what he needed to do to keep his hold on the citizens of Rough World. Nobody had ever managed to use the chamber, of course. Nobody had yet defeated him and moved on to Rough World Two. And he would make sure nobody ever did. He would do anything at all to make sure of that. *Anything.* He smiled.

The citizens of Rough World feared him, and with good reason. That thought made him smile even more. It wasn't just that he was evil. It was that he loved being evil. It resonated in his soul. Evil was his calling, and he had answered it. He took another slow puff on his cigar.

His pleasant thoughts were interrupted by his assistant.

"What is it now?" he barked.

The assistant was beaming. "I've spoken to the rival gangs on Level 10 and the Ender Dude, sir. They are setting a trap for the boys as we speak."

"Perfect! Let me know when we have eliminated this threat," Mr. Eville replied.

"Will do, Boss—er—I mean, Mr. Eville." The assistant quietly closed the office door as he departed. He had a confident air and a smile on his face.

* * *

The rival gangs continued their battle, and to the boys it started looking more and more contrived. Then, like a snap of your fingers, it was over. The Minute Hours retreated up the street, and the Skins reassembled and left slowly in the opposite direction. They left silently, with no shouts of celebration and no apparent winner. It was an odd sight and not the urban warfare the boys had expected. Something wasn't adding up.

Tannic and Some Random Guy followed the Minute Hours this time, keeping their distance. "Okay, I've been thinking, and I think I have a plan," SRG whispered to Tannic. "We're smarter than a Minotaur, right?" Tannic gave him a curious look. "And we're smarter than a bunch of Minotaurs. We're even smarter than two bunches of Minotaurs, right?"

"Sure, ok. I'd say so. They're not that smart. They're more like playground bullies, all muscle and no brains. Nothing above the neck to brag about," Tannic agreed.

"Right. So I've been thinking. We need to use our advantage. We need to outsmart them. It can't be that hard."

"How do we do that?"

"We draw them into a trap. I'm willing to bet you can run on top of the Quickphalt. It's like quicksand, which is just sand and water. So we need to locate an asphalt trap. You draw them into it and keep their attention until they're stuck. While you're doing that, I'll sneak into the headquarters, defeat the Ender Dude, and get the Rainbow Star. Then it's 'Hello Mr. Eville, meet my little friend Mr. Fortran Sword.' What do you think? I think it could work."

"Okay, I'm following your idea. But I think it's risky, and it depends on two things we don't know. Number one, we don't know if I can run on the Quickphalt. And number two, we don't know if you can defeat the Ender Dude with the Dragonwrigley. It wasn't very effective against them on the other levels."

"Do you have a better idea?"

"Nope. I think we have to go with it. As long as I can run on the Quickphalt, it might work. Then you'll just have to defeat the Ender Dude by yourself.

The gang marched purposefully up the street and took a left turn. This area had the feel of a manufacturing district from long ago. Some of the buildings were brick and some were sheet metal, but they were all burned relics, and all their windows were broken. The sidewalks were littered with potholes and broken concrete.

After two blocks, the street ended and at an abandoned building made of sheet metal. It looked no different from any of the other buildings. Its few windows were covered with dust and cobwebs. It had a large garage door with a regular door next to it. It had been painted once but now it was faded and rusty. There was a faded spot above the door, forensic evidence of a business sign long-since gone.

The Minute Hours were walking in single file up the middle of the street. Just before they reached the last building, however, each of them turned left and marched to the sidewalk, took the sidewalk the rest of the way to the building, and then turned right again and marched back to the door. They looked like ants marching single file back to their nest, but they all took the long way around the pavement in front of the building.

"That was weird, why did they do that?" Tannic asked.

"Ha, that was perfect! I think they just showed us their headquarters *and* a Quickphalt patch right in front of it. This makes our plan perfect! You draw them out into the Quickphalt, and I'll sneak in and find the Rainbow Star. If anything goes wrong I'll come back and get you out with the grappling hook."

"Uh, Compadre, the Ender Dude?"

"Oh yeah, that could be the problem. I'll figure it out. Are you ready? This is our last level, let's do it!"

"I'm right behind you, Compadre!" Tannic answered.

"Go get them, Good Buddy! Just keep moving!"

Some Random Guy and Tannic moved unnoticed, they hoped, up the left side of the street. They stayed close to the buildings, trying to blend in. Near the end of the street, SRG picked up a loose brick, looked at Tannic, and heaved it into the middle of the street. It bounced a couple of times on the asphalt and sat there. Nothing happened. Then it slowly settled right into the asphalt, deeper and deeper until it was completely gone. The asphalt closed back up again, and there was no sign the brick had ever existed.

"Well, that's a Quickphalt patch," Some Random Guy confirmed. "It was like the ground just swallowed the brick."

"Yeah. Scary stuff," Tannic added. "I don't have a good feeling about this, but here goes nothing."

While Some Random Guy hid in the shadows, Tannic continued up the street and stopped in front of the building. He started yelling and jumping up and down to get the attention of the Minotaurs. In seconds they started coming out of the door like angry hornets out of their nest. They headed straight for Tannic. He let them get as close as he dared and then he ran straight onto the Quickphalt. The Minotaurs started to follow him but stopped right at the edge.

Some Random Guy crept undetected past them to the front door. It was pretty messy inside. There were tables and chairs and a lot of boxes and old junk. You could tell that somebody lived there, though. Minotaurs apparently didn't care much for cleanliness and order. SRG could hear Tannic yelling outside while he scanned the interior. There was no obvious place to hide the Rainbow Star, and there was no Ender Dude. He was about to give up when he spotted the stairway against the far wall.

It led to an office space on a mezzanine level overlooking the ground floor. At one time it had held the offices of the small factory, with interior windows to let the boss observe the floor workers from above. There was rainbow-colored light coming out of the office windows. *Gotcha*, SRG thought. He ran across the room and up the stairs.

Tannic was keeping the Minute Hours occupied, but they weren't being sucked into the trap. They stood on the sidewalk and watched him with anticipation, like kids at a birthday party waiting for the cake to be cut. It was easy at first. He just ran in circles taunting the Minotaurs like he'd had done with the fish on so many levels. Then he started slowing down. The asphalt was getting stickier. He could feel it pulling more on him with each step, and it got harder and harder to move. Finally came to a complete stop. It was like his feet were super-glued to the street. He started to sink into it. He frantically tried to free himself, but each movement dragged him further in. It was up to his knees now. This wasn't going the way he and Some Random Guy had planned it. He heard some noises and looked up to see the

Skins arriving. As he sank to his waist, the two rival gangs surrounded him and started taunting and cheering him from the sidewalk. They all seemed to be on the same side now. *This wasn't in the script!*

They all laughed as they watched him struggle, sometimes adding jokes and jeers. "Har, har!" "Looks like he can't run on Quickphalt after all. Too bad!" "Oh no, look, he's sinking!" "Har, har!"

Some Random Guy stepped into the office. The Ender Dude was staring at him. He seemed to be expecting him. He was huge and powerful. He was wearing his bright red shirt, but he also had a red cape and a shiny helmet with a red horse-hair crest. His horns stuck out of its sides. For a moment he reminded SRG of a little kid in a homemade Halloween costume that was too big for him. But he had a large, shiny sword in his right hand and a confident glare on his face.

Some Random Guy advanced and swung the Dragonwrigley at him. The Ender Dude laughed, swung his sword, and hit the Dragonwrigley with more force than SRG had ever felt. The vibration ran all the way up his arm, the sword twisted, and he desperately gripped it tighter, but it slipped out of his hand. He watched in horror as the Dragonwrigley bounced across the floor and out of his reach. He was helpless. The Ender Dude laughed again and raised his sword.

With nothing else in reach, Some Random Guy angrily tossed the grappling hook at the Ender Dude. It was a desperate move but it got tangled in the beast's shirt sleeve and cape. His sword arm got tangled up as he tried to get it loose. He was momentarily confused. SRG seized the opportunity and grabbed the end of the rope and ran around the Ender

Dude's feet in circles.

Meanwhile, out on the street, the Minotaurs were thoroughly enjoying their show. They were all cheering and shouting as Tannic sank deeper into the Quickphalt. It was up to his neck, and in another minute he would be swallowed whole. He couldn't move at all. He knew he was drawing his last few breaths. Rough World really was beyond rough. He was sorry he'd gotten SRG into this mess. SRG was his only true friend. "Compadre!" he screamed. The Minotaurs just cheered louder.

Some Random Guy rounded the Ender Dude's ankles a second time and then gave him a tiny shove. His feet now tied together, and tipped over and he fell flat on his face with a crash.

The Rainbow Star was on the shelf behind him. Some Random Guy didn't even retrieve the Dragonwrigley. He wouldn't be needing it now. He took one last look at the struggling mass of Ender Dude lying on the floor, and then closed his hands around the Rainbow Star.

* * *

The assistant burst through the door to Mr. Eville's office. "Our plans failed, sir! They've captured the Rainbow Star! The boys have the last star!" he exclaimed. "This is a disaster!"

"Mobilize the team. Shift to Plan B. Hurry now, we don't have much time!" the Evil Boss commanded.

Chapter 13
The Final Showdown

"**We** made it! We made it, Compadre!" Tannic shouted. He was jumping up and down. He couldn't contain his excitement.

"Yeah, I guess we did. I feel kind of numb. To tell you the truth, I didn't really let myself think of us completing all ten levels. I didn't really think it was possible."

"Now we get to go home! Yippee!" Tannic shouted.

"Not so fast! We still have to defeat the Evil Boss, and Doc's plan with the power surge has to work. It might not send us home. For all we know, it might send us to some random place in the space-time continuum. I'm not going to get excited just yet. I still feel kind of uneasy."

"But we made it past the first ten levels, we completed World One! Anything would be better than . . ." His words hung in the air as the possibility sank in.

"Unless we get sent to World Two. I can only imagine how much worse that would be. No, Doc's plan has got to work. I want to go home." Some Random Guy bit his lip. He had a worried look on his face.

"It will work, Compadre. Have faith, don't give up now, come on, we're almost there."

"Oh, I almost forgot to ask! How did the Quickphalt go? I could hear lots of yelling. Did the Minotaurs get stuck in the Quickphalt? I'd love to have seen that!"

Tannic looked at him in relief. "It didn't go well, Compadre. I was able to run at first, but then it started sticking to my shoes and dragging me down until it sucked me in. The Minotaurs didn't fall for it. I was up to my chin when you captured the Rainbow Star. But how did you defeat the Ender Dude?"

"Let's just say he's no longer a fan of grappling hooks and ropes. And the bigger they are, the harder they fall." Some Random Guy looked around. "Dr. Denton?" he called.

"He's not here. Remember?"

"Yeah, I was just checking. Okay, let's stick to the plan. We've still got a lot of work to do. Come on, let's go!"

Some Random Guy walked over to the door with Tannic following him. Leaning against it was the Fortran sword. It was beautiful, but it looked heavy. He wouldn't need the Dragonwrigley now. Hopefully he wouldn't ever need it again. He'd probably never play Rough World again. He thought about that, and he vowed to himself to promptly throw the game away if they ever got back home. He picked up the Fortran. It felt light in his hand. The blade was well polished and shiny. He could see his own reflection as he admired it. He swung it sharply through the air a couple of times. It had the finest balance he could imagine. It was a far superior weapon to the Dragonwrigley. It was astonishing. He was still staring at the sword, lost in thought, when Tannic spoke.

"So what's the plan, Compadre?"

"I don't know. Obviously bring all the Rainbow Stars. We put them into the slots next to the Evil Boss's door, then we go in and defeat him. We get into the Transport Chamber and hope Doc's plan works. It should be pretty straightforward. All we need is a little luck." Some Random Guy looked at his friend. "Come on, Tannic, it's time to go home!"

Tannic thought briefly about his own home, his parents, and his sister. He felt a tug at his chest, but he quickly dismissed the thought. He would never see it again. He would never see his parents again. He thought about his little sister and worried about her. But his real home now was with Some Random Guy and his family in Albany, Oregon. He wanted to go there now.

Some Random Guy held the Fortran Sword tightly and Tannic had his arms loaded with Rainbow Stars. They were a ragged sight. Their clothes had gotten dirty and torn during the ten levels. They really could have used showers, but there wasn't time. They were eager to finish the game and leave it behind them. SRG opened the door with his left hand, and the two of them stepped into the hallway leading to the final showdown.

The hall was brightly lit. At the end of it was a large wooden door. A sign above it read "Mr. Eville. Evil Boss, Ruler of Rough World." The door was carved with hieroglyphics, and it reminded Some Random Guy of the door in the Valley of the Caves. He wondered if there was a connection. To the right of the door there were ten vacant holes in the wall, just the right size for Rainbow Stars. Tannic led the way and started placing the Rainbow Stars one by one into their homes. Some Random Guy stood in front of the door with the Fortran Sword at the ready. He wiped his brow. He took a deep breath. He was ready.

Tannic fitted the last star into place, and the door opened to reveal a huge office. It was a beautiful space with dark paneling and a plush carpet. On the far wall was an elevator door that must be the Transport Chamber. A desk sat facing the door. Sitting at the desk waiting for them was Mr. Eville. He had a confident smirk on his face.

"Come in, boys. Be my guests. Don't be afraid, come right in! Congratulations on a job well done! You're the first players to ever complete Rough World One. That's quite an accomplishment, you know. You should be proud. Now what can I do for you? What brings you here?" he asked innocently, as if he didn't already know.

Some Random Guy and Tannic tentatively stepped into Mr. Eville's private realm. The door closed itself behind them. The next thing SRG noticed was a skull-and-rose tattoo on the back of Mr. Eville's left hand. He shot a worried glance at Tannic.

"What?" Tannic whispered.

"Never trust a pirate," Some Random Guy mouthed to him silently.

He turned back to Mr. Eville. "Thank you, sir, but if it's okay with you, we'll just get into the Transport Chamber and move on now."

"Oh, I hate to disappoint you boys. I really do," he sneered. "There are lots of things that are going to happen right now, but that is definitely not one of them!"

"But we won the game. We get to move on," SRG stammered nervously.

"Oh yes, but you see, you didn't defeat me," Mr. Eville pointed out. He laughed out loud.

"Well in that case, you leave me no choice!" Some Random Guy responded. He lifted the Fortran sword, stepped toward Mr. Eville, and swung hard. He put everything he had into it. He and Tannic had completed all ten levels, and he was going home. The Fortran swung power-fully, gracefully toward Mr. Eville, who had now stood up, but he was just looking on in amusement. He made no attempt to avoid the blade. He had a smile on his face. As the sword reached him, there was a sudden flash of light and a loud clang. Sparks flew everywhere. The Fortran vibrated in SRG's hand and all the way up his arm. He barely kept his grip on it. Unfazed, Mr. Eville smiled wider and looked at them mockingly. Tannic stood silently with his mouth agape. SRG was confused. He lifted the sword up again and shot a worried glance at Tannic.

"What's the matter? Haven't you seen an electromagnetic force field before? I'm disappointed in you two. I thought you'd know better than that." He smiled evilly. "Did you little snot-nosed punks think you could just waltz in here and defeat me with some stupid sword? Ha!" he laughed. "You amuse me! I've enjoyed our little visit, I really have, but this conversation is now over. Leave! Both of you! Be gone! I don't want to ever see your faces again!" He was shouting.

"But the game. We defeated all ten levels and got the Rainbow Stars. That's how the game ends. We get to move on. Dr. Denton said . . ."

"Oh yes! My dear friend Dr. Denton, I'd almost forgotten about him." Mr. Eville yelled toward the door. "Men, please bring in the good doctor. He should see this too!"

The door opened and two Minotaurs half-escorted, half-carried Dr. Denton into the room, one on each of his arms. He looked bedraggled. His head was down and his feet were dragging on the carpet. He looked at the boys with sadness written all over his face. Then he looked down again and sighed. One of the Minotaurs spoke first. "We caught him at the power plant. Whatever he was doing, he was up to no good for sure! But we captured him before he managed to do anything."

Some Random Guy's spirits sank. He felt sick inside. He looked at his hero, standing head down and defeated. They were all defeated. It was over. He and Tannic both looked down at the carpet. This wasn't how they had planned it. They'd come so far. They'd survived too many close calls to count and collected all the Rainbow Stars. They were the first gamers ever to do that. It wasn't fair. They'd given it everything. Was there no end to this stupid nightmare called Rough World? He was trembling and on the verge of tears. He bit his lip to keep from crying. Anger was welling up inside of him.

He looked one more time at Dr. Denton and saw a glimmer in his eye. Then Doc turned his head almost imperceptibly, looked directly at Some Random Guy, and winked. Then he straightened himself up, cleared his throat and addressed Mr. Eville.

"You have to let the boys go. You know that. Those are the rules of the game. It's written in the digital programming code. They completed all ten levels and captured the Rainbow Stars. You have no choice. They get to move on." He spoke with absolute confidence.

Mr. Eville looked surprised, but he recovered quickly. "Yes, well, unfortunately my force-field changed all of that, now didn't it? They have to defeat me to move on. You know that much. And they didn't defeat me, did they? So it seems I can do whatever I want. Our little conversation is through here! Unless . . ." Mr. Eville paused.

"Unless what?" Dr. Denton asked.

"Maybe there's room for a deal. Maybe we could negotiate a settlement of sorts. I give you something you want and you give me something I want," Mr. Eville replied.

"And what do I have that you would want?" Dr. Denton asked. He glanced casually at his watch. They were running out of time. This was going to be very close. He'd set the power surge on a timer and allowed them to catch him so they wouldn't realize what he'd done. Two minutes and counting; they needed to work fast.

"Don't insult me, Dr. Denton. We both know the answer to that. You've been working on ways to generate cheaper electricity just like I have, but I know that you're light years ahead of my scientists. My informants even tell me that you've found a way to draw electricity from the clouds. This will reduce the cost of producing electricity to a fraction of what it is. I know that and you know it too. And if I control it, the cheaper production cost will make my profit margins huge! I'll have even more control over Rough World and its pathetic little inhabitants!" he gloated. "So. If you share your discoveries with me, I will let the boys go. I'd say that's a fair trade."

"No, Dr. Denton," Some Random Guy pleaded. "That's your life's work. Don't give it to somebody as evil as him! It's not worth it! Please don't do it!"

Dr. Denton looked at SRG and Tannic. He thought for a long moment and then seemed resolved. "I'm sorry, boys, but I must see that you get home. I promised I would do that. I have no choice." He looked back at Mr. Eville.

"It's a deal," he said begrudgingly.

He glanced at his watch again. "But they both go, and they go right now, or there's no deal."

"Agreed! I'm so glad you see it my way, Dr. Denton." Mr. Eville chuckled, pleased with himself.

The Transport Chamber really did look like an elevator.

Mr. Eville pulled out a small key with a skull-and-rose design, and slid it into a slot on the wall. He twisted it, and the door slowly creaked opened. The inside looked like an ordinary elevator too, except there were no buttons. Some Random Guy stepped inside and Tannic followed.

Dr. Denton looked at his watch. The boys were furiously waving goodbye, and he waved back. He wore a satisfied smile, but there was a tear in the corner of his eye. He looked at his watch again. Mr. Eville turned the key again and the door began to close. The power surge would happen any second. If it worked, it would send the boys home. If it didn't, they would end up in World Two. Or at any random point in the space-time continuum. Or, worse yet, they might pixelate and cease to exist altogether. He couldn't contemplate that outcome. He closed his eyes and hoped for the best. He'd done his calculations and redone them, and he'd come up with the same answer every time. He was confident in his work, but this was life and death. He focused on the thought of the boys going home.

The door was almost closed. Then Mr. Eville unexpectedly grabbed Tannic by the collar and yanked him out, as the door shut solidly behind him.

Tannic screamed, and Doc opened his eyes in surprise. Mr. Eville had a firm grip on Tannic's collar. The boy looked helpless.

"I think you'll be staying with me," Mr. Eville declared. "Let's just nickname you 'Collateral'."

"What are you doing?" Dr. Denton demanded. "You lied! You agreed to let them both go. You can't do that! You're a liar and you're evil! I don't believe this!"

"Oh, Dr. Denton, you flatter me!" he gloated. "Yes, being evil is beautiful, isn't it? Now you have no choice but to give me the information I want. This boy is my guarantee that you won't cheat me. Yes, I truly am evil! Har, har, har!" he added with a sinister laugh. "And I love it!" Tannic looked at Dr. Denton in desperation.

In the silence they realized Some Random Guy was pounding on the door and shouting. Suddenly there was a vibration, a kind of muted whirling sound deep inside the chamber, and a flash of light and a wisp of smoke came from the seams of the chamber door. Mr. Eville, Tannic, and Dr. Denton all watched the chamber door, but nothing else happened. There was only a deafening, ominous silence.

"Huh. It's never done that before. But then again, it's never done anything before. Nobody's ever made it to the Transport Chamber. That's the first time it's actually been used." Mr. Eville inserted the key and opened the door. The chamber was empty. "Well, I don't know where he went, but he's gone, and that makes me happy! Now let's get down to business, shall we Dr. Denton?"

* * *

It had taken SRG a second to realize what had happened. "Tannic! Tannic!" he'd screamed. There was a brilliant flash of light and a thunderous boom, and he covered his ears and shut his eyes. When he opened them, the air smelled heavy again and he was surrounded by fog.

Chapter 14
Home Sweet Home?

The last thing he remembered was the flash and the noise. The air had a funny smell to it. He would have described it as heavy. And there was smoke, or thick smoke-like fog, and he couldn't see anything. He couldn't even see the walls of the Transport Chamber. But as it began to dissipate, he realized the walls of the Transport Chamber weren't there. He was sitting on the couch in the family room. He was home! Could it be real? Was he really home? He thought about Tannic, suddenly, and felt empty inside.

His thoughts were interrupted by a familiar sound. His mom was putting her key in the door. He jumped up and ran to greet her, tears in his eyes. He ran into her open arms.

"Oh Honey, I'm so glad you're safe! Mrs. Kibbitch called and said that lightning had struck our house! I left work as soon as she called, and I tried to phone you of the way home, but you didn't answer! I've been worried sick. I'm glad you didn't try to mow the lawn in this storm. I'm so glad you're okay!" she rambled on, fighting back tears. She was so happy that she didn't even notice that his clothes were dirty and torn.

"Mom! Mom! You won't believe what happened! Tannic

and I were playing the game and got transported into Rough World for real. We had to fight for our lives to get back home. Only I made it back, but he didn't! He's stuck in Rough World! You won't believe what we saw! And we met Dr. Denton for real and he helped us. It was unbelievable! I can't believe I'm actually home. I didn't I think I would ever see you again!"

"Oh Stevie! I appreciate your vivid imagination, I really do. Your adventure sounds amazing, but Honey, you know Rough World is a video game. It's not a real place, and Tannic . . . well, you know he's not real either." She patted his head. "Now, go clean up for dinner." She stopped and looked at him. "What did happen to you? You're filthy! Wash up and put on some clean clothes. You father will be home in a few minutes and we're taking you out for pizza! We were both worried sick about you."

"But Mom, it *was* real, and Tannic, Tannic . . . is stuck . . ."

"Stevie, Honey, hurry. Scoot along, your dad will be home any minute!"

Some Random Guy walked dutifully up to his room. How would he explain this to anybody? Who would believe him? Suddenly, he was overwhelmed with emotion. He was really home. He wasn't in Rough World anymore. This was really his house. He blinked away tears and took a deep breath. He loved the smell of his house, and he loved his room. He couldn't wait to see his dad. He'd listen to him more carefully in the future. He would appreciate a lot more things from now on. He was going to be a different person. He'd grown up so much on this strange day. He thought for a second about the Dragonwrigley. He was going to miss that sword. The thought almost made him laugh, then he realized he would never wield it again, and he was okay with that. He'd rather stay home any day and not have to worry about Minotaurs and man-eating plants.

They went to Pizza King that night, his all-time favorite restaurant. He played video games and they ordered his favorite pizza. He loved that dinner, and he especially loved the three-cheese pizza. It had never tasted so good. He was starving by the time it arrived. He couldn't remember when he had eaten last. To his parents' amazement, he ate the entire thing and told them he could probably eat another one. He couldn't remember when pizza had ever tasted so good, either. He smiled.

At bedtime he went to his room without any argument. He loved being home and being in the safety of his own room. There would be no Minotaurs hiding in his closet or under his bed. He took off his clothes and folded them neatly on the floor. He put on his pajamas and crawled into bed and turned out the lights. He pulled the covers up over himself and soaked in the comfort of being warm and snug in his own bed. He laid his head down on his pillow. He loved his own bed and his own pillow. He was exhausted. It had been anything but a random day. It was a day he would remember for the rest of his life. He closed his eyes and fell quickly into a deep sleep.

But he dreamed of Tannic and Dr. Denton, and of Rough World.

The End